ABANDON INDIANA

3246-HENS

ABANDON
INDIANA

Amy Hensley

To order additional copies of this book, contact:
Xlibris Corporation
1-888-7-XLIBRIS
www.Xlibris.com
Orders@Xlibris.com

CHAPTER ONE:
JONAH—SEPTEMBER 8, 1957

They buried Chester Lee Reece on the hottest September day the town of Abandon had seen in eighty-one years, which was exactly how old Chester Lee Reece was when he finally expired. Many folks in Cullen County took that as some sort of sign, figuring that only the devil himself could have brought a man like that to Abandon in the first place and that only the devil could come to take him back home again, bringing the boiling heat of hell with him both times. Because surely it was a sin to write such bad poetry as Chester Lee Reece did, or to do those other things with the young boys which were only rumors but which eventually passed into local legend as the tight and tidy truth.

Eighty-one years ago that whole summer of 1876 was a scorcher, so hot that Chester Lee Reece's mother nearly perished giving birth to her only child in the back bedroom of a white clapboard farmhouse just outside of town, all the windows nailed shut to keep out any germs or stray animals during the delivery, just like her mama had when she herself was born nineteen years before, and she'd turned out alright. Her son died in a rocking chair on the porch of that very same house, turned brown years ago from a hundred humid summers and a hundred bitter winters. The house, of course, not Chester Lee Reece, whose complexion was more yellow, like that pulpy paper on which he scribbled his poems.

In the years in between he sat on the front porch (which his mother liked to call the veranda, because she was from the South and that's what her mama had always called it) or in the loft of the barn or under the low-hanging shade of an elm tree and composed poems of questionable literary merit. His poetry became known beyond the ten square miles of Cullen County when in the summer of 1928 he managed to get a few of them published in the local newspaper by giving the editor, Whiskey Winslow, a bottle of his favorite stuff, at the rate of one bottle per poem, this being especially impressive at the height of the long dry season in which the United States found herself. Then that fall a newly-emerging figure on the literary scene happened to come through town on the train on his way from a small plantation in southern Alabama to a lecture in New York City.

This author, besides being a fine writer of fiction, had also dabbled in poetry and fancied himself not too bad of a bard. He was also quite a drinker.

So it followed that with an hour or two to kill in Abandon he should seek out the local watering hole, and while on this quest he made the acquaintance of Whiskey Winslow. The editor had no idea who this short, funny-talking fellow was but did recognize his own kind when he saw him, and escorted the writer to his office where they shared one or two of Chester Lee Reece's bottles. As the afternoon wore on Whiskey Winslow related the story of how he came upon these treasures, and soon pulled out some back issues of the Abandon *Abandon* (which was the name of the newspaper) in which the poems appeared and showed the southern gentleman the price of the day's high spirits. The writer was quite impressed with the depth of Chester Lee Reece's ability in meter, rhyme and ambiguity, and when the train whistle blew he stuffed the papers under his arm and promised Whiskey Winslow that he would make famous the name of Chester Lee Reece, one of the finest poets that he had ever read.

A brief example:

> *All over this town, over hill and dale*
> *They will hear her cry, they will hear her wail*
> *At the precise moment she opens the gift*
> *That I have brought; then her spirits will lift.*

The subsequent publication in 1929 of Chester Lee Reece's first book, *Laundress on the Levee,* would have cost the author from Alabama his burgeoning literary career, if not for the publication a few months later of his own critically acclaimed, though highly ambiguous, novel. His success guaranteed in perpetuity the published poetry of Chester Lee Reece who, during the next twenty-five years, issued five more volumes of poetry and was known forevermore in the publishing world as Chester Lee *Reeks.* But in Abandon fame was fame, and Chester Lee Reece was now a *famous person.*

But when they laid him to rest on Sunday, September 8, the cemetery was nearly empty. Chester Lee Reece may have been a *famous person,* but some things in this world a person should not do, regardless of how famous he becomes. Of course those things with the young boys were only rumors, but they eventually passed into local legend as the downright truth.

Only three people were in attendance at the funeral: Rev. Calder, who performed the service; Dr. Riley, whose name appeared on the death certificates of every deceased person in town and who therefore felt it was his professional obligation and duty to attend their funerals; and my father, Asa Dollar.

He'd waited until my mother had returned home with the car from the Joshua's general store, then told her he needed to drive over to his friend Baldy's house to borrow some tools so he could finally start repairing the roof on the old barn. Mom didn't believe him, of course—she knew he was going to the graveyard. For one thing, it would've take an act of intervention, divine or otherwise, to get Asa up on the roof of that barn. And for another, she knew exactly where he was going because every day for the last three years she'd had to dust around Asa's beloved copy of *The Collected Works of Chester Lee Reece,* [and before that his copy of *Dream On, Golden Night,* and before that *Alone But Not Forgotten,* and before that *Come Now, Rising Tide*], all of which in their time lay tattered and dog-eared on what he called the mantel but since they had no fireplace was really just a shelf nailed crookedly to the wall.

So late on Sunday afternoon he drove to the cemetery by himself. He had wanted my sister Reece to come along with him, but as usual Mom wouldn't let her go. Instead he stood there alone between Rev. Calder and Dr. Riley with his head bowed so they wouldn't notice the tears bubbling up in his eyes, and I couldn't believe what I was seeing because at my funeral almost six years ago he didn't even pretend to be holding back the tears. He just stood there, apart from the family, his arms down at his sides looking straight ahead past my casket to the woods beyond. I couldn't understand it, but at that point I was still getting used to all this up here.

It's strange, but up here is not exactly how I thought it would be. I thought I would lie back, kick off my heavy combat boots and put my feet up on a fluffy cloud, alternately napping and keeping an eye on my family, especially my little sister, Reece. Of course I also thought I'd storm across the 38th Parallel with guns blazing and walk out a hero like Audie Murphy. I was on the MLR, the Main Line of Resistance, for less than a day when I realized I'd made the biggest mistake of my young life. So I should've known better than to expect too much of this place, but I figure a man without hope is nothing but a hopeless man. Even though inside I don't feel like a man at all.

There are no clouds here, nor angels playing divine music on golden harps, nor even a place where you can put on a white robe and meet the members of your family who came here before you. It's mostly just dark. No, not dark, really—more of a twilight. In fact, now that I think about it, it's very much like the golden dusk in which I met my fate. Maybe that's just what it's like for me. Maybe it's different for everybody, depending on how they came to be here.

I was looking forward to watching the world from this place, high above the earth yet still a part of it. But it takes things a long time to get here. I remember in the Germ Man's science class one day he told us that if there were people on other planets millions of light years away, peering at us through highly advanced tele-

scopes, they would just now be seeing Christopher Columbus dis-
covering America. It takes that long for light and sound to travel
that far. I could hardly believe it when he told us then, but now I
can see that he was probably right. Because when I peer through
the half light down at Abandon, the town where I was born and
lived for eighteen years, I can only see what's already happened.
I'll be living in the past for the rest of my afterlife.

At the end of the service, as the sun began to slip below the
horizon, Rev. Calder sprinkled a handful of dirt onto the coffin
and said the same words he'd said over me a few years earlier, and
he and Dr. Riley nodded to Dad and left him alone in the muggy
dusk. He stepped up and whispered, *"Before the beginning, there
was the end/And so there shall be a beginning again,"* the only Chester
Lee Reece lines he could remember that seemed appropriate at the
moment, then tipped an invisible hat and walked away. Rev. Calder
and Dr. Riley were already out of sight, heading back to their
homes and their television sets to tune into the Sunday night epi-
sode of The Blackie Harmony Show.

Blackie Harmony hosted a regional talk show out of Cincinnati on weekday afternoons, but on Sunday night his show reached
a national audience. Interest in the September 8, 1957 show was
especially high in Abandon—it marked the national television debut
of Halo Truly, a nineteen-year-old singer who had graduated from
Abandon High just a year earlier and who already was driving girls
wild with his thick, wavy blond hair and enigmatic blue eyes, his
gelatinous voice that literally coated the insides of their hearts and
wouldn't let go, and his certain way of caressing his guitar, pulling
it tight against his chest and then popping it out again on lyrics
like LOVE or YOU or BABY, that literally left the girls breathless
as they sank woozily to the floor and made them forget all about
that Elvis Presley fellow.

Since my family didn't have a television, or even electricity,
Dad was in no hurry to go home. He knew he should drive over to
Baldy's and borrow those tools, like he told Mom he would, but
he didn't think she'd believed his story in the first place, anyway.

She was too smart for that. He considered driving out to Patsy's Place in Falling Star, to maybe have a beer and watch that Truly boy everyone was talking about, but that was too far to go and besides, he'd stopped drinking years ago. Rebecca would smell it on his breath before the car even pulled into the driveway, and that would cause a whole set of grief that just wasn't worth it. He wished he'd brought his book of poems with him, but he'd left it up on the mantel, next to the kerosene lamp. His options exhausted, he drove through the weedy gates and out of the cemetery. It must've slipped his mind to visit my grave while he was there, even though he was just a few steps away.

*

As they are burying Chester Lee Reece, Halo Truly stands in front of the mirror in his dressing room backstage at The Blackie Harmony Show. His left knee jitters back and forth as he forces a comb through his impenetrable blond hair, laminated by a heavy layer of grease. On the orange vinyl couch behind him two hired musicians—a stand-up bass player and a drummer—rehearse by tapping out the rhythms to his big hit, "Love Me in the Morning," which tomorrow is expected to enter the American Top 10.

"Would you guys knock it off?" Halo Truly growls. "I'm trying to concentrate." He hikes up his silver-lamé jacket by its sparkling collar and lets it re-settle on his shoulders, all the time practicing his enigmatic stare. The older men seated behind him watch him for a moment, smirk at each other and roll their eyes. The drummer resumes his tapping on the sofa cushion, even louder than before. Halo Truly slams his comb down on the countertop and grabs his guitar by its neck. He slings it over his shoulder and huffs out of the room. In the serpentine hallways he gets turned around and ends up circling past the dressing room three times. Each time he passes by the open door the two musicians smile sweetly and wiggle their fingers at him in an exaggerated wave. Finally a stagehand directs him to the holding area just to the right of the stage, where he is told to wait quietly until Mr. Harmony calls him out. To calm his nerves he begins humming "Love Me in the Morning," until the stagehand returns and asks him to please refrain from making any noise while that camera's red light is on, thank you. Halo Truly tries out his don't-mess-with-me sneer on the crew member and receives a now-familiar smirk and a roll of the eyes in response.

Halo straps his guitar across his chest and concentrates on the red light. The second it blinks off he is being pulled onstage in front of the hired musicians and behind a velvety, rhubarb-red curtain. Before he can adjust himself his entire body is doused in a scalding white light brighter than the sun bouncing off Cullen's Creek in the middle of summer in Abandon. Almost immediately sweat bursts from his face and neck and into his shirt collar, but he can't wipe it away because the curtain is lifting and the girls are screaming the girls girls girls are screaming screaming screaming so shrilly that he can't hear the song in his head the song that he wrote the song he has sung to himself at least a million times the song that girls that girls girls girls are singing all across the tri-state area the song the song the song that is going to make him famous and he thinks he hears his name spoken but before it registers the drummer has counted off the song the song the song and he has to play the first bar double-time to catch up and he can't remember the words the words the words to the song in his head the song that he wrote the song he has sung to himself at least a million times the song that girls that girls girls girls are singing all across the tri-state area the song the song the song that is going to make him famous love me in the morning my angel of the night cover me with kisses after dawn's first light has swept away the teardrops from the sweet earth fresh with dew oh love me in the morning and forever I'll love you and at this moment standing under the hot lights and before the screaming girls he is a *famous person.*

CHAPTER TWO:
SEPTEMBER 9, 1957

Every single day of Reece Dollar's life, her mother never fails to remind her that when she was born she took one look at her daughter's red, bawling, scrunched-up face and told the doctor to tie her tubes immediately. Every day she manages to work this into the conversation somehow. For the longest time Reece didn't know what her mother was talking about when she said this, although she got the gist of it. Last night, lying awake in the three-quarter size bed she shares with her sister, she finally got up the courage to ask.

"Dinah?"

"Hmm?"

Reece cleared her throat and swallowed hard. "What does mom mean when she says she got her tubes tied?"

Dinah didn't even open her eyes. "It means Dr. Riley fixed it so that she can't have no more kids." She turned over on her side so that she was facing away from Reece.

"*Any* more, Dinah." She thought about what her sister said. It made sense, she supposed, but it didn't sound very good for her. "How do *you* know?"

Dinah's deep sigh shook the bed. "Because Bernie Joshua told me his mom had it done after she had Roxanne. The doctor told her if she didn't, the next baby she had would kill her."

That made sense too, Reece thought, since Mrs. Joshua was so small. She was practically a midget. Mr. Joshua was, too. Maybe that's why *her* mom did it. Except that her mom was the tallest woman in Abandon. "Bernie told you that? When?"

Dinah was quiet for a long time, and Reece thought she had fallen asleep. Finally Dinah whispered, "In class one day, during a biology lesson." Bernie Joshua was a year older than Dinah, but was in the same grade because six years ago he had polio and missed almost the entire school year until he experienced a miraculous recovery that left him without so much as a limp. "We was studying the reproductive system. It just sorta come up in the conversation."

"*Were* studying, Dinah. And *came* up."

"Goodnight, Reece."

Reece rolled over to face the wall. "Goodnight." She still wasn't convinced about everything Dinah had told her. She'd ask Roxanne tomorrow. Roxanne Joshua was her best friend and was Bernie's sister. She'd tell her the truth.

In the morning Reece makes her way down the narrow, creakity stairs that connect the kitchen to the two bedrooms upstairs. Before she even reaches the bottom step her mother says, "I need water."

"I'm going to the bathroom," Reece tells her, extracting particles of sleep from between her eyelashes with her bitten-down fingernails. "Can't Danny or Dinah do it?"

"Dinah had to go into school early, and Danny started his new job this morning at Hilliard's farm. Take the bucket with you." It swings from her mother's index finger. Her other hand threatens her ample hip with a balled fist.

Reece grumbles her commentary on the situation as she takes the bucket and tosses into it the roll of toilet paper that hangs on a nail by the door.

"Don't sass me, young lady," her mother snaps.

Reece lets the wooden screen door slam behind her. The chill of the morning air slips between her body and her nearly transparent nightgown, and the stones leading to the outhouse are sharp and cold beneath her bare feet. Her father and Jonah and Danny spent two whole days that summer of the drought, pulling these limestones from Cullen's Creek and laying the path from the house to the toilet.

The creek's namesakes—Erl, Jessie, and nine-year-old Erl Cullen II—were the first family to settle in Abandon in 1807, building their homestead along the stream they named after themselves. Erl Cullen had wanted to name the whole town—what there was of it—after himself, but his level-headed wife prevailed.

"Now, Erl, we're a modest family," Jessie told him as she helped him clean and flatten the dirt that would be the floor of their home, picking out the stones and smoothing it with her hand. "I don't believe it's your place to start giving every tree and rock the Cullen na—"

"Mama!" Erl II cried, running at full speed through the door frame. "Come look what I found," he gasped, trying to catch his breath. He took his mother's hand and pulled her a hundred yards down the length of the creek. His father followed, yelling, "Come back here, son. Erl! Come back, damn ya!" He caught up to them at the base of a towering beech tree, stricken by the elements years ago, standing leafless but proud. He brushed his hand down the trunk and strips of bark crumbled beneath his fingers. "Over here, papa," Erl said. On the other side of the tree a message was carved:

We did not abandon ye
E. Wesley
1777

"Erl," Jessie said to her husband as they inspected the carving. "I think we've found us the name for our town." Jessie Cullen's attempt at humility was short-lived, however, when nine years later Indiana became a state and Abandon became the seat of the new Cullen County, named on the suggestion of Jessie herself.

Today Erl Cullen's great-great-great-great grandson, Erl VII, lives in the original house (the dirt floor has been replaced by wood) with his wife Naomi and their kids—Jessie, Gene, Bo, Erl, Toby, Tague, Casey and Noah—thought by general consensus to be the eight stupidest children in the basin. Following their hallowed family tradition, Erl VII's father (Erl VI) and grandfather (Erl V) live in the house, too, as will Erl VIII and his wife and children, and their son Erl IX and his wife and children, and their son Erl X and his wife and children, as will they all until they finally run out of roman numerals. The Cullens are nothing if not consistent—they tend to breed lots of Erls, and their wives tend to die young. Naomi Cullen, at 36, currently holds the longevity record.

Approaching the outhouse Reece takes a deep breath and holds it, her cheeks as round with air as a chipmunk's filled with nuts. Inside she stands on her tiptoes on the gritty plank floor, hikes up her gown and hovers over the seat. She does this at least twice a day, every day, and still she cannot accustom herself to the filth and the stench.

Back outside she exhales in one gasping burst, her cheeks collapsing like a deflated balloon. She strays from the stone path to the well at the side of the house. She sets the tin bucket on the ground under the spout and begins to pump. After about twenty pumps a trickle of rusty water begins to dribble out, until soon the water is pouring full blast from the spout. When the bucket is full she attempts to carry it to the kitchen, staggering along the stone path, water sloshing out and darkening the stones with each step.

Inside, her mother takes the bucket, tsking, "You've spilt half of it. I'll need more than this." She pours the water into a pot on the bottled-propane cookstove, then whirls back around to face her daughter. "And you forgot the toilet paper again, didn't you?" she says, eyeing the empty nail on the wall.

"Yes," Reece sighs, starting out the door. "I'll get it."

But she stops just outside the doorway when she hears her mother's voice. "The day you were born I knew you would be a millstone around my neck," she is saying. Reece knows she should keep walking, but her feet feel as heavy as the limestones on which she stands. She wants to keep walking until she's out of earshot, until she's out of this town and out of this life, but instead she stands there and listens.

"I awoke on that cool September morning with a premonition that chilled me to my bones," her mother continues. "And when you came out, feet first and three months early, crying holy bloody murder, I said to Dr. Riley, 'Never again will I endure such agony.

If this one isn't a devil-child, the next one surely will be. You do what you have to do.'" She dries her hands on a crusty dish towel and turns back to her boiling pot. "Go on, now."

She knows Reece has been standing there, absorbing her mother's contempt. Head down, almost blindly Reece runs, past the outhouse to the grape arbor. She dives between the luxurious hanging vines, inhaling their sweet fragrance, letting the rough leaves scratch her face and arms. She lies face down and waters the dry grass with her tears. Chiggers feast on her ankles and she lets them. A chorus of cicadas erupts suddenly, drowning out the individual sounds of the menagerie inhabiting the nearby woods, woods which are only accessible by climbing the steep hill that rises behind the house. Those who can navigate the overgrown path through these woods emerge on the other side upon a slight bluff overlooking Abandon proper; twenty sidesteps down a dirt trail and you're on Main Street, just a block from the courthouse. When Reece was seven Jonah took her into the woods for the first time, carrying her piggy-back up the bank and into the dark, cool forest. "Legend has it a fairy princess lives in a golden castle deep in these woods, among the poplar trees," he told her. "They say she spends her days brushing her long, golden locks with a golden hairbrush, waiting for her handsome prince to return. Golden hair just like yours," he said, bouncing Reece up and down on his back. As they walked he spun elaborate tales of the princess's life. "But she doesn't live there alone," he continued. "She shares the castle with her father, the kindly king; her mother, the queen—"

"The *evil* queen," Reece interjected.

"Okay, the *evil* queen; and her older brother and sister, the duke and duchess. They all miss the oldest son, the baron, who has gone off to war."

"War?" Reece asked, wide-eyed.

"Yes," Jonah said. "He departed on a beautiful white horse, armed only with a sword and a coat of armor, to fight the fire-breathing dragon that tormented the villagers—" he stopped suddenly. "Shhh!" Reece held her breath, waiting. Jonah began walking again, slowly, cautiously. "We're drawing nearer," he said. "But I haven't told you the most important thing."

"What?" Reece whispered excitedly. She squeezed her brother's neck so tightly he could barely breathe.

"You mustn't look directly at the princess's castle," he told her, "or it will disappear in a blinding flash of light. Instead, close your eyes tightly, and when I say so, open your eyes slowly and concentrate on the giant poplar that guards her home. You'll be able to see the castle's reflection on the tree."

Reece swung her legs in anticipation as they approached the golden palace. "Are your eyes closed?" Jonah asked every few steps. Reece nodded briskly. "Okay, then, keep them closed. We're almost there." They walked a few more yards, but she couldn't stand it any longer and opened her eyes as wide as they would go. She swears to this day she saw a flash brighter than the fiercest lightning.

"Jonah! It's gone!"

Jonah set her down hard on the ground. "I told you not to look!" he said, shaking her shoulders. "You made the princess and her castle disappear." Reece burst into tears as he attempted to soothe her. "I'm sorry, Reece," he said quietly. "Maybe you can see her tomorrow."

"No!" Reece sobbed. "I want to go home." So Jonah hoisted her onto his back once again and she rubbed her snotty nose on the collar of his shirt. They made the long journey through the woods and down the hill to their little home, where he deposited Reece into bed for an afternoon nap. "Can we see the princess tomorrow?" she murmured to Jonah, drifting into sleep as he smoothed her hair. But later that year he was gone, and she often found sleep at night thinking of her older brother, carrying a knapsack filled with all the necessities of combat in an unknown land thousands of miles away, as he had carried his sister into the woods that day.

"Jonah!" Reece cries, awakening to find herself being carried piggy-back into the house.

"Shush, m'dear, you're dreamin'.."

She blinks a few times until the back of her father's head comes into focus. "Doodle!" She squeezes his neck and nuzzles his crew cut. "How was work?"

"Hard, m'dear," he says. "But not as hard as carryin' you 'round. You're gettin' too old for this." He sets her down and takes her hand in his. "Do ya wanna tell me why you was sleepin' under the grape arbor in your nightgown at eight o'clock in the mornin'?"

"*Were*, Doodle. *Were* sleeping."

"Awright, *were* sleepin'."

Reece scratches the sole of her foot against the sharp ridge of a stone. Suddenly too embarrassed to look at him, she studies the formation of tiny rocks and miniature fossils embedded in the stone on which she's standing. She tries to imagine the animal that stopped in Cullen's Creek for a drink of water, perhaps, or a bath, and ended up a stepping stone to an outhouse a million years later. She wonders if, a million years from now, a posthistoric girl will step on her fossilized remains on her way to the toilet.

Her father bends down to Reece's level. "Did your mother say somethin' to upset ya?"

Her foot is rubbed raw, so she shifts her weight and scratches the other one. "No."

He sighs and stands up. "Okay. Why don't ya go on inside and get dressed."

She moves forward a few steps, then stops abruptly. "The toilet paper. I—"

"I'll get it, m'dear. Go on, now."

Reece runs into the house, the wooden screen door banging against the door frame. She takes the narrow stairs two at a time, bursts into her and Dinah's bedroom and quickly shuts the door. Out of breath, she slides to the floor and draws her knees to her face to catch the tears that are trying to come between the gasps for air. She reaches under the bed until she feels the familiar canvas beneath her fingers. She pulls out Jonah's olive knapsack and inhales its stale odor of sweat and blood, insect repellent and Korean soil, eighteen-year-old bravado and plain old-fashioned fear. Her mother wanted to throw it away when the government sent it back to them in a box along with his dogtags, watch and handkerchiefs, knife, razor and chrome Zippo lighter, but Reece wouldn't let her. So her mother told her to put it away, far from her sight, so that she would never know it was in the house.

The knapsack comforts Reece, and after a few minutes she quiets down enough to hear them in the kitchen, discussing her again. "Mother, what did ya say to her this mornin'?" Reece hears her father ask.

"Asa, I'm only trying to teach her to be responsible," her mother replies.

"Well, you're doin' a piss-poor job of it. All you've done is upset her."

"Your language, Asa, please. As for upsetting the girl, she has a nervous disposition, that's all. There's nothing I can do about that."

"Well, I don't know what dipso—disposition means exactly, but I do know ya can try a bein' a little nicer to her."

Reece hears her mother sigh and clatter the pans. "You're tired, Asa. You've worked all night. You go on up to bed."

He climbs the stairs as though retreating from a lost battle and pauses in front of Reece's door. She shoves the knapsack back under the bed and jumps up. She quickly peels off her nightgown and slips on her school dress and shoes and splashes her face with lukewarm water from the bowl and pitcher on the washstand. She pulls her hair back into a ponytail and rushes into her parents' room, but her father is already in bed, asleep. She pulls the threadbare sheet up to his chin and kisses him lightly on the cheek.

She tiptoes away from the bed and back into her room. She scoops up her schoolbooks from the dresser and climbs out the window and down the trellis her father built onto the side of the house so the wild roses would have a place to grow. The blooms stop just short of the window sill, and on summer nights the perfumed air drifts through the open window until Reece and Dinah are nearly nauseous. Only recently she realized that if she could use the trellis to climb *out* of the window, any soul passing by could easily use the trellis to climb *into* the window and into their room. But she had immediately shaken the idea from her head, trying to remember the last time a crime of any sort had occurred in Abandon. She couldn't think of a single instance.

Once on the ground she wipes away the spots of blood on her legs where the thorns pierced her bare skin, sucking each drop from her fingers as she goes, tasting the metallic tang of her own insides. She crosses the railroad tracks that run in front of the house—nearly under her bedroom window—and makes her way down the twisting, one-lane road that crosses Cullen's Creek before doubling back toward Abandon.

Just over the tracks the ground drops off precipitously, forming the flat basin where Erl Cullen first put down roots, and where ten ramshackle houses line the curving, nameless road. On the Dollar side of the tracks this road dead ends at their house, at the narrow gravel-and-cinder path that runs parallel to the tracks and which is, in effect, their driveway, as long as no trains are coming. Reece's Grandpa Dollar built the house exactly between the tallest hill in the hollow and the railroad tracks, and people flying over the hollow or seeing it from above would notice that the land is shaped like a giant throne. They would see that the hill leading to the woods forms its tall back, the drop-off forms the legs, and the Dollar's property forms the seat. Then they would see the railroad tracks cutting through the land and think perhaps the little house was only the depot.

Reece is the first one to arrive at the creek, where all of the schoolchildren in the hollow meet, then walk the two miles to school together. She sets her books down on the grooved-out spot where the Wesley Tree used to stand. In 1817 twenty-five townsfolk uprooted the tree and moved it by horseteam to a newly-erected memorial on the courthouse square, to commemorate the town's ten-year anniversary, and every September fourteenth since then the town has held a Founder's Festival. Main Street is closed to automobile traffic, and booths are set up right in the middle of the road. The women sell their baked goods and needlework, the men hawk their carpentry, and the children play games of chance for crumbling chocolate chip cookies or scrawny goldfish. But the highlight of the day is the Harvest Parade. At precisely 6:00 p.m. the townspeople leave their booths and scatter to their homes to prepare for the procession. Everyone meets back at the school, which stands at the opposite end of Main Street from the courthouse, then marches together to the monument. They carry the bounty of their fall harvest—vegetables, fruits, flowers, whatever they can spare—and place it around the base of the Wesley Tree in honor and remembrance of their town's original inhabitants, in thanks for another prosperous year and, the cynical and the superstitious of the town have said, to ensure future prosperity. After that one of the Erl Cullens gives a little speech, and then the all night dance begins on Main Street. This year's festival is five days away.

Reece patrols the creek bank, occasionally stooping to sift through the dirt and mud when she thinks she might have found an unusual rock or fossil to add to her collection. Then she takes off her shoes and wades into the water, still searching for a new specimen. She's ankle-deep when the other kids start arriving at the creek.

"Hey, rock girl, ya findja any di-no-saurs in there?"

Reece recognizes Bo Cullen's nasal twang and doesn't turn around. Most of the boys in Abandon can't seem to resist Bo Cullen's long auburn curls, soft ashen eyes, turned-up nose and high-pitched giggle, but most of the girls in town, including Reece, see right through her.

"Actually, I've found numerous examples of prehistoric life forms within the sedimentary deposits of this creek," Reece says.

"You're weird, Reece Dollar," Bo Cullen says, scrunching her turned-up nose.

"Hey, Reece," hollers Bo Cullen's older sister, Gene Cullen. "Didja watch Halo Truly on Blackie Harmony last night?"

"She couldn't, Gene," Bo Cullen yells back, even though they're standing next to each other. "Them Dollars don't have e-lec-tric-i-ty."

"At least we have teeth!" Reece says. The other kids collectively hush to hear how the sisters Cullen will respond.

"Come on, Bo, let's go," Gene Cullen huffs, turning on her cheap patent-leather heel.

Reece slips a sandstone she found into the front pocket of her dress, squeezes into her shoes and picks up her books. She scans the crowd for her best friend Roxanne and sees her walking away from the crowd, searching for Reece. They spot each other simultaneously and join up.

"Hi," Reece says. "I need to ask you something—"

"Come here," Roxanne says, pulling her off the side of the road and into a patch of trees. "Be quiet."

"Roxanne, what—"

"Shhh! Follow me."

They creep about fifty yards into the woods until they come to a red oak large enough for both of them to stand behind without being seen.

"What are we doing?" Reece whispers.

Roxanne leans around the tree trunk and points to a small clearing a few yards away. "Look."

Reece peeks out from behind the oak and sees two figures wrestling in the grass. "Are they fighting?" she asks.

Roxanne stifles a giggle. "*No*, Reece. They're—you know . . ."

Reece squints until she notices that the person lying flat on her back is her sister, Dinah; the person kneeling over her is Roxanne's brother, Bernie; and they're doing something she's vaguely heard about from whispers at school but never in a million years imagines she'll ever do, let alone see her own sister do, in the wide open, in broad daylight. She jumps back behind the tree, stunned.

"Can you believe it?" Roxanne squeals. "I saw them doing it one other time, in our barn. They'd spread out a big pile of hay and their clothes were thrown all over the place. I'm sure they did it some other times, too, that I didn't see, 'cause they sure act like they know what they're doing."

"Roxanne, be quiet! That's my sister!" She can't help but sneak another look. "Is he hurting her? It looks like he's hurting her."

"God Reece, you sure are dumb sometimes. Come on, we're

gonna be late for school." They tiptoe back to the road, then break into a run until they catch up with the others. They walk for a long time without speaking. Climbing the steps to the school Roxanne finally says, "Isn't this neat? If they get married, we'll be sisters! Bye!" Roxanne sprints toward her locker and Reece shuffles toward her own. Dinah, married? she thinks. That will never happen, she's not even sixteen. Then she remembers she didn't ask Roxanne about her mom getting her tubes tied. She'll ask her at lunch. She reaches her locker and sees Danny hanging up his letterman's jacket in his locker, next to hers in the alphabetical rows. He wears the jacket every day, regardless of the weather. Already this morning it's eighty degrees.

"Hey Reece," he says. "Seen Dinah?"

Reece can feel her face heating up and pokes her whole head inside her locker, pretending to look for a book. "Uh, no, haven't seen her." She slams the door and turns away from him. "Bye." She scurries down the hall, sees Dinah coming toward her from the other direction, and ditches into a classroom until she passes. Should she tell Doodle? she wonders. Would he know what to do about such a thing? Would he even know what she meant? The warning bell rings and she nearly jumps out of her shoes. Her heart is beating so loud and so fast she's sure everyone around her can hear it. Head down, in tears, she makes her way to the nurse's office. "I don't feel so good," she tells the nurse.

"Do you want to call your mother, dear?" she asks.

"No! No. Can I just lie down for a bit?" The nurse directs her to a table with a red plastic cushion on top. Reece curls up on the table and immediately falls asleep. When she finally awakens she peels her sweaty legs from the cushion and learns that it's already lunch time. "Feeling better?" the nurse asks, but Reece just puts her chin down and heads for the cafeteria. She sees Roxanne at a table across the room and sits down next to her.

"Hi Reece. Here, I'll save your seat if you want to go get—"

"I'm not hungry. I need to ask you about something—"

"Hi Dinah," Roxanne says to the figure standing behind Reece's chair. She turns around and sees her sister holding a lunch tray of half-eaten food. Below the tray Reece sees a grass stain on Dinah's gray wool skirt, and a distinct image of this morning's scene flashes through her mind.

"Reece and Roxanne, the Boobsey Twins," Dinah says. "Listen, Reece, will you tell Mom I'm staying after school today? I need to go to the library to work on a report."

Roxanne begins giggling uncontrollably.

"What?" Dinah asks.

"Nothing," Reece answers, glaring at Roxanne. "Yes, I'll tell her."

"Thanks. Bye." She takes her tray to the conveyor belt that will send it to cafeteria purgatory and leaves the room. Reece sees Bernie Joshua standing just outside the door, waiting for her.

"Be quiet, Roxanne," Reece says to her friend, who had begun laughing harder once Dinah had left the table. "I need to ask you something—"

"Why weren't you in class this morning?" Roxanne asks, calming down and taking a sip of her milk. "Miss Corliss said you were sick?"

Reece nods. "I went to the nurse's office to lie down. I fell asleep."

"Oh. Do you feel better now?"

Reece nods again. "I want to ask you—"

"Roxanne, did you see it!" squeals Barrie Spingle, the class president, sitting down at their table. Three members of her entourage, including Bo Cullen, join them, all speaking at once.

"Isn't he cute?"

"I just love that 'Love Me in the Morning' song."

"Did you see the way he moved? I was so embarrassed, with my parents sitting right there."

"I thought the bass player was kinda cute—"

"Who's looking at the bass player? You're supposed to be looking at *Halo*, Charmain! Gee!"

"What did you think about him, Reece?"

"What did Danny think? I bet he wants to be just like Halo, don't he? All the boys do."

"I have to go," Reece says, hustling to put her tray away. The girls are speaking so loudly that she can hear what they're saying even out in the hallway.

"Reece's family don't have a television," Roxanne explains to the girls.

"Oh," they say together, nodding. Bo Cullen smirks.

"She's weird," Helen Silven says. "Last week in the Germ Man's class, he went around the room askin' us all what we wanted to be when we grew up, and you know what she said? A pale—palo—

"Paleontologist," Roxanne says. "Or maybe an archaeologist."

"Yeah, that was it. Weren't nobody even knew what that was, not even Mr. German. And she sat there, all pleased with herself, actin' like we was stupid or somethin'."

"It means she wants to go around diggin' up dinosaur bones," Bo Cullen says. "She's already dug up half of Cullen's Creek!" All the girls laugh but for Roxanne, who smiles faintly.

"She might be weird, but her brother is cute!" Charmain Jannings says. "And so tall. Funny how a brother and sister can be so different."

Roxanne sighs. She's explained this to them a dozen times, at least. "Reece is so much smaller than the rest of her family 'cause she was born three months early. They didn't keep her in one of those incubator things long enough, so she quit growing for a while. Plus you've got to remember, she don't even turn fourteen 'til this Saturday."

Barrie, Helen and Charmain gasp. "Reece was born on Founder's Day?" They all look at Bo Cullen, who's fuming. "That girl'll do anything to get attention," she says, standing up, as the members of the contingent follow suit.

"Well, that doesn't explain that dirty dishrag face of hers," Charmain mutters as they file out of the cafeteria. Roxanne empties her tray and goes to find Reece.

She's hiding in the last stall of the girls' bathroom, crying for the third time that day. Usually Reece holds in her tears until late at night, after Dinah's gone to sleep, clutching to her chest her

father's little transistor radio (which he bought to listen to Cincinnati Reds games, and which his wife doesn't know he owns), letting out her daily frustrations on her pillow, then allowing herself
to be soothed to sleep by the warm molasses voices of Halo Truly
and Elvis Presley coming through the earpiece from what seems
like a million miles away. But today she can't hold it in—it's been
an unusually trying day, and it's only noon.

Roxanne jiggles the lock on the stall door. "Let me in." Reece
releases the hook and Roxanne pushes the door open. She bends
over and puts her arm around Reece's shoulders. Reece dabs her
cloudy eyes, then blows her nose on a square of toilet paper and
tosses it into the bowl.

"Roxanne," she says, sniffling, "can I watch Blackie Harmony
at your house next Sunday night?"

"Of course you can," her friend says, squeezing her arm, "if
your mom says it's okay."

Reece looks at her and Roxanne knows it never will be.

"Is that you've been wanting to ask me all day?" Roxanne asks.

Reece stands up and shakes her head. "It's not important," she
says, her eyes much clearer now. "Come on, we'll be late for class."
She leads Roxanne through the frosted-glass door of the restroom
and out into the hallway. There leaning against his locker is Mark
Isaac, in all his black-leather-jacketed glory, talking up the utterly
enraptured Bo Cullen. Reece wipes the back of her hand across her
eyes, which by now are dry but red and irritated, and she is aware
that everyone, especially Mark Isaac, will know she's been crying.

"Reece? Are you coming?" Roxanne asks, pulling her by the arm.

Reece bows her head as she slips past Mark Isaac, trying to
catch just one flash of a jacket zipper or a whiff of Bryl-Creem to
hold her over until tomorrow, and follows her friend through the
crowd to their next class. In the afternoon she goes through the
motions of math and history and science, trying to calm the tide
of conflicting thoughts roaring inside her head. Would Mark Isaac
like her better if she tossed her hair around like Bo Cullen? Would
he want to do to her what Bernie Joshua did to Dinah? Eww, she

hopes not. At least not yet. Does Mark Isaac even know she exists? Why does her own mother wish she doesn't exist? These are the thoughts that cause her, during a lecture on the Boston Tea Party, to throw her head down on her desk in misery. No one even notices. Soon she finds herself at Cullen's Creek and crossing the railroad tracks to her house without even remembering how she got there. Walking down the gravel path she expects to see her family's garments flapping on the clothesline in the back yard, as they do every Monday unless it's raining or snowing, in which case the clothes are hung throughout the house to dry. But today is sunny and warm, and the clothesline is empty. Then Reece sees a large truck in the driveway, with a bucket attached to a hydraulic arm in the back and what seems like miles and miles of cable wound around wooden spools. Her father comes around the side of the house with two men wearing blue uniforms and sagging tool belts. He shakes each of their hands as they climb up into the truck and roar out of the driveway, tooting their horn at Reece as they pass.

"Reece! Come here, m'dear!" her father says, throwing open his arms. She runs to him and he lifts her up, grunts and groans and little, and puts her back down on the ground.

"Who was that, Doodle?" she wants to know.

He takes her hand and leads her to the backyard. He points out a tall wooden pole with black wires stretching to the house.

"M'dear, the Dollars are now the proud owners of electricity."

Reece gasps and throws her arms around her father's neck, squeezing tight. She stops suddenly and drops her arms to her sides.

"What's wrong?" her father asks.

She feels herself starting to cry again and swallows it back. "If only we'd had—if you'd—"

"What, Reece?"

She sniffs and swallows again, harder. "All the girls at school—all they talked about was Halo Truly on The Blackie Harmony Show last night. And I—"

Her father puts an arm around her shoulder and wipes away the single tear that has escaped from her eye. "I'm sorry ya didn't get to see Halo," he says gently. "Maybe—"

"That Truly boy is nothing but poor white trash," her mother says, carrying a basket of wet clothes from the front of the house, where she's washed them with rainwater from the cistern. "She didn't miss anything special."

"Halo's family has electricity, at least," Reece says, hiding her face in her father's chest.

"You march upstairs to your room, young lady, and you stay there until you're ready to speak to me with respect," her mother says.

"Mother—"

"Asa, don't you go taking her side again. As for this electricity you've gone and put in without telling me, these new sockets in the walls do this family no good at all without anything to plug into them. And how do you expect to pay—"

"Now, Mother, I'm takin' care of all that." He winks at Reece. "Go on up to your room now, m'dear."

Reece goes into the house as her mother emits a *hrrumph* and turns to the clothesline. She watches through the screen as her father sneaks up behind her mother and grabs her waist, pulling her towards him. She wriggles free and sets the basket on the ground. She begins hanging up the clothes, oblivious to her husband. "I guess I'll go get washed up for supper," he says, turning away.

*

Reece has been lying face down on the bed for almost half an hour when her sister walks in and flops down next to her. "I saw you in the nurse's office today," Dinah says.

Reece props up on her elbows and tries surreptitiously to wipe the tear streaks from her face. "This morning?"

Dinah rolls over on her side. "Yeah. You looked like you was asleep, so I didn't say anything to you."

"*Were* asleep. And I was. Why were you there?"

"I felt like I was going to throw up," Dinah says. "I did, twice. But after I did I felt a lot better, so I only missed my first class. So why were *you* in there?"

Reece turns over and lies on her back, studying the brown stain in the corner of the ceiling where rain leaks in sometimes and dribbles down the newspaper on the walls, smearing advertisements for shiny refrigerator-freezers and long, flared skirts. "Same reason," she says, "but I didn't throw up."

"Maybe we caught a bug or something," Dinah says.

"Mmm," Reece says.

"But don't tell mom," Dinah says. "I don't want her to worry."

Reece nods her head in agreement. "Dinah?"

"Yeah?"

"Do you know who Mark Isaac is?"

"Sure, that greaser guy?"

"Well, yeah, I guess." Reece takes a deep breath. "Don't you think he sort of looks like Halo Truly? Except that Mark has dark hair?"

Dinah laughs. "I'd say Halo is a lot cuter than Mark Isaac." She jumps up off the bed and takes a school book from the stack on the dresser. She pulls out a sheet of paper from beneath its cover. "Look at this."

Reece takes the paper from her sister's hand. At the bottom of a torn-out page of photographs is a headshot of Halo Truly, his face twisted somewhere between a come-hither stare and a sneer.

"Dinah, where did you get this?"

"Found it in a yearbook in the school library today."

"You stole it?" Reece says.

"They'll never miss it," Dinah says. "Take it. It's yours."

"Dinah, I can't—"

"Take it, Reece. I bet Bo Cullen doesn't have one."

"Well—" She traces Halo's face with her finger. "Okay." She carefully slips the photo under her pillow. "Thanks."

Dinah shrugs and returns the school book to its place on the dresser. She turns to look at her little sister. "Do you want me to say something to Mark Isaac?"

Reece's eyes grow wide. "No!" she says.

Dinah laughs. "Okay, then. Maybe later."

Reece scoots to the side of the bed and throws her legs over until they touch the floor. "Dinah?" she asks, studying her long, sockless feet.

"Yeah?"

Reece exhales deeply. "What's wrong with me?"

Dinah sits down next to her sister. "What do you mean? Nothing's wrong with you."

Reece stands up and looks at her reflection in the scuffed, milky surface of the mirror. "Look at me!" she cries. "I have this ugly, dirty blonde hair and these pale gray-blue eyes that keep changing color and blending in with the rest of my face. I'm shorter than all the other girls in my class but my feet stick way out. It's not fair! You look like Audrey Hepburn and I look like—like—"

"You look like Grace Kelly," Dinah says, coming over to the mirror and putting her arm around her sister. "And think—she just married her prince. You will too, someday. I promise." When they hug, Reece detects the odor of another person on her sister's blouse, and she pulls away.

"Supper!" their mother's voice says from the kitchen below. They race each other down the stairs and sit down at the table in their usual seats.

"Slow down, girls!" their mother scolds.

Their father comes in and takes his place. "Where's Danny?" he asks.

"He started working for Baldy today. Against my wishes, as you know."

"I thought that was just in the mornin's, before school. Evenin's, too?"

Their mother takes off her apron and joins them at the table. "Yes, Asa. Even though I don't approve of him working for that man and that . . . *son* of his—" she says the word distastefully— "this is a good way for him to save some money for college. You certainly won't be able to provide the tuition, room and board."

"What for?" Dinah says, spooning mashed potatoes onto her plate. "He'll get him a basketball scholarship to someplace far away. He told me he was gonna use that money from working at Hilliard's to buy a car."

"He'll get him a car when I say he can," their father says.

Reece takes the bowl of potatoes from her sister. "Can I start earning some money for college?" she asks.

"There's no need for that," her mother sneers. "College is no place for a girl like you."

"But I want to be a—"

"That's enough!" her mother says.

"Mother—"

"Don't 'Mother' me, Asa. That girl doesn't have the sense to know what's good for her."

They all look to Reece for her reaction, which is to continue eating as if the conversation never took place.

"Reece, m'dear, if you want to earn a little spendin' cash, you can help me—"

"Asa, I said *no*. Now eat your supper, all of you."

The remainder of the meal is eaten in total silence, save for the clinking of forks against plates, until they're nearly finished and Danny whooshes through the door.

"Did you save me some, Mom?" he asks, taking his seat at the table. He spoons the rest of the potatoes and corn onto his plate as his mother gives him the chicken leg she's been keeping back for him.

"There you go, dear. How was your first day of work?" she asks.

"Thanks, Mom. Work was okay. I think Baldy's going easy on me the first few days."

"Mr. Hilliard, Daniel."

"Sorry, Mom. I didn't even see *Mr. Hilliard* today, except for a few minutes this morning. I'll be working mostly with Addison, feeding the animals, things like that."

Mrs. Dollar stands up abruptly and begins gathering up the empty bowls. "Give me your plates, girls, Asa. Daniel, you hurry and finish up so I can get these dishes done. Dinah, go get me two buckets of water."

The kids glance at each other with furrowed brows. "Give the boy two minutes to eat, Mother," their father says.

"I want to get this kitchen cleaned up," she says. "I'll just get the water myself." She takes two buckets and heads out to the well.

"What's wrong with her?" Danny asks.

"What's *ever* wrong with her?" Reece says.

"Reece!" their father snaps, then adds gently, "Be nice." He turns to Danny. "What's this I hear about ya spendin' your hard-earned money on a car? You've never driven anything but a tractor your whole life."

"Thanks, Dinah!" Danny says to his sister. "I suppose now I'll have to tell Mom how you and Reece were *both* in the nurse's office this morning."

"What's that all about?" their father asks.

"Nothing, Doodle," Reece says. "Just a stomach bug. You won't tell Mom? You either, Danny."

"Okay," they say, Danny more reluctantly, although the look in his father's eye convinces him to remain silent on this one.

Dinah stands up. "I'm going to my room to do homework," she announces, but no one pays attention, as she says this every evening after supper.

Danny stands up as well and says, "I'm going out to the barn," which means he's going to shoot baskets at the netless rim attached to the side of the old barn. No one pays attention, as he does this every evening after supper. He's done this ever since he was old enough to hold a basketball. He and Jonah would take turns hurling their under-inflated ball at the bent hoop after school, after their chores were done, and after supper well past the time that the evening light had faded and they couldn't even see the rim. Through the years, though, something began to happen: Danny became a better player than Jonah. Although at six foot two Jonah had the height for basketball, he just didn't have the hands. But he continued his nightly practices with

Danny, seeing in his little brother the vast potential that was there. Soon Danny was better than everyone on the junior varsity team, and at the beginning of his seventh grade year there were rumors that he would be named to the varsity team, the first underclassman ever to do so. By age twelve he was taller than most of the senior boys, and had been taller than Jonah was when he left. Now, at the beginning of his senior year, he is already a unanimous pick for the all-county and all-state teams, and a virtual shoo-in for the coveted "Mr. Basketball" title as the best high school basketball player in the state.

Asa stands up and says, "Reece, I'll get the lamp, you get the book." He says this every evening after supper, but only Reece pays attention. He takes the extra kerosene lamp from atop the pie safe, lights the wick, and carries it into the living room, where he sits down in his favorite easy chair. Reece takes a book of poetry, *The Collected Works of Chester Lee Reece*, from the mantel and squeezes into the chair next to him.

"What do we read tonight, m'dear?" he asks.

"You pick," Reece says. "He's your favorite."

"Yes, m'dear, that's why I named ya after him."

"At least you didn't name me Chester!" Reece giggles. They go through this routine every night.

"Okay, let's see," her father says, flipping through the pages. "How about this one?" He opens the book wide so the pages lay flat and begins reading in a low, hushed voice.

> *I never thought I'd see the day*
> *When everyone had gone away*
> *And all the streets were bare*
> *And there was no one standing there*
> *Except for one wee girl*
> *With the blondest hair in curls*
> *And the bluest of blue eyes*
> *Who looked at me, surprised*
> *To see another human face—*

Seems we're the last ones of our race.

But yet that day was here

And in my heart I felt the fear

Of living life alone

With no one to share my home.

Until the girl with the blue eyes

Much to my great surprise

Said she would be my wife,

Took my hand and changed my life.

When he's finished he closes the book and hands it to Reece. "Until tomorrow," he says. She replaces the book on the mantel. She doesn't really understand most of the poems her father reads, but she pretends to like them because he does. "Now it's off to work, m'dear. You're sure you're feelin' okay? No more stomach bug?"

"Yes, Doodle, I'm fine. Goodnight." She kisses him on the cheek.

"Goodnight, m'dear. I'll see ya in the mornin'." He goes into the kitchen to kiss his wife goodbye and Reece goes upstairs to her room, where Dinah is finishing up her homework. Danny soon follows, pulling down the collapsible stairs from the ceiling outside his sisters' room and climbing up to his room in the attic. "Hey, Danny," Dinah hollers before he pulls the stairs back up. "Did you know we have electricity now?"

"We do?" he asks. "Then what good are these new sockets in the walls without anything to plug into them?"

Dinah and Reece roll their eyes at each other and burst out laughing. Dinah extinguishes the kerosene lamp next to their bed. "Goodnight, Danny."

"Goodnight, Dinah. Goodnight, Reece." He pulls up the stairs.

"Goodnight, Danny," Reece says, but she knows he doesn't hear her. He's bouncing his ever-present basketball on floor above them, and soon the rhythmic thump . . . thump . . . thump lulls her to the edge of sleep. Just before she teeters over it, she tries to picture what Halo Truly is doing right that very instant. She imagines him standing in the center of an adoring crowd at a fancy cocktail party somewhere important like New York or Los Angeles or Indianapolis. He is wearing a silver lamé jacket, which she heard he wore on The Blackie Harmony Show last night, holding a martini glass in one hand and slicking his other hand through his wavy blond hair at regular intervals. The women there are beautiful and laugh at his jokes, whether they're funny or not, and the men are handsome and slap Halo on the back and plead with their eyes to let them be his new best friend, because that would be the next best thing to actually *being* him. In the background a single piano is softly playing the sort of music played at cocktail parties, until suddenly from out of nowhere the opening bars of "Love Me in the Morning" are heard and the room is charged with electricity. Halo Truly freezes for an instant, picks up the beat, then drains his martini and tosses the glass aside. He shrugs his shoulders once, twice, then starts to sing the first song he ever wrote and which today climbed to number nine on the American charts. When he finishes the entire room erupts with applause and congratulatory handshakes and complimentary drinks and offers from a number of the women to go upstairs with them. And all of this is happening to Halo Truly, according to Reece's last waking thought, because he left the town of Abandon the first chance he got and he never looked back. *Lucky*, she dreams.

*

Halo Truly and his hired band come off the cramped stage in Lexington and, without knocking, immediately enter the office of the club promoter and demand payment. They know if they don't walk out of this office with the cash in their hands they won't get paid at all, and their old Chevy is sitting on empty. He wishes he had a manager to do this dirty work for him, but he can't afford one just yet, and his record company won't spend the money. And as much as he hates Roger "Rog" Reynolds and Kick Freestone, and as much as they hate him, he's thankful to have the older men along to handle things like this. They have to settle for fifty dollars less than they originally agreed upon, but Halo is too tired to argue, even if he does have the number nine record on the American charts this week. They squeeze the guitar and snare drum into the trunk, strap the bass on top, fill up the Chevy at the gas station across the street, and drive two blocks to the motel. They have to share one room, which means Rog and Kick each take a bed and Halo sleeps on the floor between them. If he's lucky, one of them will at least give him a pillow. Before he closes his eyes Halo consults their itinerary, which he's folded and unfolded and refolded so many times that holes are forming in the creases, and sees that they're due to play at a high school auditorium in Nashville tomorrow night. He can't wait until Saturday, when he can finally go back home. He falls asleep with thoughts of blackberry pie with fresh cream, and the highest, fluffiest biscuits in the county, and the crispy fried chicken and fried potatoes his mother is sure to make for his homecoming, thoughts which cause such a rumbling in his stomach that in the dark Kick jerks Halo's pillow out from under his head and throws it at his face, and it's still there in the morning when he wakes up on the floor.

CHAPTER THREE:
1893—1932

Asa Dollar's mother and father, Arden and Leda Dollar, crossed the Ohio River from Kentucky to Indiana in the spring of 1893. Through the summer, until Arden built their little house by the railroad tracks, the two of them slept at night under a haven of trees through which the stars and moon shone, a hazy ring sometimes enveloping the lunar orb, portending a thunder shower. Leda didn't need to look at the moon to know when it would rain—she could smell it in the clouds two days before.

By her twenty-ninth birthday Leda had given birth to six healthy daughters: Anna, Betty, Connie, Dorothy, Edna and Fanny. After Connie was born Leda's husband stopped sleeping in their bed, disgusted by his wife's increasing girth and by the fact that she seemed capable of producing only girls, who were about as useful to him as a three-legged pair of pants. He returned only three more times, each after an evening spent imbibing hard liquor, to give her another chance to provide him with the son he thought he needed in order to live as he needed air in order to breathe. Soon after Fanny was born, Arden came into Leda's room one night, climbed on top of her and pushed himself into her so hard that the bed literally broke down and afterward she bled for nearly two days. When eight months later Leda gave birth to a boy Arden rode his horse up the hill that rose behind their little house, through the woods to the bluff overlooking the town and proclaimed at the top of his voice to all those who would listen that Arden Dollar had a son, a boy named Asa.

The boy was named after Arden's own father, who fought bravely and proudly in the Civil War, defending the great state of Kentucky and the even greater Confederate States of America, surviving the Battle of Gettysburg and returning home only to find his young wife dead of a smallpox epidemic that had exterminated practically the entire town. The elder Asa waited nearly ten years to marry again, and in 1871 his new wife gave birth to their only child, a son. Thirty-three years later Arden stood high above the town of Abandon, sorry that his father had not lived to see his only grandson—his namesake—and wishing that he had followed his instincts and gotten rough with the woman years ago: he could've saved himself a whole lot of trouble, had the boy already and been done with it all. Because he sure as hell was done with her now.

Asa's sisters had more of a hand in raising him than his own mother did. Every time she touched him or even looked at him she relived that night when the bed frame shook and collapsed and she thought she would bleed to death, and she would hand him off to one of her older daughters and go for a walk through the woods or along the railroad tracks. When Arden wasn't away looking for work, for an odd job to tide them over until he could find something more permanent, he would take the boy fishing or rabbit hunting, or teach him to plow a field or whittle a rough-edged whistle out of soft beech wood.

Then in 1917, when Arden was forty-six and Asa was thirteen, the call came through the county for men to sign up to go to France and fight the war to end all wars. So they went down to the recruiting station set up in the largest town for fifty miles, Broulet, a town in the next county over that was settled by the French in 1734. Everyone pronounced it *brew*-let instead of brew-*lay* because, after all, that was the way it was spelled. Before they walked in Arden told Asa to just go along with whatever he said, because it was their patriotic duty to serve their country like his grandpa did in the war between the states. So Arden told the recruiting officer that he was thirty-eight and the boy here was eighteen, but just then Erl Cullen V walked in and slapped Arden on the back and said in a loud voice *Dollar you old dog, you mean to tell me the army's gonna take an old man like you and a boy barely weaned off his mama's tit?* and the recruiter pointed the Dollars to the exit. Arden walked Asa home, his step a slow shuffle and his shoulders hunched over in a way his son had never seen before. The next morning Arden was gone and his family never saw him again.

Asa quit school soon afterward and got a job working for the town blacksmith, eventually learning to shoe a horse faster than anyone in Cullen County. One by one his sisters married and moved away, each seeking greater fortunes in various points west of the Mississippi, leaving Asa and his mother alone in a house which now was too big for just the two of them, and much too quiet since she wouldn't speak a word to her son. The day he turned eighteen he went back down to the Army recruiting office in Broulet, which they'd never bothered to shut down at the end of the first world war. They took him in the back and gave him a physical exam and when it was over the doctor marked a big black X on his chart and told Asa that he and his flat feet would never be a member of that or any man's army. That night he did what his father had done: he packed a bag and left the house an hour before dawn. He headed north to Indianapolis, where he heard there might be work making automobiles—every day those horseless carriages borrowed piece after piece of his shoeing business with no intention of ever giving it back.

In January 1932 Asa received a telegram from his sister Betty informing him that their mother had passed away a week before. Her dying wish was that her only son not be notified until she was already buried in a corner of the Abandon cemetery. Betty told him that the old house was his now because none of them—his sisters and brothers-in-law—wanted it. So he returned to Abandon with no more than what he left with ten years earlier and settled into the house his father built, and it was as if he had never left.

*

Rebekah Wündermann was the only child of Gunther and Hannah Wündermann, formerly of Beidenburg, Germany, just *süden* of the Danish border. Gunther believed zealously in the absolute rights of women, of the poor and the downtrodden. In his backyard workshop he tinkered with homemade mechanical contraptions that might someday permit him to fly to the moon, or London, or at the least to his neighbor's house across the road. As will happen with a man well ahead of his time, his ideas were not appreciated in his hometown, let alone in his native country. He wanted to go to America, for he was sure that in the United States, the land of opportunity and hope and freedoms unimaginable, all Americans would understand and admire him. He taught himself to speak English and, after selling off most of his belongings, earned enough money to book two passages to America on a ship departing Hamburg in April. His last order of business in Beidenburg was to ask the father of the woman he loved, Hannah Weiss, for her hand in marriage. He wore down the old man with a litany of complex, rational arguments which knew Mr. Weiss could barely comprehend, much less dispute. And so in 1900 twenty-five-year-old Gunther Wündermann married fifteen-year-old Hannah Weiss in a small ceremony in the Lutheran church attended by both of their families, and the next day the newlyweds boarded a ship to America.

Immediately upon arriving in the United States Gunther bought two train tickets to Pennsylvania, where he had heard many Germans were settling. Reaching the settlement, however, he was appalled by their old-fashioned views regarding everything from education to religion and decided his family would have no part in it. He inquired in the community as to where to procure a horseless carriage like that one he'd owned in Germany, so he could leave this place as soon as possible. When the laughter finally stopped one fellow told him about a gentleman in Indiana named Haynes who made a gasoline-powered automobile called the Pioneer. With his last few dollars Gunther bought two more train tickets, this time to a place called Kokomo, where the man Haynes was said to have lived, and set off to commune with men on his own intellectual level.

Gunther never was able to find the Haynes fellow, but he did buy himself a horseless carriage and even found a job in the factory that manufactured the cars. It was only a temporary position, he often told his wife, until he could find something more suitable to a man of his superior intellect. Hannah wanted to begin having children, but Gunther presented her with a number of birth control methods and devices that he had concocted himself, convincing her that they should not commence their family until he had attained a more suitable position. What Gunther failed to notice, however, because Hannah took great care to hide it from him, was that she indeed had become pregnant on four separate occasions, each time finding a way to terminate the pregnancy before her stomach began to swell, each time concealing any evidence such as sheets speckled with blood. When she became pregnant for the fifth time, though, she decided finally to stand up to her husband. She was, after all, twenty-one years old, and she had begun to learn to speak some English, although she spoke not nearly as well as Gunther, who had lost almost all traces of the accent of his homeland.

She carried the baby to term, careful not to gain too much weight to arouse her husband's suspicion. Their daughter Rebekah was born in February 1906, in the middle of a cruel winter storm. Due to the blizzard the town doctor could not reach the Wündermann's home until two days after the birth, just in time for him to watch Hannah bleed to death, the infant cradled in her arms. Upon examining the dead woman the doctor turned to the stupid German and berated him for not summoning him sooner, and for allowing his wife to give birth at all. Stunned, Gunther asked why.

Because she's scarred, the doctor sneered. *It's obvious she'd miscarried before, she's suffered terrible wounds. Some of them appear to have been self-inflicted. It's a wonder she survived two days.*

With the words *two days* still hanging in the air, the doctor pulled a large bottle of disinfectant from his bag, handed it to

Gunther, pushed his hat onto his head and trudged outside into the snow.

Gunther took his daughter from her mother's arms for the last time and set her on a pile of blankets near the wood stove in the kitchen. Using the disinfectant the doctor had given him he cleaned his wife's body, carried her outside wrapped in a sheet and buried her in a snow bank. Then with the remaining antiseptic he scrubbed every inch of the floor and walls and furniture inside the house. He wrote a letter to Mr. and Mrs. Weiss to inform them that their daughter had died as a result of giving birth to their granddaughter Rebekah. Then he packed one suitcase full of clothes and one suitcase full of books and papers, picked up his daughter from the kitchen floor, bundled her into the front seat of his automobile and drove out of the driveway in the tracks made by the doctor's carriage. He didn't stop until the car ran out of gasoline in a place called Muncie, which seemed to Gunther as good a place as any to raise a newborn, and that is where he decided they would live.

He found another factory job, this time making glass jars, and a neighbor lady watched Rebekah during the day while he was at work. This arrangement remained even after the girl reached school age, since at night Gunther educated her himself, teaching her all the things she would *need* to know to get by in the world, and not the things the teachers thought girls *ought* to know, which wasn't much because it seemed to him like all girls ended up doing anyway was get married and have a lot of children and die before they were thirty. But not his Rebekah. Her level of education and superior intellect would insure that she wouldn't *have* to get married and have children and die before she was thirty. Together they studied the great scientists; he taught her how to speak the language of his home country, although by now he considered America his home; and they read great literature, especially literature that civilized people weren't supposed to read because it was a bad influence on proper young ladies, like Dreiser's *Sister Carrie*. Gunther appreciated the fact that the author of such a scandalous tome was born in Indiana, even though he hadn't lived there for years. Between that book and the Haynes Pioneer, he was finally becoming impressed with Indiana, and was glad he left that restrictive and repressed place called Pennsylvania.

Rebekah was seventeen when Gunther arranged for her to attend the teacher's college in town, presenting her with the necessary tuition money in exchange for her promise to live at home instead of on campus. Upon earning her degree she wanted to teach mathematics at the high school or even at the college level, but was hastily informed by the college that arithmetic was not an appropriate area of study for women. Wouldn't she be more comfortable in the English Literature section? they suggested. Wouldn't she be more comfortable wearing long skirts on campus? Wouldn't she be more comfortable sitting in the back of the Latin class and keeping her mouth shut so that the men could learn without being humiliated? For four years she fought this and other injustices, such as the ridiculous sorority girls who buried any appearance of intelligence and used their affiliation to lure the equally ridiculous fraternity boys into the marriage trap. The few men who approached her were denied, deemed as minor distractions. She never danced the Charleston nor sipped bathtub gin.

Rebekah graduated in 1927 as a fully licensed teacher of English Literature. She was twenty-one years old, the same age her mother had been when she had died. Gunther drove them home from the ceremony in his brand-new Ford and told her to wait in the car, that he had a present for her in the house. When after a few minutes her father hadn't returned, Rebekah opened the front door to hear a loud popping sound. She rushed to her father's bedroom in the back of the house to find he'd shot himself in the head with his pistol, clutching in his hand a photo of his wife taken on their wedding day in Germany. She pulled the quilt up over his face and whispered her good-byes, knowing his life without Hannah had never been fulfilling, even as he attempted to fill that life by guiding and shaping her own education.

On the bed beside him she found a large stack of money, what she figured to be his entire life savings, and next to that a pile of what appeared to be various homemade birth control devices. She scooped up the money and the prophylactics and carried them to her own bedroom, where she put them in a suitcase along with her clothes and her college diploma, climbed into her father's new Ford and drove until she ran out of gasoline in a town called Abandon. She found the school and walked into the office and five minutes later Rebecca Wonderman had a teaching job.

Rebecca taught English literature and grammar at the school in Abandon for six years. The town had not advanced far beyond the one-room schoolhouse—all twelve grades were educated in the same building, although the classrooms were separated by grade and occasionally by subject.

Rebecca worked in Abandon but refused to live there. She felt that being seen by her students shopping for groceries at Joshua's general store or getting her hair done at the Klip 'n' Kurl undermined her authority. So she rented a bungalow along the river in Falling Star, just a few miles southeast of Abandon. Her landlord, Mr. Hoffman (she never knew his first name), only charged her ten dollars a month for a two-bedroom house with indoor plumbing and an exceptional view of the Ohio River and the green Kentucky shore. He mowed her grass in the summer, raked her leaves in the fall—piling them high at the edge of the yard and burning them in a black cloud of smoke that lingered for three days—and shoveled her snow in the winter. He re-shingled the roof and re-painted inside and out, all without being asked and without asking anything in return—until the night he knocked on her front door, the faint odor of cheap whiskey on his breath.

By Mr. Hoffman's account, and by that of most of the menfolk of Falling Star, Rebecca Wonderman was a fantastic specimen of womanhood—nearly six feet tall, with deep mahogany hair that she kept corralled in a suitable schoolteacher's bun at the nape of her neck and which half the men in town dreamed of unloosing in a fit of passion and wrapping around their naked bodies. And her legs! They were the longest, most *majestic* legs anyone ever hoped to see, floating there between the folds of her ankle-length skirts.

Sometimes as she stepped up into her '27 Ford the shape of her knee, like an apple ripe for plucking, strained against the fabric. Other times the hem of her skirt wafted up and there, above the top of a boot, a sliver of unstockinged flesh burst from its laces, implying that as the leg wished to be freed from its shackles, so did the woman. That night Mr. Hoffman decided he was the man who would set her free and charged up her steps.

Rebecca met him at the door and before he could speak grabbed his left arm and twisted it sharply until he was forced to turn around. Holding the arm behind his back, she marched him across the porch and down the steps and shoved him into the front seat of her Ford. It all happened so fast and Mr. Hoffman was so drunk that he went right along without a struggle. And when she drove to the little boat ramp just down the street, pulled right up to the edge and pushed Mr. Hoffman out of the car and into the water, he just whooped and hollered and rolled around in the mud for a while and said, "Miss Wonderman," (for he never knew her first name, either), "you are one hell of a woman. Whooo!"

The next morning he woke up on the river bank, his clothes damp and stiff and his throat drier than a haystack in winter. Despite his hangover he unstuck himself from the muck and walked a mile and a half to the general store, bought a whole sack of groceries, carried them to Rebecca's house and set them on the front porch where she'd find them when she got home from school. After that he continued to mow and rake and shovel and paint, just like before, except now he only charged her seven bucks a month rent instead of ten. And now every night at six o'clock when he'd go down to Patsy's Place like he always did, like all the men in town did when they got off work (although no one could figure out just what it was that Mr. Hoffman did, exactly, besides collect rent), the others would gather around him and make him tell the story again and again, of how he was the only man to nearly tame that amazing Wonderman woman.

One night a new man walked into Patsy's, a man they didn't know. He sat down on the other side of the room and ordered a

Coke, but after a few minutes Junior Wilcox motioned for him to come over and join them.

"What's yer name?" Junior asked the stranger as he borrowed an empty chair from a nearby table.

The man offered his hand to Junior. "Name's Asa Dollar. I just moved back down here from Inda'nap'lis. Got me a job over at the iron forge." The other men at the table nodded and murmured and slurped from dark bottles labeled root beer, but which Asa suspected correctly contained something more potent and illegal.

"You say you come back?" Mr. Hoffman said. "You from 'round here?"

"Hm mm," Asa said, having been caught mid-sip. "Got me a place over in Abandon. My dad built it. He's dead now, and my mom too. So I'm livin' there." He looked at the men seated across from him. "Ya fellas look familiar. Ya work at the forge, too?

The men nodded and continued their conversation. "Don't mind them," Junior said. "Takes 'em a while to warm up to strangers." He motioned toward the other men. "Rest of us, we all work at what used to be the distillery up river. We're making 'apple cider' now, but that's just 'til this whole mess blows over. Least that's what we tell the government. We all come here most nights after work." He took a long swallow of beer and set the bottle back on the table. "If the cops come, just follow us. Patsy's got a tunnel that'll lead us out. Don't worry, though—the cops never come here." He looked around at the men and they all laughed. "Patsy's husband was a cop," he told Asa. "Killed a couple years back in a shootout with a moonshiner. This was their place, his and Patsy's. Hers now."

Asa nodded again and finished his drink. "Let me get ya somethin' else," Junior said, gesturing to Patsy. "Hoffman here was just tellin' us for the forty-seventh time how he turned Miss Wonderman into the woman she is today." Everyone but Asa laughed; some banged the tabletop with their palms and fists. Patsy brought Asa one of the dark bottles and scowled, not unkindly, at the men.

"Who's Miss Wonderman?" Asa wanted to know.

"Well, I'll tell ya," Mr. Hoffman exclaimed, standing straight up and then leaning into Asa's face. Even with Asa sitting and Hoffman standing they came up to about the same level. "She's about the finest woman in Falling Star. Schoolteacher in Abandon, over there by you, I reckon. And let me tell you what that woman done!" He straightened up and strolled around the table, recounting his tale as if telling a ghost story to rapt boy scouts huddled around a campfire. "I'd just barely knocked on her door when she came out onto the front porch," Mr. Hoffman began.

"Tell 'em how much of that corn whiskey of yours you'd had that night," hollered Junior. The men erupted.

"A little," Hoffman said as the noise died down. "Then she wrapped her arms around me in a big ol' bearhug and lifted me a good three feet in the air, straight up." Asa frowned skeptically. "Oh no, it's true," Hoffman said, resting his hand on the back of Asa's chair before moving along again, continuing his circuit around the table. "And with my feet danglin' she carried me a good hunerd yards, down to the ol' boat ramp. You fellas know which one I'm talkin' 'bout?" The men all nodded, even Asa, who had happened to notice it on his way to Patsy's that evening. "I was cursin' and strugglin' and tryin' to get free of her, but that woman had her mind set 'bout what she was gonna do!"

"Don't they all, Hoffman?" Junior interjected, and again the men roared.

"Maybe yours does, Junior, 'cause you don't know how to handle her!" said one of the other men, whose name Asa didn't know.

"Hey, I know who wears the pants in my house, and believe me, they fit her just fine!" Junior said. The men doubled over in agonized laughter as Junior slapped Asa on the back. "You got you a woman?" he asked.

"Naw, not yet," Asa said.

"Damn lucky, you are!" Junior said.

"So like I was sayin'," Hoffman continued, "she lifted me up over her head and threw me into the river! Threw me 'bout five foot in and left me there to sink or swim, ain't that what they say? Can't remember much after that, 'cept wakin' up on the river bank, soakin' wet." He made his way back to his seat, sat down, and with the back of his hand wiped a line of sweat from beneath the band of his cap, even though it was February. "Whew, I am in love with that woman!"

"You're in *lust*, that's what it is!" Junior said. "Don't you think, Asa?"

"I—I wouldn't know," he said. "Ya say this woman rents a place from ya?" he asked Mr. Hoffman.

"Yep. She lives right next door to me on Church Street. In fact, the Catholic church's on the other side of me. It's bad enough they let their bingo games and Monte Carlo nights and fish fries or whatever the hell it is they do over there go on 'til all hours of the mornin', then come strollin' in the next day all pleased with themselves, like it's okay what they done the night before as long as they make up for it today, but then they go and get the town to rename the street just so them folks can be sure to find their way back in the mornin'—" Asa stood up as Mr. Hoffman continued to rail against his neighbors and slipped out of the place before anyone noticed he was gone. He stepped into his car and drove directly to Church Street, remembering having seen the Catholic church earlier that night. He passed it at the corner of First Street and stopped the car in front of the second house down. A yellow light shone through the front window, but the porch was dark. A 1927 Ford filled the driveway.

Asa cut the engine and walked up onto the darkened porch. Before he had a chance to knock the porch light came on and the door opened, and he found himself staring down at the most stunning woman he had ever seen. For once the exaggerated stories of a drunken man in a bar were no exaggeration. But while this woman was even more beautiful than he had imagined, she was not quite as tall as he had thought she would be. At six feet four Asa could see the top of her mahogany hair.

Usually when he tried to speak to women he fumbled for the right thing to say, and it came out sounding like two squeaky gears grinding against each other. But this time he looked directly into the woman's amber eyes and said, "I've come to meet the incredible woman who threw that Hoffman fella in the river." He extended his hand as if offering to shake. She stared at him for a moment before seizing his hand with both of hers and attempting to twist his arm behind his back. He grabbed her forearm with his free hand and twisted until she was completely turned around, her back to him.

"Is that what ya were tryin' to do?" he whispered into her ear, still grasping her wrist. She didn't answer but he noticed the pace of her breathing had quickened. He reached his right arm around her waist and said into her neck, "My name's Asa, Miss Wonderman. What's yours?"

She gripped his fingers with her free hand and said in a low voice, "Rebecca."

Asa chuckled. "I didn't think ya had a first name. No one in town seems to know it."

She turned around to face him, letting him put both of his arms around her. "No one ever asked."

CHAPTER FOUR:
SEPTEMBER 10, 1957

Reece is jolted awake by the deep, prolonged blast of a locomotive's horn. Ordinarily she sleeps right through the low rumbles and clacking wheels; thirteen, almost fourteen years of living next to the railroad tracks have made her oblivious to the sound. But this sound—cutting through the thick silvery dawn in that precarious moment when the sun readies itself for the coming day, balancing just below the horizon, waiting impatiently to push the stars and the moon up and over the arc of the sky into the still blackness of the other side of the world—this sound is new, unfamiliar, and scares Reece nearly out of bed. Just before she was awakened, she had dreamed her only dream of the night, or at least the only dream she could remember, that she was walking home from school with Mark Isaac, his arm slung casually around her shoulders, and she tried to act just as casual even though her insides tingled and were tangled. As they crossed the bridge over Cullen's Creek a lumbering locomotive rounded the bend and came toward them at a hundred miles an hour, going too fast, too fast, too fast. She tried to scream but could only whisper. Mark Isaac scrambled up the short incline that led to the tracks and stood there between the ties, arms held up, palms forward, entreating the train to stop. As it came within a few feet of the boy suddenly he wasn't Mark Isaac anymore but Jonah, who turned his head to look at his sister as the engineer pulled down on the horn and the blast jolted Reece awake, and it was as if her subconscious knew the real-life train was coming and designed a custom-made dream just for that circumstance, timing the two train whistles in perfect synchronicity, knowing the whistle would cause her to wake up with a pounding heart and sweaty palms from a dream that seemed to go on forever although it probably lasted only a few seconds.

Reece lies on her back and fans herself with the sheet. She realizes then that Dinah is gone. She reaches across Dinah's empty place and feels around on the nightstand. She picks up the old watch their father gave them to use as a clock and squints in the dawn until she can make out the hands. It's still an hour before they have to be up for school. As the roaring train recedes she hears a sound by the bedroom window. Peering in that direction, allowing her eyes to adjust to the light, she sees Dinah slumped on the floor, her head thrust out the window, vomiting down the side of the house and onto their father's wild roses.

Dinah feels her sister's stare and turns toward her, wiping her mouth with the hem of her nightgown. "Don't tell mom, okay?"

Reece nods and slips back under the covers. She hears Danny unfurl the stairs that lead to and from his attic room, climb down slowly, fold up the steps, and tiptoe downstairs. Their mother is already in the kitchen fixing his breakfast. In a few minutes Dinah joins her in their bed and they spend the next hour feigning sleep, each one knowing the other one is awake. Eventually they rise, brush their teeth with water from the bowl and pitcher, and dress. Dinah takes the remaining water in the pitcher and pours it out the window and over the roses, rinsing away whatever the birds haven't already picked clean.

"Remember, Reece, don't tell."

"I said I won't."

Downstairs their mother is seated at the kitchen table, working the crossword puzzle in last Friday's newspaper. When their father gets off work each morning he picks up the previous day's paper from the table in the break room and brings it home. The news is always old, but better than no news at all, Asa figures. His wife always waits until the following morning to do the crossword, so she can immediately look up the ones she missed when he brings her the next edition. But she never misses a single clue—all the squares are always filled in neatly and correctly, and she never bothers to double-check her answers.

She's already set out their breakfast plates—fried sausage and biscuits, both cold, since they've been sitting out since Danny ate his breakfast more than an hour earlier. Dinah moves the food around on her plate and covers her mouth with her hand. Reece makes a sandwich from the meat and bread on her plate and swallows it in three bites. She races toward the door with Dinah right behind her. "Bye, mom," they call out.

With a quick, steady hand their mother pulls Dinah back by her skirt. "You girls get back here," she snarls. "You know you are not permitted to leave this house until your father gets home." The girls shuffle back to the table. Reece surreptitiously swaps her empty plate with Dinah's full one and eats her sister's breakfast before their mother notices.

Mrs. Dollar finishes the crossword, folds the paper neatly and goes to the window. She checks her watch, then walks outside and listens for the sound of his car, of tires crunching along the gravel path. The family car is just another in a series of embarrassments to the Dollar children, a black, no-nonsense, '47 Ford when everyone else in town drives sleek, fin-tailed, pastel-colored coupes. Reece had heard that Halo Truly bought his mama a pink Cadillac like Elvis did, but she couldn't imagine it.

Their mother returns to the kitchen and finds the girls gone. She stumbles toward the table. "Girls?" she calls out, weaker now. "Dinah? Reece?" She sits down and holds her head in her hands. "Girls?" she says again as they bounce down the stairs.

"What, mom?" Dinah asks.

Their mother explodes. "Don't ever do that again!" she screams. "You stay in this kitchen until your father gets home!" Trembling, she rises and gathers the breakfast plates. "Reece, go get me some water so I can wash these dishes."

"But you said to—"

"Do it, young lady!" She slams the plates down on the table. Reece takes the bucket and heads out to the well.

"Where *is* dad?" Dinah murmurs.

Her mother sits down again and exhales hard. "I don't know." Walking to the well, swinging the empty bucket beside her, Reece can remember what the mornings were like before she and Dinah entered school, when their father still worked the day shift at the iron forge. After he had left for work and Jonah and Danny had left for school, their mother would lock all the windows and pull down the cheap paper shades so that it was nearly too dark to see in the house, then drag the pie safe across the door as a barrier. She would make the children sit at the kitchen table and snap beans or shell peas or stir cake batter or knead bread dough as she paced the floor. Sometimes she would move the shade aside with one finger, her alert eyes scanning up the hill and across the railroad tracks and down into the basin and back again, as if she were waiting for something to happen. At these times she became oblivious to her children, even as they begged for her attention by calling out to her and pulling on her skirt. Finally Dinah would hold Reece in a headlock and drag her to the floor as Reece, crying the entire time, struggled to free herself from Dinah's grasp. Hearing the ruckus their mother would snap out of it and pull Reece away from her sister and say "Stop that fighting, ladies," to which Dinah would reply, "We're not fighting, we're wrasslin'!" and their mother would say, "I don't care what you call it, I'll have none of that in this house. Reece, you leave your sister alone," and plop them both back down in their seats at the table, where they would sit quietly for a while until Dinah began punching Reece in the arm when their mother wasn't looking. Sometimes they would try to sneak upstairs to their room, but their mother would chase after them and drag them back down by the arms and whop Reece on the butt and make her read whole books of the Bible as punishment, while Dinah received a mild rebuke. And if they had to go to the bathroom, and swore they couldn't wait any longer, Mrs. Dollar would drag the pie safe away from the door and take her husband's shotgun from behind the stove and make the children run as fast as they could to the outhouse where she would stand guard, holding the gun on point until they were finished, then they would all run back to the house and she would lock the door, drag the pie safe back over the peeling linoleum and replace the gun. Then in the afternoon, just before everyone returned home, she would put the pie safe back in its place in the corner and raise the shades and everything would seem perfectly normal again. Those were just the times Reece could remember; she wasn't sure what it was like when they were babies, but it was probably much of the same.

It finally came to an end late one morning just before lunch, only because their father wasn't feeling well and came home early. When at last he was able to enter the house, after their mother had moved the pie safe away from the door, he demanded of the children what was going on. Dinah told him they were just playing a game, that was all, just as their mother told her to say, but Reece told him the truth, that it was like that every day. When Jonah and Danny got home he asked them as well, and Jonah said no, she'd never acted that way as far as he knew, but Danny said sure, he could remember mom doing stuff like that ever since Reece was born, but he never thought too much about it. Their mother never said a word, never offered any explanation, even though their father asked her about it almost every day.

Very soon after his discovery their father started working the night shift, allowing him to be home with his wife during the day. It actually worked out better for the family, since the night shift paid a bit more, but it wreaked havoc on their father's body, as he tried to learn to sleep during the day, so that even on weekends he had to stay up all night, usually reading the poetry of Chester Lee Reece by candlelight.

The water bucket is nearly full when Reece hears her father's car pull up in the driveway. "Reece!" he calls to her. "Come over here and help your ol' Doodle." He takes a large cardboard box from the backseat and sets it on the ground. "What is it, Doodle?" she asks, running up beside him. "You'll see, m'dear." They each lift one end of the box and carry it toward the house.

"Shouldn't you be in school now?" he asks Reece as they approach the door.

"Yeah," she says. "But mom wouldn't let us leave until you got home." Her father frowns and starts to say something when her mother meets them in the yard.

"Asa, what in the—"

"Mother, now we can put all that new electricity to good use. Reece, you get the door." She holds it open while he carries the box through the kitchen into the living room and sets it down in the middle of the floor. Using his pocket knife he slits open the top and pulls out a black and white television set.

Reece wants to shout and throw her arms around her father's neck, but her mother's reaction prohibits it. "Asa, how in heaven's name could you do such a foolish thing?" she roars, standing there over the box, fists on hips. "There are so many other things we need, like a refrigerator, or light fixtures. What were you thinking?"

"Now Mother, there'll be plenty of time to get those things," he tells her, assembling a t.v. tray with thin, gold metal legs and a gaudy landscape scene on top, setting the television on it and plugging it in.

"Girls, go on to school now," Mrs. Dollar says quietly, barely moving her taut lips.

"But we're late. We'll need a note," Reece says.

"Just go!" their mother shouts.

They scramble outside and decide to take the shortcut through the woods. When Reece reaches the giant poplar, the tree her brother Jonah told her guarded the princess's castle, she closes her eyes. After stumbling along for a few steps she trips on a branch and lands face down on the dirt path. "Come on, Reece," Dinah says, exasperated, pulling her sister up by the elbow. As they walk she helps Reece brush dead leaves and grass from her dress.

They emerge from the woods onto the bluff overlooking the town and stop for a moment to catch their breath before descending the steep, rocky bank. "Do you think mom'll let us keep the t.v.?" Reece asks.

Dinah snorts and shakes her head. "Of course not," she says. "When does mom *not* get her way?"

Reece considers this, but can't think of a single instance. "I hope we at least get to watch it tonight," she says. "What's on Tuesday nights, anyway?"

"I don't know," Dinah says, beginning to climb down the hill. "There's Erl Cullen," she shouts up to Reece. "We can ask him."

At the bottom they fall in step behind Erl Cullen VIII, who'd taken the long way around. "Hey Erl, you late for school too?" Dinah hollers in his ear. He twitches with surprise and whirls around. When he sees Reece there, red splotches dot his neck like countries on a relief map.

"Um, yeah," he squeaks. "Hi Reece."

She walks alongside him as Dinah follows. "Hi Erl. Listen, you know what's on t.v. tonight?"

"Why?" he asks. "You guys don't have a t.v."

"Yeah we do," Reece says. "My dad just brought it home this morning, and we're gonna watch it tonight. What's good?"

"Well, on Tuesday nights we usually watch *Wyatt Earp*. It's pretty neat." He notices the brown stains on her dress. "What happened to you?"

"Daydreaming again," Dinah interjects. "Thinking 'bout some dinosaur sitting on a big rock somewhere in Africa and tripped over her own feet."

Reece glares at her sister. "At least I'm not lifting my skirt with a boy like Bernie Joshua," she blurts out.

Erl's embarrassment spreads to his face which instantly becomes as mottled as his neck. Dinah's face catches fire with rage. "You little sneak!" she screams.

"I'm gonna tell mom what you've been doing," Reece says.

"No you're not, damn you." Dinah reaches for Reece's neck but she slips away and takes off, running full speed down the sidewalk.

"Oh, and I'm gonna tell her what you just said," Reece shouts with glee over her shoulder.

Dinah pushes Erl into the street and begins chasing her sister. Just in front of the school steps she has to stop, doubled over with a stomach cramp. Erl finally catches up with her, but Reece is long gone inside the building, its weighty, ornate door closed behind her with a ponderous, echoing boom.

"Dinah?" he says in a hushed voice.

She gasps, then answers, "*What?*"

Erl fumbles in his pants pocket, then pulls out a wadded piece of paper. "Can you—will you give this to Reece?" The red wave of embarrassment has now flooded his ears, and his hand trembles as he passes the note to Dinah.

The look she gives him could bring down the brick walls of the school. He mumbles *thanks* and rushes inside. She smirks and starts to throw the note on the ground, then opens it up and reads it. Her smirk becomes a full belly laugh as she stuffs the paper into her history book.

*

"It'll be okay," Reece assures Roxanne as they follow the gravel path to the Dollar's house after school. She points to the base of the hill in the distance. "See, she's in the garden. She'll never know you were here."

Roxanne shrugs. "Maybe," she agrees as they turn into the driveway. She stops and takes Reece by the arm. "Hey, your mom's out here by herself. I thought she didn't go outside alone."

Reece squints at her mother's form bent over a row of potatoes and sees the shotgun propped against a nearby tree. "She's not alone," she mutters. They continue walking until they reach the house, where inside they find Mr. Dollar, Dinah, Bernie Joshua, and Erl Cullen VIII gathered around the television set. Dinah is standing with her hands on her hips, looking completely disgusted; Bernie is jiggling the mass of black wires protruding from the back of the t.v.; Erl is beating its top with the side of his fist; Mr. Dollar is stomping various spots on the floor, as if squashing a bug. After each stomp he looks up at the screen, sees no change in the gray squiggles snaking across it, shakes his head, makes a noise not quite human, studies the floor with deep concentration and stomps again.

"Doodle, what's wrong?" Reece cries, her face twisted in near-horror, her voice higher-pitched than usual.

Bernie looks up, a bouquet of wires in his hand. "I tried to tell your dad that without an antenna he's not gonna get a good pitcher, but he won't listen."

"*Picture*, Bernie," Reece says, exasperated. "Doodle, can you fix it?" She's frantic now, near hysteria.

"Al . . . most . . . got . . . it," he grunts, preparing for the *coup d'stomp*. "Everybody get back." He raises his foot and plants it with such force that the windows rattle, the walls shake, plaster flakes from the ceiling, a shell-shocked mouse scurries across the length of the baseboard into a tiny hole in the corner, and the television teeters on its makeshift stand, nearly falling off before rocking back into place. They stare at the screen, edgy with anticipation. The gray squiggles straighten into horizontal lines, begin to fade and rise to the top like a windowshade being lifted. The strained face of Blackie Harmony, the tri-state area's favorite, and only, afternoon talk show/dance party host, appears on the screen like a heavenly apparition.

"Yea!" they cheer in unison. Reece hugs her father. Dinah links her arm in Bernie's, then remembering herself, steps away from him. Erl moves over to stand by Reece as she's disengaging herself from her father's grasp. She looks down at him. He's the only person in her class she literally can look down upon. "What are you doing here?" she asks, not unkindly, but not interested either.

He points to Dinah. "She invited me." Reece's questioning stare is met by Dinah's smirk. "She said you liked my note," Erl continues.

"What no—"

"Erl Cullen, don't you have to be getting home?" Dinah interrupts, whisking him into the kitchen. She whispers in his ear and pushes him out the door. She turns around and finds Bernie standing behind her. He pulls her aside so that they can't be seen from the living room. He puts his arms around her waist. "I better be goin', too," he whispers. "'Cause I can't stand bein' 'round you tryin' to act like we aren't—"

She cuts him off with a peck on the lips and shoves him toward the door. "You better hurry before my mom comes in," she tells him.

He tries to hold her eyes with his, but she won't cooperate. "Come on, Roxanne," he calls.

"Bye, Reece. Bye, Mr. Dollar." Roxanne passes by Dinah, studying her from eyebrows to ankles. "Bye, *Di-nah*," she sings, then hurries out the door to catch up to her brother. Dinah runs upstairs to her bedroom window to watch Bernie walk home.

Squatting down in front of the television, Reece and her father peruse the snowy channels—he turning the knob number by number, round and round, she yelling *Stop!* or *Go!* or *Yes!* or *No!*—not realizing for a while that they're seeing the same few stations over and over. With every revolution each one is less visible than the last, and no amount of stomping seems to correct the problem. Only Blackie Harmony's show comes in clearly, so they settle on that. Reece's father eventually relaxes in his easy chair; she climbs up next to him and they sit completely silent for the next half-hour, watching the images in front of them in light and dark shades of gray and white. Their reverie is finally broken by Reece's mother, who sets on the kitchen table a large tub of potatoes, freshly washed at the well, and returns the shotgun to its place behind the stove. In the living room she finds her husband and her younger daughter asleep in the chair. She snaps off the monstrous box and they awaken simultaneously.

"Mom, we were watching that," Reece whines.

"Turn it back on, Mother," her father says.

"Look at the two of you, lying around in the middle of the day like sloths. Asa, I made quite a mess out there in the garden and I need you to go clean it up. Young lady, you come out here and help me peel these potatoes. I swear you give me more trouble than all of my children put together. You have ever since the day you were born, when I told Dr. Riley to put an end to my child-bearing misery."

Reece's father helps her out of the chair and steers her toward the kitchen. "You help your mom now, m'dear," he murmurs into the top of her head. He takes his cap from atop the pie safe and fits it over his flat-top as he goes out the door, letting it slam hard. Her mother has to light one of the oil lanterns so they can see not to slice off a finger in the peeling process, which is hindered even more by the near-rotten state of the potatoes that were left in the ground too long. The sky has darkened considerably in the last few minutes, and the rusty windmill that guards the old barn creaks and spins in every direction, trying to keep up with the spontaneous, whirling gale. Raindrops that look to Reece like giant gobs of spit hurled by the adolescent boys in her class slam against the windows, drawn out at first, then more and more frequently until a full-fledged rainstorm is in progress. Reece puts down her peeling knife and peers out the window, trying to glimpse her father. A brilliant stroke of lightning shoots down from the black sky in a halo of white and strikes the old windmill. Reece watches it topple in slow motion, crashing against the side of the barn in a junk heap. "Mom—" she starts to say, but is drowned out by an explosion of thunder, a reverberating sonic boom that makes her heart quiver inside her ribcage, and she feels the undulating waves of sound rumble through the ground, up through the floor into her feet and legs and body until she can barely breathe. Just then she sees her father, bracing against the storm, making his way to the house. He rushes through the door and shakes off the wet like a frightened pup.

"Lost the windmill," he says, removing his soaked shirt and holding it near the warm stove.

"I saw it, Doodle. Lightning hit it."

"You saw it? Why didn't you say anything?" her mother demands.

"I tried—" Another thunder crash interrupts her yet again.

"Go upstairs. I'll call you when supper's ready."

Climbing the stairs she hears her father unbuckle his belt and take off his pants to dry them. Her mother's voice drops. "Daniel . . . do you think he's okay? He's out there on his bicycle some-where . . ."

"Now Mother, Baldy wouldn't let him ride in this. I'm sure he's fine."

Danny! Reece is ashamed that she'd forgotten all about him, and hopes he makes it home all right. She opens the bedroom door and finds Dinah lying on the bed in only her slip, her hands gripping her stomach, grimacing in agony.

She quickly shuts the door behind her so their mother won't see. "Dinah, what's the matter?" She sits on the edge of the bed, one arm wrapped around her sister. A flash of lightning illuminates her pale, drawn face, and the rain is coming down even harder now, pounding the roof like a million angry fists.

"My . . . stomach."

"Are you going to throw up again?"

Dinah shakes her head. "No. It's like . . . like a stabbing pa— Ow!"

Reece stands up, worried. "Listen, Dinah, I'm gonna have to tell—"

"No!" Dinah tries to sit up but is forced back down. "Reece . . ."

Reece bends over, putting her face near Dinah's.

"I need to go to the outhouse, but I can't . . ."

"Tell me what to do," Reece says. The house sways in a sudden gust of wind. Dinah cries out in distress.

"Get a . . . bucket."

"Dinah, Mom'll see me—"

"Reece . . . please."

Reece sighs. "Okay." She takes her raincoat from the closet and formulates a plan of diversion on the way downstairs. Fortunately her father is trying to distract her mother from thinking about Danny by showing her, wearing only his underwear, the many features of the new television. Reece sneaks around the table, grabs the empty potato tub and the roll of paper towels from beside the propane stove and races back upstairs. She helps Dinah lift up her slip and squat over the tub, and when she's finished she helps ease her back onto the bed. "Better," Dinah breathes.

"Dinah, what am I supposed to do with this?" Reece asks, wrinkling her nose and trying to hold her breath.

"Oh . . . out the window . . . I guess . . ." She's drifting off to sleep.

Sure, Reece thinks, forcing the window open. *The wild roses could use more fertilizer, on top of what you gave them this morning.* Blasted by sheets of stinging rain, she dumps the contents of the tub and notices blood. A lot of blood. She slams the window shut and hides the bucket in the closet—she'll wash it out later.

"Dinah?"

"Mmm?"

"Are you okay?"

"Mmm . . . feel better . . ."

"Dinah, do you know you're bleeding?"

Dinah's eyes flash open. Tears pour out as fast as the rain falls from the sky outside.

"I think you need to see Dr. Riley."

Dinah nods and lets her baby sister hold her in her arms. "You . . . can't tell Mom," she rasps.

"Dinah, I—"

"Please, Reece. Will you go with me tomorrow?"

In her mind Reece tries to sort out the scattered pieces of this mystery, some of which she can't comprehend, yet somehow inherently understands. "Yeah, I'll go with you," she whispers. "Now you lay down and try to sleep."

"Girls, supper," their mother calls.

Dinah grips Reece's arm. "I can't go down there. You have to tell her something. Make something up."

Reece stands and opens the bedroom door. "Don't worry." She hears a train coming in the distance. She thinks nothing of it at first, but as she descends the stairs she realizes it isn't time for a train. She knows the rail schedule like she knows her own name. And this train is moving much too fast. She looks at her father, who's trying in vain to hide the fear in his eyes.

"Reece, where's your sis—" Her mother is interrupted by the kitchen window blowing apart, spraying tiny glass shards into the creamed corn.

"Get down!" her father shouts over the din, the roar growing louder and louder by the second. He pulls his wife and daughter under the table, shielding each one under an arm, for what feels like a day and a night. Reece desperately wants to look out the window, to watch nature at work, to glimpse a real funnel cloud, but her father's grip is unbreakable. She sends a mental message to Dinah to hold on, hoping she's sleeping through it all. Reece shuts her eyes so tight they feel as if they're turning inside out. She hears her mother mouthing a prayer, she assumes, of deliverance. The house shudders and sways and Reece is sure she can feel the roof closing in on them. At that moment all she can think of is, *Good thing Doodle put his clothes back on before the storm hit. How awful to be found dead under the rubble that was your house wearing nothing but your underwear.* Reece considers these thoughts bizarre and inappropriate, but lost in them, she's distracted until she realizes, as fast as it began that it's over, just like that. The room is quiet, and the rain and wind have stopped. An occasional lightning bolt streaks through the sky far away, which is becoming lighter despite the onset of dusk.

The three Dollars emerge from under the table. "Well, my supper is ruined," Mrs. Dollar says, stirring the creamed corn, then dumping it in the trash can.

"Forget about supper for tonight, Mother," Mr. Dollar says. "Let's take a walk and look for damage until Danny comes home. Reece m'dear, go check on your sister."

But Reece is already halfway up the stairs, and is relieved to find her wish has come true—Dinah slept through the whole thing. She covers her sister with the quilt and takes the soiled tub from the closet, using this opportunity to wash it out at the well while her parents are on their reconnaissance mission at the back part of the property.

An hour later, with the homestead surveyed and only minor damage found, the Dollars hear a vehicle pull into the driveway. In the fading light they see Archibald Hilliard and his son Addison drive up in their old farm truck, with Danny squashed between them in the front and his bicycle in the back.

As soon as he's able to climb out Mrs. Dollar clasps Danny to her and whisks him into the house, muttering to him in loving tones and smoothing his damp hair. Mr. Dollar walks around to the driver's side and shakes Hilliard's hand.

"Baldy. How 'bout that? A tornado this late in the season. Thanks for bringin' the boy home."

"Asa. It weren't no problem." From where he stands he inspects the Dollar's property. "Looks like you survived pretty good. Made out better'n we did." He puts his arm around Addison's shoulders as he comes to stand next to his father.

"Aw no, Baldy. Ya lost everythin'?"

The two Hilliards nod their heads in unison. "Just 'bout. House is pretty much flat, but the truck made out alright. We'd picked 'bout half the corn, but the rest is prob'ly in Kentucky by now."

"I'm sure sorry to hear that, Baldy," Asa says.

"Thank ya. Saved the barn though, and the animals. You know that blasted storm cellar Sarah made us build that one spring? It's the only reason we're here talkin' to ya now. Me and Addison and Danny got down in there just in time—could hear everythin' blowin' 'round up above us. Then it got real quiet all of a sudden, and we figured it was over, so we come up and seen—" Emotion overcomes him and he can't continue. They stand in heavy silence for a minute or so until finally Asa says, "You got you any insurance over there?"

Baldy nods. "A little. Prob'ly not enough to get back to the way we was, though." He begins to compose himself and flushes a little, embarrassed. "We'll be all right," he proclaims, lifting his head and squeezing Addison to him. "Right, son?"

"Yeah pa."

"Yeah. Well, we best be gettin' on." The Hilliards release their grip on each other and get back in the truck. Mr. Dollar starts to walk back to the house, then stops and turns around.

"Ya got a place to stay tonight, Baldy?"

Baldy revs the engine and flips on the headlights. "Thought we'd stay at my sister's for a day or two. That's where we're headed right now."

"Where's your sister live?"

"Oh, 'bout seventy miles from here."

"Seventy miles! That's too far to drive. You two stay here tonight, and in the morning me and Danny'll help ya get your place cleaned up. I've got to go to work here pretty soon, but Mother'll help ya get settled in."

Baldy shuts down the engine and kills the headlights. He and Addison get out of the truck and follow Asa into the house.

"Mother!" Asa calls. She comes into the kitchen carrying her bible, which she and Danny had been reading in the living room by lamp light. Rebecca has devoted the last few years of her life teaching Danny which parts of the book are true and which, in her experience, have been proven utterly ridiculous, implausible and untrue. That which she formerly took as the ultimate gospel she now approaches merely as a work of literature. "Baldy and Addison're gonna stay here tonight. They lost the house in the storm. I told 'em ya'd help 'em get settled in."

The squeaking sound of her fingers squeezing the imitation leather cover fills the room. "But Asa, where in the world will they sleep?" she asks, calmly, commandingly.

"Well, I suppose the couch, Mother. It's just for one night."

Baldy interjects. "If it's a problem, we can stay with my sister—"

"Yes, that would be a fine idea," Rebecca says.

"You're stayin' here Baldy, end of story," Asa says. "Now I need to get goin' to work; I've just got to say goodnight to my girls first." He starts upstairs, then adds in a stage whisper, "Don't ya worry 'bout Mother. Ya know that she likes to act all rough and tough, but she *loves* it when I act rough right back to her." He exaggerates a wink. "She's all bark and no bite, ain't that what they say?" The three of them laugh. Asa, still chuckling, looks at Rebecca. "Mother, you'll get the extra blanket?"

She slams the thick bible down on the kitchen table but can't bring herself to follow her husband upstairs.

"Bal—Mr. Hilliard, Addison. Come in here and see our new t.v.," Danny says to them from the living room. Baldy walks into the next room but Addison stays behind. He moves next to her and whispers in her ear, "How come you never invite me over anymore?"

Rebecca bristles. "I have never invited you into this home, and I never will," she seethes.

"Well, that's not how I remember it," Addison continues, his breath heavy with chewing tobacco. "It's been a long time—"

"I don't know what you're talking about," Rebecca says, her voice tight and small.

"Addison, come on," Danny says.

"Go on," Rebecca says, slipping away from Addison and upstairs to get the blanket.

Already upstairs, Asa knocks on Reece and Dinah's door. Dinah's asleep, but Reece is sitting on the bed, doing homework. He sits down beside her. "Sorry m'dear, no poems tonight. Kind of an unusual night, it was."

Reece nods her head. "It's okay."

He squeezes her against him. "Listen, Mr. Hilliard and Addison are stayin' here tonight. Their house got blowed down in the storm."

"*Blown* down, Doodle."

"Aw right, got *blown* down. So you be nice to them, okay? You and your sister be on your best behavior."

Reece sighs. "We will."

"I know ya will. Goodnight m'dear." He kisses her on the cheek and stands up.

"Goodnight, Doodle."

He meets his wife at the top of the stairs, a pilly blanket in her arms. "I do not want those people staying in our home," she seethes.

Reece, hearing the commotion outside her door, steals from the bed and squats down to peek through the keyhole.

"Baldy's been my best friend for twenty years, Mother, and Sarah was yours. He'd do the same for us and ya know it. Now ya treat him right while I'm gone, and his son too. They're our guests for tonight."

"And only tonight," Mrs. Dollar says, turning her back and descending the first two steps.

Asa doesn't move. "Why do ya have it out for them?" he wants to know.

She turns to face him and says loudly, "Something's wrong with that boy. Thirty two years old and still living at home. It's just not natural. They're poor white trash and I don't want them in my house or near my family."

"Keep your voice down!" he commands in a heated whisper. "Reece will hear ya."

"Reece is too stupid to know what we're talking about," she says even louder.

Asa rolls his eyes. "What gives ya the right to judge people like ya do? Your own daughter, for christ's sake—"

"*Don't you use that name in this house.*" Little spit globs fly from the corners of her mouth, and she's breathing hard and fast. "I'll tell you what gives me the right. Who do you think runs this house while you're working all night and sleeping all day? At least your schedule means I have the bed to myself. And you've always got some frivolous scheme, like buying a pocket-sized radio, a television set—"

"I told ya Mother, don't use words I don't under—"

"I'll use whatever words I please, you ignorant, impotent hayseed."

He pulls back his hand, loading it with his boiling rage, and heaves it with all his force at her sneering countenance. The blow lands against the blanket she holds up at the last second to shield her face. She grabs his quivering limb and twists it, her eyes boring into his, those eyes telling him everything he needs to know. She releases his arm and with it releases all traces of a struggle. She glides down the stairs, arranging her face in a peaceful expression to receive her guests. Asa shuffles downstairs through the kitchen door out into the still, cool evening.

In the middle of the night the girls' bedroom door opens. A tall figure slips through the shadows and stands over the bed. *Reece*, it whispers. Hearing her name through the murky cloud of sleep enveloping her, she bolts upright and stares through the dark at the closed door. As her eyes adjust to the light she convinces herself that no one is there; she's dreaming. She lies back down and is asleep again before her racing heart can return to its normal rhythm.

*

In Nashville tonight their rhythm was off, bad. He blames Kick, since as the drummer it's up to him to keep time, but Kick swears that Halo was rushing every song, like all he wanted to do was just get off that stage. But that wasn't true—he was just nervous. All week he had been looking forward to returning to Nashville, the town where he got his big break.

The day after his high school graduation, Halo packed a bag with his good pants, two shirts, three pairs of underwear, three pairs of socks, a razor, deodorant, and his church shoes and slung it over one shoulder. On his other shoulder he carried his father's guitar, which had become his own when his father died four years ago in an accident at the forge. No one would tell him straight out what had happened; they must have thought he was too young to understand. But he had been fourteen, the same age his father had been when he quit school and lied about his age to get hired on at the forge in the first place.

At the visitation they kept the casket closed, which scared Halo and put all sorts of wild thoughts in his mind. For most of that day he had hidden out in the little kitchen area of the funeral home, constantly stepping out of the way of the old ladies who came in to make fresh coffee and went out again with more plates of cookies, although he couldn't imagine ever being hungry again after that day. It was while he was sitting in the corner, blending into the wallpaper, that he overheard exactly how his father had died. A cauldron of molten iron they were pulleying overhead tipped over and poured onto his father, then cooled and hardened almost immediately. He couldn't believe it at first, since the information came from the two most notorious gossips in Cullen County, until Mrs. Cullen whispered, "And they say it weren't no accident."

Mrs. Spingle gasped. "How could that be?"

Mrs. Cullen leaned closer. "They say that Rollie Riker caught that fox Henderson Truly in his henhouse, if you know what I mean. When word got around at the forge they all decided to teach Henderson a little lesson about messing with other men's wives."

Halo felt he would be sick, but he couldn't move from his chair. If he stood up and went to the bathroom the women would see him and know that he heard everything. He swallowed hard and tried to think rationally. He knew it wasn't true what they said, it couldn't be. Yet he had heard his father talk about Rollie Riker in passing, that he worked second shift while his father worked first shift. And his father *was* gone a lot of evenings . . . Still, he refused to believe it. And if his mother ever found out, it would kill her. It would literally kill her and he would be an orphan, with absolutely no family to call his own. He decided right then and there he would do whatever it took to protect his mother for the rest of her life.

The following night, when they had returned home from the funeral, Halo's mother brought out his father's guitar and placed it across her son's lap. She had a dreamy look on her face, like she was somewhere else, and Halo was afraid she might have gone into shock. Then she began to speak in a voice Halo had never heard before, low and throaty.

"The first time I ever saw your father, he was playing this guitar," she said. "He was eighteen and had already been working at the forge for four years, but he had a little band on the side that played at weddings and such. That night they were playing at a dance at the high school. I was seventeen and had gone to the dance with Jerry Feldon, who was set to enter the Navy in a few weeks. Needless to say, Jerry left the dance alone and I left with your father." She slid her fingers along the neck of the instrument. "He stood off to the side of the stage, almost to where you couldn't see him, and still you could tell he was the handsomest man there. All of us girls were wild about him, which drove our dates crazy. But we didn't care. I remember Nellie Riker made such a fool of herself that night—she was Nellie Saunter then—and tried to make Rollie look the fool too. But he wouldn't stand for it and dragged her out of there by the arm." Mrs. Truly smiled at the recollection. "She was jealous of me for weeks after that."

The realization hit Halo and he tried to change the subject. He put his hand over his mother's. "Mom, you don't have to talk about this right now."

"Oh no, I'm fine," she said. "It makes me feel better to talk about it. You know what happened next: we got married, had you, and lived a wonderful life until—" She pressed her hand over her mouth to suppress a sob. Halo started to move the guitar from his lap and put his arm around her but she motioned for him to stop. "I'm fine, really," she said. "Anyway, I know he would have wanted you to have his guitar. It was his most prized possession."

Halo picked up the instrument and twirled it in his hands, studying it from all sides. "I didn't even know he owned a guitar," he said. "I never heard him play it."

His mother smiled again, so slightly Halo almost missed it. "He played for me," she whispered, "almost every night." She patted her son's knee and stood up. "I'm going to bed," she said. "Don't stay up too late." She walked to her bedroom so slowly Halo thought she would never get there. As soon as the door clicked shut he heard the inevitable weeping and carried the guitar out to the front porch so he wouldn't have to listen to her. By the time he went to bed he had figured out four chords.

So the day after his high school graduation his mother gave him one hundred dollars, which he tried to refuse because he knew she couldn't afford to waste that kind of money. But she said that it was his inheritance from his father, and that he had earned it by being such a comfort to her these last four years. She didn't have to say it, but Halo knew that he was the spitting image of his father, and when his mother looked at him through the tears in her eyes she saw Henderson Truly at age eighteen, and for a moment she was eighteen again too, and all the pain of the last four years was wiped clean away.

In the morning she drove him to the bus station, and as he boarded the 8:15 to Nashville she gave him his dinner and supper wrapped up in brown wax paper. She stood there waving to him as the bus pulled away, and when he couldn't see her anymore he ate his dinner and half of his supper before they left the county.

His first night in Nashville was spent at what he kindly called a fleabag motel next door to the bus station. Early the next morning he carried his suitcase and his guitar to a place down the street from the Ryman Auditorium where you could make acetate recordings, two for fifty cents. He'd only written one song, a country and western tune called "Love Me in the Morning," but the man in the control booth told him he needed another song for the flip side of the record, so why didn't try a more revved-up version of the song he'd just recorded, like Elvis did with "Blue Moon of Kentucky." Halo told him he preferred Eddie Cochran to Elvis, and the man said whatever, just give it a little kick. So he made up a new rhythm on the spot and ten minutes later, when the acetates popped out of the machine, the man in the control booth said son, you have a bonafide hit in your hands there. Halo bought ten copies.

Immediately he took the records around to eight different radio stations, keeping one for himself and one to send to his mother back home. Then he thought better of it, afraid that it might remind her too much of his father and upset her, and put both copies in the bottom of the suitcase. Then he waited in his motel room for the record companies to start calling.

After a month of no one calling but his mother, and not having heard his song on any of the eight radio stations, he tried another course of action. He called each radio station fifty times a day and requested that they play "Love Me in the Morning" by

Halo Truly. Of course the disc jockeys knew it was him calling all those times so they purposefully *didn't* play the song.

One evening soon after, walking back to his motel room from supper at a brightly-lit diner down the street, he noticed a club called the Juice Harp which offered "Open Mike Night" every Tuesday and Thursday. It was Tuesday, so he ran to the motel, grabbed his guitar, and ran back to the club. He didn't overwhelm the drunken crowd, but he was invited to come back on Thursday. That night the reception was a bit warmer, and so he came back the following Tuesday and Thursday. The club owner noticed how the women in the place were starting to take notice of the young man and offered to pay him if he wanted to play every night from one to three a.m. Halo took the opportunity, since his one hundred dollars was down to thirteen and his motel bill was due next Friday.

It was two months since Halo had come to town, and he had already decided that if he hadn't made it by the end of the summer, he would return to Abandon and get a job at the forge like his father had. But every night until then he played the country and western version of "Love Me in the Morning" to whoever still occupied the Juice Harp from one to three a.m., and he played a few other songs, mostly Hank Williams tunes, since they were easy to learn. At the end of his first week he casually mentioned from the stage that he'd made a record of "Love Me in the Morning," and if folks liked it, well they could call up their favorite radio station and request it.

That was all it took. By his second full week at the Juice Harp he got moved up to the eleven p.m. to one a.m. shift, and the week after that, the prime nine to eleven p.m. shift, completely displacing the house band, featuring Roger "Rog" Reynolds on bass and Kick Freestone on drums. The funny thing was, the fans didn't know there were two versions of the song, and every one of the radio stations took to playing the revved-up version all on their own. So by mid-August Halo Truly was the newest rock and roll sensation in the country music capital of the world. Halo signed with the first record company who called, not even bothering to read the contract on which he put his signature. He didn't care what it said; he only cared that they were going to press thousands and thousands of his record and send them to stores and radio stations all across the country, and by fall he would be a *famous person*, the most famous person Abandon had ever seen, more famous even than Chester Lee Reece.

With his first advance royalty check he moved to a better fleabag motel, called his mother to tell her he would be on The Blackie Harmony Show on September ninth, and began practicing his sneers and poses in front of the mirror. It had all happened in Nashville.

Being back in Nashville tonight has made Halo remember the events of four years ago—especially his father's death—and to think about the past three months of his life and how far he's come in such a short period of time. Standing on that stage tonight, all he could think of was that his father had been eighteen—the age he was now—when he met Halo's mother at the school dance where his band was playing. Looking out into the audience he had wondered if his future wife, the mother of his children, was out there somewhere, and the thought had humbled him in a strange sort of way. He knows he was preoccupied and that he probably did rush the songs. But he also knows that Rog and Kick wanted to hurry up and get off the stage too, so they could hook up with their buddies at the Juice Harp and drink themselves stupid well into the next morning. He had held his tongue, though, as he always does, because he knows it's no good to contradict those fellows. And besides, their rhythm may have been off, but he still looked good. The girls had screamed even louder than they had the night before in Lexington. He thinks it must be the silver lamé jacket.

CHAPTER FIVE:
1932—1937

The collective population of that rough, curved heel of Indiana that trod the banks of the Ohio River were relatively insulated from what was happening in the rest of the country in 1932. Most folks had steady jobs that paid enough to put a roof over their heads and food on the table. The prohibited liquor was in plentiful supply if you knew the right people, and life progressed as normally as it always had. But the night Asa Dollar drove from Patsy's Place to Rebecca Wonderman's house on Church Street and stepped up onto her shadowy porch, he had no idea what he was walking into. He was like an innocent child stumbling into a stranger's car, lured by the promise of candy, and he never knew what hit him.

Rebecca's father had convinced her that if she had sex she'd get pregnant, and if she got pregnant she'd die during childbirth. He'd instructed her on the use of the prophylactics he'd concocted, but her years of education told her they certainly couldn't be very reliable. So she lived a life of voluntary celibacy, which was difficult to maintain during college. It seemed to her young men lurked around every corner and behind every tree, just waiting to pounce on the unsuspecting women. But Rebecca was able to emit an aura, an icy shield that deflected the attention of the men without a word or even a look, so that by the end of her senior year the abstinence was less voluntary than she liked to admit.

It wasn't as if she were totally naïve or unknowledgeable of these matters—she understood the principles of biology and chemistry and even the strange alchemy that sparked between men and women, and during lunch at the school in Abandon when the other female teachers spoke of their experiences Rebecca nodded and smiled and sometimes even lied. As the years passed, though, the desires she had so long suppressed stacked themselves inside of her until they pressed against her skin, seeped from her pores, out through the tips of her fingers and the ends of her hair, and began to melt the wall of ice she had erected around herself all those years ago. She started to make eye contact with men again— lingering glances she infused with as much meaning as possible. But when Marvin Weakly, the only bachelor teacher at the school, asked her to go dancing one Saturday night, she refused him. She realized that if she were alone with this man she wouldn't know what to say or do, and she'd probably end up looking down at the top of his head either on the dance floor or later, at her house, and at a loss for words would start telling him things about herself, secret, private things that no one else knew, that maybe she didn't even know herself until she'd whispered them in the dark. And after she'd given him everything that was in her mind and soul she would give him her body, and the next Monday she would carry her tin tray into the teacher's lunchroom and walk over to the table where he was sitting with the other male teachers and their mouths would snap shut when they saw her coming and instantly she would be turned inside out, and for the rest of her life everything about her would hang heavily in the air between them, always visible, as visible as the ice shield had been before. Except now *they* would control it, not she.

So that was what awaited Asa behind Rebecca's door that night. Weeks earlier she had decided that she was through living that way, that she wanted what everyone else in town had, that despite all the risks and all the reasons she had turned over and over in her mind she would take the ultimate chance and give herself to the first man who presented the opportunity. The very next evening Mr. Hoffman presented himself on her doorstep, and after depositing him in the river she decided she would have to set some parameters. Nothing that could be enumerated or even explained—

she would just know when the moment arrived. And so on that February night when the tall stranger with the dark hair and firm grip pulled her hard against him and asked for her first name in an aching whisper, the criteria had been met. Rebecca trembled when Asa simultaneously kissed her and undressed her and nudged her backward down the hall to her bedroom, but he acted as if he didn't notice. When it was over she turned her head away from him into her pillow and cried in pain and joy and embarrassment and relief, and he touched her shoulder and rolled her into his arms, and she thought that she could grow accustomed to this.

Finally, despite their best efforts, the inevitable happened, and Asa proposed to Rebecca on the porch steps as soon as she told him what she had known for weeks and what the doctor that afternoon had confirmed. Asa could tell by the way Rebecca's jawline tightened and her eyes turned dark when she broke the news that she had already made up her mind about what the next course of action would be—an unmarried schoolteacher in *that* condition would be a scandal and a shame to the teacher, the students and the town. So the next day, Thursday, Asa took the afternoon off from the forge, picked up Rebecca after school and drove to Dr. Riley's in Abandon, where they had their blood drawn. Then they drove on down to the limestone courthouse at the end of Main Street and applied for the license, and the clerk there told them there was a three-day waiting period before the license would be valid, which meant the earliest they could get married was Sunday. As they left the building Rebecca told Asa that that was unacceptable, that she would not be married on the lord's day, and that was that.

For most of her life Rebecca had never put much faith in religion. The premature death of her mother, and the years of her father's instruction on the practicalities and the serious nature of life, had convinced her that one's lot in life was determined solely by one's own sacrifice and struggle and not by the whimsical decisions of an invisible, not even mortal, being. Would such a divine power allow a girl to grow up without a mother, to walk into her father's bedroom on the day of her college graduation to find bits of his gray matter splattered against the headboard? Would this omniscient, omnipotent being allow a woman at the height of her youth and beauty and intellect to spend all of those years alone, with no one with whom to share these secular gifts but adolescents with more appreciation for the exploits of Al Capone than for the grace of a Petrarchan sonnet; a balding, sour-faced math teacher; and a lonely, overstimulated landlord? She would throw herself headlong into the muddy Ohio before she would cast her fate to the bitter wind of a imperceptible deity.

But the morning after her first encounter with Asa, when she awoke to find a shard of sunlight slashing across his face and illuminating one sharp, unshaven cheek, she nearly had to shield her eyes. At that moment the rational, the logical, the skeptical and the cynical all fell away and what was left was more luminous than the mahogany tresses that spread across her pillow and more graceful than Petrarch on his best day. The heat of the bed became too intense for Rebecca and she flung the covers from her body and knelt naked by the side of the bed, her elbows resting on the mattress, her tingling scalp perched in her hands, and behind her closed, burning eyelids she saw a translucent hand sweep her up and cast her fate into the arms of this man beside her, and she accepted this turn of events without question. The next Sunday she asked Asa to accompany her to the Baptist church (she certainly wasn't going next door to that Catholic church) and at first he said no, that he wasn't the church-going type, never had been, never would be. But that evening when he came over for supper Rebecca refused to feed him or even let him through the door, telling him that any man who spent his Sundays sleeping late and listening to the radio and drinking at Patsy's Place instead of worshiping the lord would not step foot in her house, let alone her bed. And so they were apart for a week, until the next Sunday morning when Asa pulled up in front of Rebecca's house wearing the only suit he owned and drove her down to the Baptist church and sat beside her in the pew, all without saying a word, for there was nothing to be said. And it was needless to say that Asa never visited Patsy's Place after that, and when the fellows at work asked why they didn't see him there anymore, his inability to look them in the eyes told them all they needed to know. In empathy they nodded and slapped him on the shoulder as they filed out of the forge and said *we've all been there, brother*, as well they all had.

And so now Rebecca refused to be married on a Sunday, until Asa shook her by the wrist and explained as gently as the impatient rage boiling inside of him would allow that the longer they waited, the more time the busybodies in town would have to calculate the weeks and months and soon everyone in Falling Star and Abandon would know what a slut she was. She raised her arm as if to strike him but he blocked the blow, gripped both of her wrists and forced her into the front seat of his car. He dropped her off at Dorthea's Dress Shop and told her to pick out her wedding dress, he would be right back. He drove to the Baptist church and found Pastor Alberts and told him they'd be needing his services on Sunday afternoon, then went back and picked up Rebecca and her dress, drove them to Falling Star, let them off at the corner of First and Church Streets and didn't come back until Sunday morning.

There was never really any question as to where they would live as a married couple. Rebecca had only once visited Asa's house on the outskirts of Abandon, at the bottom of a hill and practically sitting on the railroad tracks. Asa had fixed supper on the propane cookstove, and they sat around the oil lamp as he read to her (from a book he lifted from the break room at the forge) the putrid poetry of the one-syllable wonder Chester Lee Reece, which she despised but tolerated because they were about the only things the one-syllable wonder Asa Dollar could understand. Early in their relationship she had tried to engage him in serious discussions of literature and art, of politics and current events, but he would simply wave off her attempts with a shrug and a grin and a claim that he didn't really follow all of that stuff, now let's go to bed.

Rebecca spent that evening at Asa's house in great discomfort, not because she was forced to endure two hours of *Laundress on the*

Levee by Chester Lee Reeks, but because she absolutely refused to use the fetid outhouse. So the day they were married Asa boarded up his house in Abandon, the house his father built, and moved his things into Rebecca's house on Church Street in Falling Star, the house with a glorious view of the Ohio River, two doors down from the Catholic church.

*

Jonah came into the world on February 12, 1933, and with his birth the Dollar family began in earnest. Rebecca's father had told her all the details of her mother's home childbirth and subsequent death, so upon the first pangs of labor she demanded that Asa drive her to the hospital in Broulet, where they were met by Dr. Riley. Asa wanted to name his son Asa Junior, but Rebecca chose the name Jonah and told her husband that Asa could be the child's middle name, and so it was.

Rebecca had quit her teaching job at the end of the first semester to prepare for the birth of the baby. She turned the second bedroom into a nursery and lurched her way through her first year of motherhood. She never expected to become pregnant, let alone survive the childbirth, and when she *did* survive she realized she had no idea how to raise a child. She searched for the elusive maternal instinct she had heard about, and felt its pull once in a while, but relied mostly on her education, common sense, and the understanding gained from five and a half years of teaching. She kept her firstborn clothed and fed and bathed, and some days while she was changing his diaper he would smile at her in recognition and she would feel a tingling sensation in her chest and know that everything would be alright.

Rachel was born almost four years after Jonah, on Christmas Day 1936, and the first month of her life was the most pleasant month Rebecca had ever known. The first time Rebecca looked upon Rachel's red, wrinkled face, she experienced a sense of peace she hadn't felt since that morning she knelt beside her bed and saw the hand of god behind her eyes. She had never really understood men, either in body or mind, so Rachel's birth came as a relief. She knew what to expect with a girl.

Rebecca quickly discovered that her daughter was as different from her son as Keats was from Eliot—not that one was better or worse than the other, just different. They even smelled different— where Jonah had mostly smelled like pee and whatever he had eaten that day, Rachel always gave off a scent of sweet honeysuckle and rainwater.

Jonah was old enough to help Rebecca with Rachel, although he would often watch the two of them together with bitter jealousy in his eyes. Rebecca never looked at Jonah the way she looked at her new baby, as if Rachel was a rare and precious jewel.

In the late afternoons of that first month of Rachel's life Asa would come home from work to find the house clean, the pleasant smells of dinner cooking drifting through the house, the children bathed, fresh from their naps and wrapped up inside a warm blanket, one under each of Rebecca's arms, listening as she read bible stories aloud and watching the snow falling faster and faster and piling up against the back door. Rebecca wouldn't even hear Asa come in; her face would hold a rapturous look as if to say she was finally, *exactly* where she was meant to be, there and nowhere else. Some days she would even allow Asa to sit with them and read from Chester Lee Reece's newest book of poems, *Come Now, Rising Tide*, which Mr. Dollar had acquired by trading in *Laundress on the Levee* at the bookstore Patsy's sister owned in the basement of her house.

The title proved most prescient, for at the end of January the melting snow was washed away by days of unstoppable rain. Rebecca and Asa kept watch on the river from their back window, taking turns at night while the other slept. On the second day the river spilled over its banks and continued to rise. On the third day their entire backyard was flooded. By the fourth day the river was lapping against the porch, licking the rotting wood with a quick, muddy tongue.

On the fifth day they started evacuating the town of Falling Star and sending the residents to the Presbyterian Church, up the hill on higher ground. They set up cots in the sanctuary and Patsy brought over sandwiches and coffee, and for the little ones, milk. Asa's foreman at the forge told the men they could go home early that day, to see that their families got out safe, but he was sorry to say they wouldn't get paid for the hours they didn't work. Asa couldn't afford to give up half a day's wages, not with two children, so he held out until the regular quitting time. He knew Rebecca would gather up the kids and get them to a safe place.

When Asa tried to drive home that evening he was stopped about a mile from his house. The whole street was flooded, and his heart started moving up into his throat when he saw how high the water had risen since just that morning. The most he could see of the houses along the road were the tops of the roofs. The police made him turn around and told him to drive on up to the Presbyterian Church; that was where all the folks who lived on that street had been taken.

So Asa drove up the hill to the church through almost three feet of water, but even then he felt as though the water was rising behind him so quickly he could hardly keep ahead of it. He stopped the car in the church parking lot, picked up his copy of *Come Now, Rising Tide* from the front seat and stuffed it into his coat pocket, glad he had taken it to work with him that day. He knew Rebecca would never remember to bring it with her in the rush of evacuation.

At that point the water was beginning to creep up the steps to the church, but not nearly as fast as it was sweeping through the town. Inside was like a convention, all sorts of folks talking and milling about. He was surprised to see Pastor Alberts there. Asa couldn't imagine the clergyman liked the Presbyterians much, but figured in a situation like this people probably put those things behind them best they could. The pastor walked up to Asa as if he were in a hurry, with a worried look on his face.

"How are Rebecca and the children?" he asked Asa right off, without even saying hello.

"Um, that's what I've come here to find out," Asa told him.

The pastor grabbed Mr. Dollar by the shoulders. "They're not here, Asa," he said.

Asa wasn't sure he understood what the pastor was saying. "Do ya think they're still at home?" he asked, picturing in his mind their flooded street, the submerged houses.

"Could be, Asa," he said. "Let me talk to the fire chief. I think he has a boat we can use."

So Pastor Alberts and Asa borrowed the chief's lifeboat and floated down to Church Street. When they arrived at the house they just kept floating on in through the front door. In the living room there was a little attic reached by pulling down a set of collapsible stairs that folded up into the ceiling, and that was where they found Rebecca and Jonah and Rachel, sitting at the top of the folding stairs.

"Rebecca, what are ya doin' up there?" Asa shouted up to her. "Why didn't ya leave?"

She was holding the children on her lap, one on each leg, and gripping them so tight Asa was afraid she might choke them.

"Rachel is sick," Rebecca said, calm as ever. "I think she has a fever. I didn't think it was wise to take her out in this incessant rain." She bent her head to look out the front window, to check on the status of the rain, and the whites of her eyes turned gray when she saw instead the raging water stirring outside, as if she was finally seeing it for the first time.

"I'm sorry, Asa," she said, not so calm now. "I thought I would just wait until you got home. I didn't know the river would—"

"It's alright, Mrs. Dollar," Pastor Alberts said. "We're here now. We'll help you." He steered the lifeboat over to the immersed stairs and stood up in the boat. He felt around in the water for the steps and climbed halfway up. "Hand me Jonah," he said. Rebecca shook her head frantically.

"Do it, Rebecca," Asa said.

She scooted to the edge of the top step on which she was sitting, shifted her weight, and handed her son over to the Pastor. He snatched the boy, turned and gave him to his father. Asa was getting Jonah situated in the boat when he heard Pastor Alberts say, "Now Rachel."

Asa looked up when he heard Rebecca shriek. Then he heard the river gulp and splash and swallow their daughter whole.

"*No! No! Rachel!*" Rebecca was screaming. She was already down the ladder, wading, diving, treading through the river that had overtaken the living room.

"Rebecca!" Asa shouted, trying to keep Jonah in the boat with one hand and paddle with the other.

Pastor Alberts was clinging to the side of the ladder and reaching out half-heartedly to Asa's wife. "I'm sorry, my child," he whispered, over and over again. Asa wanted to push him off that goddamn ladder and hold him underwater for about ten minutes, to feel him flailing and gasping under his hands. Instead he reached out to Rebecca and grabbed the only part of her he could see, that marvelous mahogany hair. He yanked her up out of the water and she fought for breath, then fought her husband for the right to dive down again and search for her lost child.

"*NO!*" she bellowed so loudly it shook the house. Then Asa realized the house was shaking because it was breaking loose from its foundation, being washed away by the out-of-control river. The force of the water swept the boat through the front door and back into the street, although by now the street and the river were inseparable. Still gripping Rebecca's hair, Asa pulled her up into the boat. Pastor Alberts leapt desperately into the craft with them; Mr. Dollar resisted the urge to kick him square in the chest so that he would fall backwards into the rapids. Instead the four of them bobbed as if on the ocean until they were met by a rescue team about half a mile down the road. They guided them back to the church, which was being evacuated as well. Asa and Rebecca's house passed them on the way.

If Jonah was scared he never showed it. He sat quietly in the boat that whole time, never saying a word. Asa figured when Rebecca regained her breath she'd start hollering and kicking and screaming, but she just sat there, nearly comatose.

At the church the three remaining Dollars headed straight to the car. Pastor Alberts tried to say something, but Rebecca managed to slam the door in his face. They drove away from Falling Star as quick as they could, the river chasing them, and rode in silence all the way to Asa's old house in Abandon. There the land was mostly dry, except for right around Cullen's Creek.

"We can rebuild the house in the same spot," Asa said as they pulled into the driveway. When Rebecca didn't answer he looked over at her and although the twilight had faded to near darkness, he could see that she was staring down at her breasts, leaking and heavy with milk.

He left her sitting there, with Jonah asleep in the backseat, and went to the barn. He found a crowbar, pried the boards from the windows, used them to start a fire in the woodstove, and tried to make their new home habitable, as uncontrollable sobs escaped from his body.

Asa never saw Rebecca cry, or mourn, or grieve in any way. He figured she took care of that business during the day while he was at work.

CHAPTER SIX:
SEPTEMBER 11, 1957

D r. Riley's office takes up the first floor of his house, a two-story aluminum and wood dwelling purchased from the Sears and Roebuck catalog thirty years earlier. Patients wait in the living room not on hard metal and plastic chairs, but instead relax on the deep, soft cushions of a floral print sofa. They get their blood drawn and have a cup of coffee in the kitchen, give their urine samples in the bathroom where they dry their hands on real towels instead of scratchy paper, and are examined on folding tables covered with bed sheets and separated from the other patients in the room by thin quilts hung between them, a workable arrangement since Dr. Riley typically has only one patient in the room at a time.

But he's unusually busy this morning, mostly folks with minor tornado injuries. He'd come downstairs at seven o'clock to have a cup of coffee and read his newspaper, and they were already waiting for him on the front porch even though they knew he didn't open for two more hours, standing there wrapped in home-made bandages and makeshift splints, groggy and woozy and leaning on the porch rail. So he'd let them come inside and made them all coffee and asked them to wait just a few more minutes while he went upstairs and changed his clothes and he never did get to drink his coffee, so by eight-thirty his hands were shaking and he had a thundering headache but he couldn't understand why since coffee certainly wasn't addictive—he was a doctor, he would know something like that.

Reece and Dinah are among those waiting for Dr. Riley on his porch, feeling conspicuous due to their lack of any apparent malady.

For three hours they fidget on the sofa, Dinah leaning her head against an understuffed pillow on which the late Mrs. Riley had needlepointed the lord's prayer in garish yellow thread, getting up only to pee in a cup and have a prodigious amount of blood drawn from her arm, until finally at ten o'clock she is called back to the examining room. Reece stands up and starts to follow her into the dining room, but Dr. Riley's nurse Alfie stops her and gently nudges her back to the couch. Dinah's eyes never leave Reece's as she joins the doctor in the other room.

Reece sinks down into the threadbare cushions and closes her eyes. In her mind she can still hear her parents fighting in the hall just outside her bedroom door, as clearly as if they are sitting next to her now. Earlier this morning, slipping out to the toilet before anyone else in the house had awakened, she had glanced into her mother's room and seen the shotgun lying in the bed next to her, and a chill had raced through her body and made her shudder. Downstairs she had tried to walk noiselessly, to open the door without creaking so as not to wake their houseguests, but when she had sneaked a peek into the living room the Hilliards were gone and their pickup truck wasn't in the driveway. She'd wondered if they'd even stayed there at all.

Dr. Riley's front door flies open, bounces off the wall and slams shut again. "A wop bop a loo la la la la la la la la la la la la la BOOM!" Reece jerks her head up off the back of the sofa and watches Vernie Cletis burst in, singing, screaming, slurring and swaying. "Ah wop a wop a wop a la de la de la de BOOM BOOM!" Her gray hair is darkened by grease and grime and clumps together so that her scalp shows in places. Her light blue shirt, part of her ex-husband's delivery uniform and which he probably told her she could just keep rather than try to snatch it from her, stretches tight across her chest, fastened by only one straining button. Her jeans, men's size 42-28, are splattered with blood and the left cuff is rolled up to her knee. She's carrying a small object in her right hand. "I said a wop bop a bop a woo woo woo go BOOM!" She staggers toward the examining room, limping now, waving the object in the air. "Dr. Riley I go boom!" He meets her in the waiting room and tries to coerce her to an examining table, but she'll have none of that. She pulls him over to the couch and they tumble down where Reece had been sitting just a moment ago, before she had rolled away in the nick of time.

"Vernie, what happened?" Dr. Riley shouts, straddling her, forcing her shoulders down.

Vernie Cletis cackles, chokes on her own spit, gags, coughs, then finally gurgles, "I had'n acc'dent."

"What kind of accident, Vernie? With your truck?"

"No, s'lly, I go BOOM!" She flings her arms open in a mock explosion, knocking Dr. Riley away from her. She holds up her left leg and wiggles her four remaining toes in his face. "Vernie go boom," she says more softly now. The blood trickles from the chasm where her big toe used to be, down her leg toward her knee. Dr. Riley gently lowers her leg onto the couch so that the foot hangs over the edge and says quietly, but with authority, "Alfie, will you please go outside and see if Vernie's truck is there?"

She nods vigorously. When she's halfway to the door Dr. Riley says, "If it is, bring me back whatever's in it." She nods again and practically leaps outside. In stunned silence Reece and the others in the waiting room form a circle around the doctor as he tends to his patient with an almost maternal devotion, rubbing her temples, whispering soothing words. The moment ends when Alfie returns holding a shotgun in one hand and a gallon jug of vodka, empty, in the other. He motions for her to put the items in the kitchen and leans over Vernie's bloated, splotched face.

"Vernie, did you drink all that vodka by yourself?"

She closes her eyes, grins and nods, seemingly enraptured by the mere thought of the clear silky liquid passing through her.

"Vernie, did you shoot your toe off with your shotgun?"

She opens her eyes and gives Dr. Riley the kind of stare reserved for lovers and enemies. "Doc'r Riley, ya don't make house calls no more. So I had ta have a reason ta come see ya." She holds up the object she's been gripping the whole time. She takes Dr.

Riley's hand and places her big toe—its bottom crusty with dried blood, ligament, tendon and muscle—in his open palm. "You make it bet'r, wo'n you?" Her head drops to the side as she passes out against the needlepoint pillow.

Immediately a murmur rises among the other patients in the room. Suddenly Reece realizes, horrified, that Dr. Riley has left Dinah alone in the examining room while he deals with this mad-woman. She rushes to the first bed and finds it empty. In the second bed a small child with what appears to be a broken arm lies whimpering. Moving to the third bed she's met by the sight of Dinah lying on her back, her slip pulled up to her chest, naked from the waist down, her heels in metal stirrups at the foot of the table, knees bent and wide open, exposed there to the world and to anyone who should walk in.

"Dinah, what—"

"Reece, is that you?" Dinah props up on her elbows. Yellow tear streaks split her face. "What's happening out there? I didn't know what to do, I was afraid to move—" She starts to sob and lies back on the table, finally putting her knees together. Reece pulls down Dinah's slip and searches for her sister's dress and panties.

"Get dressed," Reece tells her, handing Dinah her clothes with trembling hands. "We've got to get to school."

Dinah dresses and scoots off the end of the table. Hitting the floor she winces and leans on Reece for support.

"Can you walk?" Reece asks.

"I . . . think so," Dinah grimaces, taking small, tentative steps, then halting for a moment. "Is it okay to go out there?"

Reece nods. "I think so. Vernie finally fainted."

"That was Vernie Cletis doin' all that whoopin' and hollerin'? What happened to her?"

Reece guides her sister toward the waiting room. "I'll tell you later. You sure you're okay to walk?"

They literally bump into Dr. Riley, who's dragging Vernie Cletis to the first examining table. "I'm sorry, Dinah. Can you come back tomorrow?" he asks, heaving Vernie up onto the bed.

Dinah doesn't reply. Keeping their heads down, clinging to each other, the sisters make their way through the crowd and out onto the sidewalk that leads to the school.

They've walked only a few yards when the loose rumble of an old farm truck rolls up beside them. The bed is stacked with long, broken strips of wood and shards of glass. "Hey Dollar gals!" a man's voice says.

They stop walking and the truck stops as well, idling in the middle of the street. "Oughtn't you Dollar girls be in school right now? You need a ride?" Addison Hilliard asks.

The sisters look at each other in silence, then shrug and climb into the battered vehicle. To Reece the odor of wet soil and stale cigarette smoke and pig manure is strangely comforting, but it immediately makes Dinah nauseous.

"Stop, Addison!" she blurts, leaning her head out the passenger window and opening the door halfway. She bobbles out onto the street before the truck has stopped and vomits into the peony bush in the yard of Miss Corliss, the English teacher. Addison brings the truck to a halt along the sidewalk, a little past where Dinah is retching over the flowering plant, and bumps the curb with the front tire.

"She okay?" Addison asks Reece.

Reece nods and keeps her head down, focusing on the half-rolled pouch of chewing tobacco lying on the rusted floorboard on the passenger side. She concentrates on the Indian on the label, trying not to blink, because a blink would become a tear which would become a raging river bound to wash her and this truck into Cullen's Creek and on into the murky Ohio River. The Indian's profile becomes blurry and she sees there in the fog her sister lying on Dr. Riley's table and that dark, dark chasm between her legs, open for all to witness, and she sees Bernie Joshua on top of her in the field writhing like an animal caught in a trap, out there in the open for all to witness, and she knows the two are connected in a shameful way that hurts her in her chest just to think about so that she has to cry out just to relieve the pressure, and when she does the tears do come, but she swallows them down quickly and hopes that Addison hasn't noticed, which of course he has. He reaches across her and pulls an oil-stained rag from the glove compartment.

"Here," he says, handing it to her. "The edges are pretty clean."

She wads up one corner and dabs at her eyes and nose. "Thanks," she whispers, still studying the tobacco pouch. Addison scoops it up and stuffs it in the front pocket of his plaid shirt.

"I'm tryin' to quit. Smokin', that is. So I chew this once'n a while."

Reece nods slightly and transfers her gaze to the open glove box. Inside she sees the pointed end of a pinkish rock protruding from beneath a precisely folded road map. She reaches over and removes a perfectly shaped arrowhead. She rubs her thumb from its flat end to its sharp point and back again, up and down, up and down, feeling its cool smoothness in her hand, imagining a young Miami Indian shaping this tool a hundred, two hundred years ago, working for hours and hours to fashion a hunting knife or an eating utensil, and imagining how he must have felt when he discovered he'd lost it somewhere along the white man's trail that led his people from the only home they'd ever known.

"Found that on our farm," Addison says. "Out in the middle of the field. Stepped down off the tractor and there she was, right under my boot."

Reece nods again. "I found this near Cullen's Creek the other day," Reece says, pulling the sandstone from her dress pocket. She'd worn the same dress Monday and had forgotten to remove the stone.

Addison examines the sandstone and hands it back to Reece. "That's real nice."

She goes to replace the arrowhead in the glove box, but Addison stops her, closing her fingers over the sharp stone. "You keep it," he says.

"But it's yours. I can't—"

"Take it," he says, patting her wrist as gently as his farm-callused fingers will allow, then pulls back quickly when the passenger door opens and Dinah climbs in, wiping her mouth with the back of her hand. "How you feelin', Dinah?" he asks, shifting the truck into Drive and pulling into the street.

"Fine," Dinah mumbles, slumping down in the seat and wincing with each bump in the road.

"You Dollar gals are too quiet," Addison says after a few blocks and flicks the radio's volume knob to the right. Bill Monroe's unmistakable bluegrass mandolin cries out to Reece from the truck's tinny speakers buried deep inside the dashboard. She closes her eyes and imagines herself sitting on her father's lap in their dark living room, her pale, smooth cheek resting against the day-old stubble on his lined face, sharing the earpiece of his transistor and taking turns listening to the Grand Ole Opry. Just four days ago the Opry's high lonesome sounds had filled her ear with a joyful sorrow she didn't quite understand but felt deep in her bones. She had felt safe there in the dark, wishing for her entire life to remain just as it was at that moment, thinking Abandon wasn't such a bad place to be, at least for now. But just four days later, jostling around in the cab of Addison Hilliard's pickup truck, the noon sun pouring in through the windshield and burning her bare legs beneath her dress, the sharp end of the arrowhead stabbing her sweating palm, her sister nearly fainting in the seat to her right and Addison Hilliard's pantleg brushing against her thigh on her left, she remembers something Miss Corliss said in English class last week, that you ought to be careful what you wish for because it might come true, and she wants to scream *stop! stop!* and jump out of the truck and run away from this truck, from her sister moaning in the front seat, from the man driving who looked at her with a sad longing when he touched her hand, and away from this town that worships a tree (a tree!) every fall with a vegetable parade led by the stupidest and most fertile family in Abandon.

But she doesn't move, barely breathes, and soon Addison stops the truck in front of the school and Dinah stumbles out, immediately doubling over as she walks up the cement steps. Reece hangs back for a moment. Millions of tiny heat pellets beat against the inside of her forehead and behind her eyes and she wonders if maybe she has a bad case of sunstroke.

"Reece?" Addison says, placing his hand on her shoulder. His touch is like an alarm going off in her feverish brain and she leaps out of the truck. Addison shuts the passenger door behind her and says out the window, "I'll see ya tonight, Reece."

She turns to look at him. "What?"

He chuckles. "Well, unless my pa and I get our whole house built up in a day, I guess we'll be stayin' with ya again tonight. Your dad stopped by our place this morning. He said it was okay." He waves, makes a U-turn in front of the school and speeds toward the lumber yard.

In front of the principal's office Reece adds the arrowhead to the growing rock collection in her pocket and pulls out the tardy note she forged in her mother's hand this morning in Dr. Riley's waiting room. After stopping at her locker she makes her way to the Germ Man's science lecture, passing by the sophomore health class Dinah should be attending this period. She scans the room with a sidelong glance but can't determine if Dinah is there or not. Upon reaching the Germ Man's class she slips into her seat, only to be excused for lunch just a few minutes later. In the cafeteria she finds Roxanne Joshua, who always seems to get to the lunchroom before she does, trying to locate the beef in her beef stroganoff. Reece takes the empty seat next to her friend and lays her head down on the table across folded arms.

"Reece," Roxanne says, nudging her elbow. "You okay? Get up." Reece, swimming through a foggy ocean of confusion in her mind, lies perfectly still, unanswering, until Roxanne gives up and continues eating her lunch. Reece can't ignore, however, the scraping of metal chair legs against the concrete floor and the folding table shifting under her head as Bo Cullen, Barrie Spingle and Charmain Jannings join them. Reece appraises them with glassy eyes.

"Where's your brother today, *Reeks?*" Bo Cullen asks.

Reece yawns. "Helping the Hilliards rebuild their house, I suppose," she says. "They pretty much lost everything in the storm last night."

"Ooh, I bet Danny looks real cute when he uses a hammer," Charmain says.

Bo Cullen rolls her eyes. "Danny Dollar ain't nothin' special," she says. "None of them Dollars is."

"That's right, Bo," Reece says. "We're not special, as in special ed, like your family."

Bo Cullen stands up so hard that her chair flies out behind her. "You take that back, Reece Dollar!" she screams.

"Make me," Reece says, still seated and quite disinterested in the whole matter.

"I don't make trash, I burn it," Bo Cullen says. Barrie and Charmain gasp and stand up behind their friend.

"You *are* trash," Reece says, raising her pitch a degree, then adds a favorite phrase of her mother's, "poor white trash."

Bo Cullen's eyes catch fire. "You're the one with trash in your house. Everybody in town knows the things that creepy Addison Hilliard does, and you let him sleep under your roof like he's President Eisenhower." For a moment their eyes lock with a rage and an intensity neither has known before. Bo Cullen blinks first. Her face loses its color and she turns and flees the cafeteria before her quivering legs can give out on her. Reece looks at Barrie and Charmain, who follow Bo Cullen to the restroom. She grips the edge of the table as she thinks of Addison Hilliard's hand on her hand, his leg against her leg, the nearly weightless arrowhead sitting like a boulder in her dress pocket.

"It's time to go," Roxanne says, taking Reece by the arm. Outside the cafeteria they notice a crowd of students gathered around a man with a microphone and another man with a bright light attached to a camera. The girls and boys clamor around the man with the microphone, chattering and giggling and shouting what seem to Reece like random words.

"What's going on?" Reece asks.

"I don't know, let's see," Roxanne says, leading the way. Reece can see now that the side of the camera reads WHFM-TV Channel 1. "It's the guy from t.v.!" Roxanne erupts and forces her way into the circle of students. Reece strolls the perimeter and notices Miss Corliss standing next to the man with the microphone.

"Halo was just an excellent student," Miss Corliss is saying to the man. Both of their faces are overwhelmed by obviously phony smiles; Reece think Miss Corliss's mouth might just blow up if she smiles any wider. "Always turned in his homework on time, always read the assigned pages in *The Scarlet Letter* or *Huckleberry Finn*, always did real well on his tests. Just a real fine, upstanding young man."

The man with the microphone nods at Miss Corliss and turns to his right, and Reece can see that his black hair is heavy with more than a little dab of Bryl-Creem and his face is orange with thick makeup. "And what do you remember about Halo Truly?" the man asks Charmain Jannings, who has managed to work her way through the throng.

"Oh, I remember how cute he was!" Charmain gushes. "Nobody knows this, but sometimes, at night, he used to sneak over to my house and stand under my bedroom window and play his guitar and sing just to me! You know that song of his, 'Love Me in the Morning?' Well, he wrote that song just for me!"

Reece shakes her head at this blatant lie and tries to walk away, but the crowd shifts suddenly and pushes her right into the cameraman.

"And how about you?" the man with the microphone asks Reece, squeezing her upper arm and pulling her to the center of the camera's lens.

"Well, uh, I, uh, never really knew him," she says. "But did you know that, um, another very famous person from Abandon died recently?"

"No, I wasn't aware of that," the man with the microphone says. "But can you tell me about Halo—"

"It's true," Reece says. "Chester Lee Reece was a great poet and the greatest man to ever come from Abandon. He died a few days ago, and Doodle—my dad—said that no one even bothered to show up at the funeral of such a great man. I would've gone with him but my mom—"

"Thank you, dear," the man with the microphone says and turns his back on Reece. "We can edit her out later," he says to the cameraman, making a cutting motion across his throat. Reece lowers her head and barrels her way out of the herd to her next class. After school Reece is waiting for Roxanne just outside the front doors when Principal Grumley approaches her. "Miss Dollar," he says, leaning slightly forward, hands behind his back.

"Hi Mr. Grumley," she says, trying for a brave grin.

"Miss Dollar, my secretary has informed me that your attendance, and that of your sister Dinah, has been extremely poor this week." Reece swallows, the last of her smile faded now. "Is everything alright at home?" he asks.

"Did the man from t.v. interview you too?" she asks.

"Now, don't you try changing the subject. I asked you a question," Mr. Grumley says.

"Oh yes, yes, everything's fine," she says, too quickly.

"No tornado damage?"

This is her opening. She debates whether or not to tell the principal about Dinah, about electricity and Mark Isaac, to ask him if she really looks like Grace Kelly. "No," she says finally, "no damage. We were lucky, I guess."

"Lucky indeed," Mr. Grumley says. "But I'm concerned nonetheless. I'd call your parents, but I'm told you have no telephone. Is that correct?" Reece nods. "So I've written them a note." He pulls a folded sheet of paper from his jacket pocket and hands it to her. "Will you please make sure that they read it?" Reece takes the note and nods again, locking her knees to keep them from swaying. Mr. Grumley places his hand on her shoulder. She feels it down to her toenails. "You're a good girl, Reece." He walks away as Roxanne arrives.

"Ooh, what did Mr. Grumley want?" she asks.

"Nothing," Reece says.

During the two-mile walk Roxanne chatters about Halo Truly and how Charmain Jannings told a bald-faced lie and she hopes they show her on television tonight so everyone will know what a liar she is, and when Reece doesn't respond she changes the subject to the field trip the eighth grade is taking on Friday to Mammoth Cave in Kentucky. "I bet you can get you some neat rocks and fossils for your collection there," she says. "Maybe even a stalactite or a stalagmite." She grins, proud she is able to use the new words she learned today in the Germ Man's class.

"Mmm," Reece says, deciding not to tell Roxanne that last week her mother had taken the shoebox that held Reece's rock collection and scattered it in their garden, burying the stones in the dirt so deeply that they were probably in China now, and that she did it for no good reason other than she knew she could and that Reece couldn't do anything about it. Instead she imagines herself breaking loose from the pack of teenagers oohing and aahing and straining their necks in awe at the limestone wonder, and hearing them shriek in horror as she grows to ten times her size and tears a giant stalactite from the fossilized ceiling, causing the cave's five levels to collapse one upon another until she alone stands triumphant atop a tower of rubble and dead teenagers, poking their eyes out with pointed end of her stalactite sword.

"Aren't you at all excited?" Roxanne asks. "You were last week."

"Mmm," she says. They walk in silence a while. Finally Reece says, "Roxanne . . . what did Bo Cullen mean about Addison Hilliard? About the things he does?"

"Oh nothing, I'm sure," she says. "Bo Cullen's just jealous of you, that's all. You know she's got a great big crush on Danny. All the girls do." She adds quickly, "Except me of course."

Reece contemplates this with some puzzlement, not able to imagine her brother in a boyfriend sort of way. Her puzzlement quickly turns to relief when she figures that if she isn't attracted in that way to her own brother then she must not be quite as weird as everyone thinks she is.

"What I mean is," Roxanne says, "is that I like your brother alright, but . . . well, you know who I think is just a dream?" She glances from side to side, making sure no one's around to hear her earth-shattering revelation. She stage-whispers, "Mark Isaac.

He looks just like Halo Truly, except for his dark hair, don't you think?"

Reece's legs are suddenly two cement pillars. She opens her mouth but before she can speak a loud, rumbling vehicle pulls up alongside them. "Hey Reece Dollar. Hey Roxanne Joshua. You gals wanna ride?" Addison Hilliard asks.

"Yeah," Roxanne says, pulling Reece's arm. Her legs won't move. "Reece, come on."

Reece shakes her head. "No, I want to walk." She extracts her arm from Roxanne's grasp and takes a small, halting step forward. She studies a crack in the sidewalk, snaking from left to right and ending at a tuft of grass sticking up through the concrete. She's trying to remember if she's ever seen Roxanne talking to Mark Isaac in school, if there's been some sign she's missed. She can't think of anything. She takes a few more steps. The pickup truck crawls along the road beside her.

"Come on Reece," Addison says. "No use in you walkin' all that way when I'm goin' right by your place." The wood scraps that filled the truck bed earlier in the day have been replaced by planks of clean, new lumber.

"Third trip today," Addison says, motioning toward the boards in the back. "Luther's takin' all the tore-up pieces from the storm and givin' us some good lumber cheap, to help us rebuild. There's a lot of folks been there today, I'll tell ya. Now why don't you come on? I gave ya a ride this mornin', I give ya a ride this afternoon."

Roxanne, already seated on the passenger side, looks at Reece. "He gave you a ride this morning? Reece, what's that all about?"

Reece is regaining strength in her legs and walking faster now. "Nothing. I'll walk, thanks." She starts to run, desperately wishing the truck would zoom past her, up the road and out of sight, and that she could just be left alone.

"Suit yourself, Reece Dollar," Addison says, speeding up and zooming out of sight. Reece slows down and inhales deeply, taking in the scent of the earth, of soil being turned up in the harvesting process and nourished by the decaying leaves, scarlet and rust and saffron and bronze, as they fall from the dogwood and tulip trees. She exhales too quickly and her head feels like a feather bed, like it would up and float away if it weren't attached to her shoulders. She stops and bends at the waist, her head nearly all the way between her knees. Above her she hears the familiar squeak of a pubescent boy whose voice is changing.

"You okay Reece Dollar?"

She opens her body into a standing position and looks down. "Yes Erl Cullen, I'm fine." She begins walking again. Erl trots for a few steps to catch up with her.

"Can I carry your books?" he asks.

Reece shifts her schoolbooks to the other side of her body, away from Erl. "No, I've got them."

Erl juggles his own books in his arms. "You didn't meet us all at the bridge this morning." Reece walks a bit faster. Erl tries again. "Any reason why you didn't meet us all at the bridge this morning?"

"I wasn't feeling well," she says.

Erl lowers his head. "Oh." He snaps his head up again. "Dinah too?"

"Mmm."

They walk, or rather Reece walks and Erl jogs, in silence for a few minutes. Finally Erl says, "I found a neat rock. You wanna see it?"

"Sure," she says, looking the other way so Erl won't see her eyes brighten.

He pulls a gray stone from his pants pocket and hands it to her. "I found it in the school parking lot this afternoon, when I was waiting for—" He cuts off his words and looks away from Reece so she won't see the fire creeping up his neck and into his face.

She takes the rock from his trembling hand, examines it and sighs with disappointment. "Erl, this is just a piece of gravel."

"No, look at this side. There's a shiny spot, like crystal."

"That's not crystal. It's just gravel. Plain old driveway gravel." She tries to hand the stone back to Erl but he won't accept it.

"You keep it, Reece Dollar. For your collection."

She sighs. "Okay, Erl." She slips the rock into her pocket with the sandstone and the arrowhead as they approach the one-lane bridge that crosses Cullen's Creek. She thinks maybe she'll find a new box and start up her collection again. "Well, I'll be seeing you," she says.

"Uh, okay. Bye. Bye Reece." He backtracks down the lane and sprints toward the Cullen house. Reece sets her books on the concrete ledge of the bridge and makes her way down the embankment that leads to the creek. She removes the piece of gravel from her pocket and chucks it into the water, trying to make it skip along the surface, but the rock is not flat enough and sinks unceremoniously. She watches the spot where it entered the creek for a long time, letting her eyes lose focus. One time Jonah brought her down here to teach her how to skip stones. He held the unofficial county record with seven skips on a single throw. Jonah searched the water's edge for the flattest stones, then he and Reece staked out a dry spot high up on the creekbank. He demonstrated a couple throws, so Reece could see for herself the effect they were after. Then he stood behind his sister, wrapping her thumb and forefinger around a smooth granite shard in just the right position, pulling her arm back and flinging the stone squarely into the water with a resounding *plop*. After a few of these unsuccessful attempts Reece became discouraged, sat down hard on the damp grass and cried the anguished cry of a child with no cares in the world yet feeling as though the world weighed down on her slight shoulders. Jonah, ever patient with his baby sister, sat down next to her, soaking his new jeans, and pulled her close, letting her wipe her runny nose on his favorite shirt. After a while he whispered in her ear, *Do you want to try one more?* and she shook her head vigorously, like a dripping dog shaking off the damp. But Jonah persisted, lifting Reece to her feet and handing her the last stone in the pile, a sharply etched piece of flint. He stepped back, out of her way, and held his breath. She rubbed the gritty surface of the stone with her thumb as if conjuring a genie, planted her

feet into the ground and let it fly. They watched it skim the surface once, twice before sinking out of sight. *Jonah!* she cried, flinging her arms around his waist. He stooped down to her level, grasped
her upper arms and looked directly into her eyes. *You did it, little
gal*, he said. *Don't you ever let anyone tell you that you can't do whatever you want to do. You hear me?* Reece nodded and took his hand
as they trudged up the bank and back home. Just outside the front
door they stopped. *Reece, you're the smartest little gal I know*, he
said. *You don't let nobody tell you different.*

Reece finds herself sitting in a muddy patch at the water's
edge, her knees pulled up near her face, her arms wrapped around
her legs. *Jonah*, she whispers, and her eyes focus again on the rip-
pling creek. She feels something wet on her cheek, lifts her hand to
her face and knocks away the tear. She blinks a few times, trying to
adjust her eyes to the waning light. She's been sitting here for at
least two hours, easy. She starts to stand up when she hears footsteps beside her. "Hey Reece Dollar, your daddy's been worried
about you," a gentle voice says. Addison Hilliard squats down next
to her. "It's suppertime. Your mom fixed up a fine meatloaf."

She looks at him with doubt. "She never fixes meatloaf."

He stares into the muddy water. "That's 'cause she never had no
meat. But this afternoon, when I's takin' Roxanne Joshua home after
school, she said her mom and dad's givin' food from their store to
folks with storm damage, so we wheeled right over there. I got a lot a
food and I give it all to your mom. For lettin' us stay with you and
all." He looks at Reece. "Hey little gal, you been cryin'?"

Reece wipes her cheek again and shakes her head. "No."

Addison wraps his arm around her shoulders and lifts her up
to her feet. He smells of freshly-sawed wood and Ivory soap. He
hugs her, loosely at first, then tighter. She studies the red and blue
plaid pattern of his workshirt, trying to ignore the heat rushing
through her, the tingly feeling in her chest and in her head. Finally he releases her and they walk down the unnamed road, over
the railroad tracks and down the gravel driveway to the Dollar's
kitchen, where the meatloaf awaits.

"There you are," Reece's mother says when they walk through the door. "You've been nothing but a worry to me since that miserable day you were born, and now I've got to worry about your sister too. Sit down." Reece looks to her father for support as she takes her seat next to Addison, but he's staring at his plate and won't meet her eyes.

"Where's Dinah?" she asks.

"We don't know, Reece," Mr. Dollar says. "Baldy and Danny went out lookin' for her. I'm not too concerned; she prob'bly just got turned around in the woods, that's all. I'm gonna eat me a bite and then go lookin' too. If they don't find her by then."

Reece takes a sharp breath that only Addison notices. He pats her knee, then reaches for the bowl of green beans Mrs. Dollar is passing to him. "Shouldn't we all be out searching for her?" Reece asks, becoming more and more alarmed as she replays the morning's events in her mind.

"There's no need for that," her mother says. "Now eat your *meat*loaf," she adds, glaring at Addison.

"My pa and I sure do 'ppreciate you lettin' us stay here and all, ma'm," Addison says.

Mrs. Dollar holds a forkful of meatloaf in mid-air. "Yes, well, hopefully it won't be for much longer. Asa, how's the work coming on the Hilliard house?" She bites the food from her fork and swallows it nearly whole.

"Oh, it's comin' along, Mother. Be another day or two before it's livable, I reckon. Wouldn't you say, Addison?"

"Mmm," Addison says, chewing. He washes it down with a long drink of milk then says, "I heard the peculiarest thing down at the lumber yard today. Ya know Vernie Cletis?"

They all nod.

"Seems she got herself drunk last night."

"Nothing unusual about that," Mrs. Dollar sniffs.

Addison goes on. "Drunk her a gallon of vodka, then took her gun and shot off her big toe."

"You're kiddin'!" Mr. Dollar says, slapping his thigh.

"No. And there's more. There's blood everywhere, she's drunk as a skunk, but she finds the toe and drives on over to Dr. Riley's, wavin' it around his office like it's a white flag and she's surrenderin'."

"Why on earth would that woman do such a thing?" Mrs. Dollar asks with contempt.

"Well, that's the kicker," Addison says. "To hear Luther tell it, and he oughta know, since his wife Alfie's the nurse, Vernie done it cause she's in love with Dr. Riley. She needed to have some ailment so she could come see him, since he don't make house calls no more."

Any more, Reece whispers to her plate.

Mr. Dollar laughs long and heartily, nearly choking on a green bean. Reece moves her food around on her plate, picturing Vernie in her mind, stumbling through Dr. Riley's door, covered in blood and smelling like a distillery.

There's a knock on the screen door. From his seat Mr. Dollar peers out into the twilight, then says, "Dr. Riley, that you? Hey, we're just talkin' about ya. Come on in."

The doctor steps into the room and removes the John Deere cap he always wears when he goes outside, even though he lives in town and hasn't farmed a day in his life. It was taken as payment from a patient, no doubt.

"Heard 'bout you and Vernie Cletis, doctor," Mr. Dollar says. "How's she doin'?"

Dr. Riley scratches his head with the hand that holds his cap. "Oh, she'll mend. I sewed her toe back on and set her down in my back room to sleep it off."

Mrs. Dollar motions to one of the three empty seats at the table. "Join us for dinner, Dr. Riley?"

"No thank you, I can't stay long." He scans the faces in the room. "Is Dinah here?"

Mr. Dollar stands up. "We don't know where Dinah is right now," he says.

"Oh my, well . . ." He looks at Mr. and Mrs. Dollar. "Can we speak in the other room?"

Mrs. Dollar lights a kerosene lamp and carries it into the living room. Mr. Dollar and Dr. Riley follow her, and all three sit on the couch.

"You see we got us a television?" Asa Dollar says.

"Yes, I see that. It's a real fine one, too," Dr. Riley says. "But I'm here to talk to you about Dinah."

"What in the world do you mean?" Mrs. Dollar asks.

Dr. Riley perches on the edge of the sofa, his elbows resting on his knees. "Your girls came to see me this morning. Dinah wasn't feeling too well, so I took some blood and urine samples."

"They came to your office?"

"Yes ma'm. I don't know how to tell you this, but to say it straight out."

"Say what, doctor?" Asa says.

Dr. Riley takes a deep breath. "I think Dinah's pregnant."

The house is completely still. Reece and Addison have stopped eating in an attempt to hear the conversation in the living room. Mr. Dollar looks at the floor, trying to take it all in.

"The whore!" Mrs. Dollar screams, jettisoning herself from the couch, through the kitchen and out into the night air. "Dinah!" she yells, stomping up the hill and toward the woods. With each step her sensible rubber-soled shoes make an *uck . . . uck . . . uck* sound on ground still saturated from the storm last night. "Dinah Dollar, you whore, you come out here this instant!" She disappears into the dark trees with only instinct to guide her.

The men stand. "I'm sorry, Asa," Dr. Riley says.

They shake hands. "Thanks for tellin' us, doctor," Asa says, showing him to the door.

"Let me know when you find her," Dr. Riley says outside. "She'll need to start coming to see me on a regular basis."

Mr. Dollar pats the doctor on the shoulder. "Thank ya." He walks back into the kitchen and looks at Reece. "Ya hear what Dr. Riley said?"

She nods and looks out the window, but sees only the reflection of a small, pitiful, scared little girl she recognizes as herself six years ago, when they got the news about Jonah and she didn't really understand what was happening. But this she understands, far too well, much more than she realized until this moment.

"Ya went with her to the doctor, m'dear? Ya knew and didn't tell us?"

Reece shakes her head. "I didn't know she was—" She runs up the stairs to her room, feeling her way since she can't see through the tears.

Mr. Dollar gets the kerosene lamp from the living room and hands it to Addison, then picks up the lamp in the kitchen for himself. Addison nods and follows Asa outside to join in the search.

*

At the same time, Halo Truly is searching the streets of Memphis for Elvis Presley. He wants to ask him if this was how it was for him at first—all of those girls screaming hysterically for you, yet you don't feel worthy of such attention, because you're just a simple boy from the country who doesn't deserve all that's happening to you.

He's heard that Elvis bought himself a mansion here, but he would feel funny just walking up to his front door like that. Yet he doesn't know where else to look. Where does someone like Elvis hang out? Does he frequent the blues clubs on Beale Street? Does he spend time with Sam Phillips down at Sun Records? Apparently not, because he's checked those places, and the Palace Theatre, and Lansky Brothers, too, where he heard Elvis buys all his fancy clothes, and come up empty-handed. So as he walks the streets of the city, he tries to find the answers on his own.

As Halo's single gained momentum across the country, his record company had suggested a short tour of the South first, in an attempt to capitalize on the popularity of other Southerners like Elvis and Jerry Lee Lewis and Little Richard. So far it seems to be working—in each city the crowds grow larger and larger, and everyone knows the words to "Love Me in the Morning." Tonight, for instance, was definitely their best show so far. For

the first time it was an outdoor venue—the county fairgrounds—
and it was standing room only. Girls stood outside the gates
behind barricades of hay bales and cried and wailed because they
couldn't get in to see him. At the end one girl even jumped up
on stage and tried to tear off Halo's silver lamé jacket, until a
security guard stepped in and escorted her backstage. Halo was
certainly surprised to see her back there when they finished the
set, and was even more surprised by what she suggested they do
in the backseat of her father's car, which she said was parked
about a half a mile away. Halo's mother had taught him to always be polite, so he told the young lady politely but in no
uncertain terms that that wouldn't be possible tonight, thank
you. Immediately Rog and Kick moved in and told her to bring
a girlfriend and meet them back there in fifteen minutes, and
that was when Halo took to the streets of Memphis.

It's after midnight when he finally returns to the motel, his
search for Elvis having been fruitless and the questions still murky
in his mind. Rog and Kick aren't back yet, so he claims one of the
beds for himself, if only for an hour or two. They'll surely force
him back to the floor when they return, but until then he burrows
himself deep into the mattress and falls asleep.

CHAPTER SEVEN:
1937—1941

It took two weeks for the flood waters of Falling Star to recede so that folks could make their way back into town, so during this downtime Asa tried to make the house livable. He plugged the holes in the walls well enough to keep out the February freeze, using plywood, newspaper, and whatever material he could get his hands on. He swept dirt and dried mud from the wooden floors, and promised himself he'd get some linoleum to put down in the spring—it would, after all, be a lot easier for Rebecca to clean and take care of. He drove to the general store and stocked up on a few non-perishables, which he stored in his mother's old pie safe. He stoked the fire in the wood stove and folded up the dust covers from the furniture he'd left behind when he moved into Rebecca's house in Falling Star.

Every morning he woke Jonah, dressed and fed him, and tried to find things to keep a three year old occupied. It didn't work. Usually Jonah followed his father around the house as he completed his chores, never crying or getting in the way, just watching. On Jonah's fourth birthday Asa went upstairs to see if Rebecca wanted to join them in town for an ice cream treat, but the way she stared up at the ceiling, not even blinking, told Asa all he needed to know. In town he wanted to buy Jonah a real present, not just an ice cream, but his wallet was nearly empty and there wouldn't be any more pay until the forge dried out and was open for business again, so they drove back home and settled into their usual routine.

Every afternoon at one o'clock Asa brought Rebecca dinner on a tray, and brought her supper up at six o'clock in the evening.

Twice every day he brought two untouched trays back down again and split the meals between himself and his son. Every night he would sit Jonah on his lap in his big easy chair and read a Chester Lee Reece poem to his son by the smoky light of the kerosene lamp. Whenever he would begin to speak the lines, he would hear Rebecca groan and turn over in her bed.

By the second week Asa couldn't stand being cooped up in that house any longer with Rebecca just lying upstairs like that, so he decided to fix up his property as best he could. He bundled up Jonah against the cold and sat him outside where he could keep an eye on him, and started by repairing the gaping slats of the barn which stood lopsided but seemed sturdy enough. He made arrangements with Gib Jackney, who lived down the tracks a ways, to buy a small load of hay for the horse he hoped to get someday. He forked the stuff into the barn under the eye of Mr. Dandy, a stray German Shepherd who survived the flood and wandered, dirty and matted-haired, across the railroad tracks and onto the Dollar's homestead, and who was named for the title character of a Chester Lee Reece poem:

> *Oh Mr. Dandy, Mr. Dandy*
> *How you amuse us night and day*
> *With your ever-present humor*
> *And songs so light and gay.*
> *Oh dandy Mr. Dandy*
> *You are pleasant and divine,*
> *We will forever love you*
> *Until the end of time.*

Asa cleared all five acres of the property by hand and plowed most of it, intending to plant corn on it in the spring. He skimmed the muck off the top of the pond that stood at the boundary line between him and Gib Jackney and waited for the frogs and dragonflies to return. He re-seeded the grape arbor and cleared away the dead brush. He gave the springhouse a fresh coat of white paint and inaugurated it with one quart of freshly-acquired milk from his newly-acquired (on credit) dairy cow, which he named Chester in honor of you-know-who, and locked the door up tight so Mr. Dandy wouldn't find the bottle and claim it for himself.

At the end of the two weeks the land was in fairly good shape and there wasn't much more he could do until spring, so he and most of the other menfolk of the county spent the next two weeks building an earthen levee around the town of Falling Star. When this task was completed he spent two more weeks helping clean up the forge so they could all get back to work. Asa was grateful for the chance to keep busy, but the hardest thing he had to do every day was drive by the place where their house had once stood, where they had lost Rachel. From the street he would look up at the red brick facade of the Presbyterian church where he had sought shelter, where he thought he would find his wife and children safe, and see the high-water mark, which they had measured at eighty feet. Even though he had been right there in the middle of all of it, he still couldn't believe it. He just couldn't imagine the water ever rising that high, and yet he had lived through it, so he knew it to be true.

For those entire six weeks Rebecca did not speak and did not leave her bed except to swing her legs over the side and relieve herself in a tin pan. Asa took care of Jonah as best he could, and took to praying that when the time came for him to start working full time again, the boy would be safe alone with his mother in that house all day. It seemed to Asa he had taken to praying a lot lately, while Rebecca's beloved bible had washed away in the flood and she hadn't asked about it yet.

Finally on the Monday morning he was set to go back to work at the forge, he just came out with it and asked his wife how she planned to take care of her house and child from the comfort of her bed. Rebecca grunted and rolled away from him, taking the coverlet with her.

Asa straddled her body, pushing her shoulderblades into the mattress as her starved hipbones poked his kneecaps. "God damn it woman, listen to me!" he roared.

"Asa, your language—"

"Shut up! Just shut up!" Asa said. "Shut up and get your ass out of his bed! Jesus, at least—"

"Don't you use that name in this house," she seethed.

"Jesus jesus jesus!" he screamed. "Jesus wants ya to get up and take care of your family!"

"Jesus killed my daughter," she whispered, turning her face into the pillow. "He can go to hell." She tried in vain to shrug her husband away from her body.

"Look at ya," Asa said. "Used to be ya could practically whup me with one hand tied behind your back." He returned to his side of the bed, against the wall. "Look what you've let yourself become."

Rebecca closed her eyes. "I've become a woman who let her baby die," she said. "Just sat there and watched as that idiot, that man of *god*, dropped my baby into the—"

"Mom? Mom?"

Rebecca felt a gentle hand nudging her arm and opened her eyes to see Jonah standing at her bedside.

"Mom, did baby jesus kill baby Rachel?" he asked. Neither of his parents answered him, so he tried another approach. "I hope not," he said. "I love baby jesus. He wouldn't do something like that."

Rebecca reached out and smoothed Jonah's light mahogany hair. "No, he wouldn't," she barely said. "Baby jesus loves you, too, and he loved baby Rachel. He's watching her up in heaven right now."

"Good," Jonah said, smiling. "I'm glad he's watching her." He ran back to his room which adjoined his parents' by a short hallway.

"*Now get out of this bed*," Asa whispered in Rebecca's ear.

She sighed heavily, pushed the coverlet to the foot of the bed and sat on its edge. She looked around the room. "Have you seen my bible?" she asked Asa.

*

At first Rebecca was very tentative around her new home. She sat on the edges of the furniture, refused to walk barefoot in the house and held the pans and pots and plates and pitchers by the tips of her fingers, nearly letting them slip to the floor on many occasions. She consented, reluctantly, to use the despised outhouse, but only during the daylight hours—never after dark. Asa chuckled to himself when she announced this, knowing from experience that circumstances far beyond her control would take care of that sooner or later.

Gradually she returned to the Rebecca of old, even renewing her library card in Falling Star so she could keep up on the literature of the day. Every night before she tucked Jonah into his bed she read him a chapter from *Gone With the Wind*, then took to her own bed and read ten more chapters before extinguishing the oil lamp, turning her back to her husband and falling asleep. She went back to her old self in every way but the one which was most vital to Asa's physical well-being. For nearly two years he pleaded, petitioned, prodded, prompted, propelled, impelled, compelled, coaxed, cajoled, beseeched, begged, bribed, sweet-talked, tempted and threatened. As months passed and her frame began to fill out she fought him off more successfully each time. Finally, though, her heft was no match for a man long denied as Asa. Remembering their first encounter at her house on Church Street, he waited until she was almost asleep to heave his body on top of hers, force her legs apart and whisper into her neck that these were her wifely duties and she *would* perform them. Teetering on the brink of sleep, Rebecca's eyes parted and her face contorted. Asa prepared for yet another rebuff as suddenly her legs flew up and around his waist, squeezing his midsection so tightly he thought his ribs would crack like walnut shells. As he writhed in Rebecca's grasp an agonized smile crossed his face, and he wished only that he had tried this approach sooner.

*

Rebecca had decided they would begin attending church again, only she would never step foot in a Baptist church, after that idiot Pastor Alberts had . . . well, she couldn't even think of it. She determined they would try the Presbyterian church, since they had after all offered shelter during the flood. She had been reading her bible faithfully every morning, but during the past couple of years had come across some discrepancies which she needed a trained professional to sort out for her. For the first two weeks she dressed Jonah and Asa in their Sunday clothes and the three of them drove to Rev. Calder's church, where the woman paid rapt attention and the boy and the man squirmed and struggled not to fall asleep during the service. The third week, when Rebecca laid out Asa's clothes, he refused to get dressed. "I've heard all I need to hear," he told her. "I don't care if ya take the boy, but I'm not goin' anymore." When Rebecca tried to protest, he silenced her immediately by letting her know which of *his* services she'd be doing without if she pressed the matter. She drove Jonah to church that morning and mentioned it no more.

Rebecca had feared that when it was time for her first born to start school she wouldn't know how to fill her days. A visit to Dr. Riley, however, gave her plenty to do and think about. There were new clothes and diapers to sew, and a crib to be purchased, and Jonah's room had to be redone in order to accommodate his new baby brother or sister. She asked Asa once a week to please consider tapping into the electricity of the neighbors across the tracks, or at least installing indoor plumbing, because she certainly didn't intend to haul herself and that baby all the way to the outhouse ten times a day. He did put down the linoleum he had been promising for two years, and swore that electricity and running water would come along soon enough. But the weather turned cold before those things could happen, and he told his wife she would have to wait until spring.

On Christmas Eve 1939 Rebecca began to feel the familiar labor pains and sent Asa to fetch Dr. Riley. A wet snow had fallen almost non-stop for the past three days, making the road to the hospital in Broulet impassable. When the doctor arrived he headed upstairs and told Asa to pump water from the well and heat it on the woodstove. Through the grate in the floor of the bedroom that brought warmth up from the living room below, the doctor called instructions down to the nervous father and his calm son. Early on Christmas morning Daniel Dollar joined the family, exactly three years after his ill-fated sister was born. Rebecca took this as a sign from god that this child would not be taken from her, but just to be sure she slipped him between her soaking nightclothes and her chest and the two of them fell asleep.

Danny spent his first night in his mother's bed, and his second and third nights as well, which soon stretched into a week and then a month's time when mother and newborn son were never parted. Rebecca carried Danny everywhere, afraid to release him from her grasp even for a second, especially on the days it rained. Her older son tugged at the sleeve of her nightgown in a plea for the attention that only a mother can give, but was shooed away for fear of disturbing his baby brother. He would not be deterred, however, having grown accustomed to her undivided affection years before when they lived in the house by the river. So he took the pillow and blanket from his mattress and made his bed on the floor next to his mother. This crowded situation gave Asa no choice but to begin sleeping his Jonah's bed each night, driven from his wife's side by a six-year-old boy and a one-month-old infant.

Though he disapproved of the sleeping arrangements, Asa had little time nor energy to remedy the situation. Orders at the forge had more than tripled, requiring he work overtime nearly every day. While the additional money came in handy, he could have used the extra hours completing his chores around the homestead. He had already decided that in a few weeks, when Jonah turned seven, he would enlist the help of his older son. He knew Rebecca would hardly stand for it, but something had to be done. Jonah could feed Mr. Dandy the dog, and Chester the cow, and the new horse, Nanny, and the two hens he had been able to purchase with his overtime money. In the spring he would teach the boy how to milk the cow and pitch hay and drop corn seeds in rows and weed between them. The boy was bright and had watched his father do these things for so long that he was sure he could accomplish these tasks.

As spring turned to summer, and summer to fall, Jonah did take over these simple chores, and performed them much better than Asa had imagined. Rebecca had been easy to convince when she realized the more time Jonah spent outside doing chores, the less time he would spend indoors bothering her as she tended to Danny. But one afternoon when Jonah was nearly eight years old, and fall had turned to winter seemingly overnight, Rebecca looked at him as he blew into the house, stomping his feet and rubbing his hands together to warm himself, and didn't even recognize her son. He seemed so much older, somehow, so mature. His form had actually filled out a little, and his flushed cheeks gave him a rather grown-up look. He had even taken to imitating his father by loudly scraping a ball of phlegm up from the bottom of his throat and spitting it out the kitchen door and up the hill as far as he could. The first time Rebecca saw him do that she smiled and set Danny down on the floor. She took Jonah's coat from his shoulders and told him to sit down at the table, and brought him a cup of hot chocolate she had been heating for herself on the propane stove Asa had recently bought. She sat down next to him and stroked his bangs, which were matted to his forehead with sweat despite the cold. "How was school today, Jonah?" she asked him, and Jonah simply smiled and looked down into his cup.

By the end of 1940 business at the forge had slowed and Asa resumed his usual working hours, but at Rebecca's insistence Jonah still helped his father with the chores. On Christmas Eve they exchanged their presents—a stuffed toy rabbit for Danny, who had taken to carrying an old sock around with him everywhere; a pair of work gloves for Jonah (which he had asked for); a new apron for Rebecca; and a new silver-plated fob for Asa's pocket watch. They didn't indulge the children in the Santa Claus ritual since the previous Christmas Rebecca had been in labor, and this year Jonah was too old and Danny was too young for such a thing. So they drank hot cider and went to bed early, and for the first time in a year Jonah and Danny slept in their own room and Asa and Rebecca slept together in their bed.

By Jonah's eighth birthday Rebecca knew she was expecting again. On October 8, 1941, Dinah was born. When Dr. Riley told Rebecca it was a girl, she shrieked in horror—she'd be damned if she'd lose another daughter. She'd been positive she'd been carrying a boy, that it was her destiny to bear nothing but sons, because only sons were strong enough to survive. When the doctor tried to hand the newborn to her mother, Rebecca folded her arms across her chest and turned toward the hospital wall. Later that week, back home in Abandon, she awoke one day to find the girl lying in her arms anyway, placed their by her husband, she suspected. She studied the pink face and tried to conjure up the maternal feeling she'd had with her other children, but all she felt was a tight, empty space settled hard at the bottom of her chest. Just then Asa brought Jonah and Danny into the room, and the three of them cooed over the baby and took turns holding her. When Asa offered her to Rebecca again she shooed them away toward the crib, but when she saw the looks in her sons' faces she relented and held the child, stiffly and away from her body. At that moment, at age thirty-five, Rebecca Wonderman Dollar swore she would never bear another child as long as she lived.

CHAPTER EIGHT:
SEPTEMBER 12, 1957

She hears her mother's voice above all the others calling her name. Each time her mother says that word, punching it with sarcasm and truth as only a mother can, she jumps as if a shot has been fired. She's been crouching behind a dogwood at the far edge of the woods since early this afternoon, after she tumbled from Addison Hilliard's truck, entered the school through the front door, exited immediately through the back door, and hiked all the way here. She scraped her legs pretty badly climbing up the embankment, but by now the blood has dried into tiny scabs dotting her legs like the chicken pox. She hasn't moved in five hours. The first fifteen minutes or so were the worst, when her limbs were invaded by legions of microscopic soldiers attacking her from the inside with weapons of needles and pins and tiny sharp swords that pricked her skin until she thought she would scream *I surrender*. Still she didn't move, not even to shoo away a mosquito that landed on her knee, and eventually the pain melted into an icy numbness and her flesh hardened so that the mosquito couldn't draw blood anymore.

But now in the night so dark it hurts, her mother's voice is coming closer and closer to her through the woods, and every time she shifts her eyes in the direction of the sound she swears she sees her mother's hulking form moving toward her, then realizes it's just a branch shivering in the wind, or even just her mind showing her what she thinks she sees. She does see several tiny points of light, however, scattered here and there, and knows she isn't imagining those, that practically everyone in town must be looking for her, and that her hiding place won't be safe for much longer. She wills her body to move and waits a minute or two for her paralyzed limbs to respond. Finally she unfurls herself, slowly, hugging the tree for balance, then gently stomping her feet to get the circulation going. Each stomp takes double the effort, not only because her legs are dead, but because she must extract her feet from the muck that has formed on the floor of the woods, a dirty black mixture of earth and rain and forest debris, and soon her ankles are splattered with the stuff. When she's regained about half the feeling in her arms and legs she takes a few tentative steps, then starts to run. She's shaky but mobile until her momentum is stopped when she twists her ankle. It doesn't hurt, but she turns and searches the ground to see what she stepped on. She picks up a hunting knife, rusted almost clear through with age and the elements, the iron oxide flaking off on her hands and on her dress, but still quite a sharp weapon. She squeezes her fist around the handle and takes off running again, with more energy now, emerging from the woods at the spot where the embankment is not so steep. She slides all the way down on her backside until she reaches the bottom of the hill, then without pausing stands up and keeps going, running down the middle of the street. A disabling cramp sears her side yet she continues running until she reaches the courthouse square.

The Founder's Festival starts in less than three days, and preparations have already begun. During the day workers strung multi-colored lights on the courthouse and on the trees that line the street leading to the square, and tomorrow colorful flags will be hung from the streetlamps. Storefronts have been scrubbed and sidewalks swept, and in twenty four hours the street will be closed to traffic so vendors can spend all day Friday setting up their booths. But the workers and the storekeepers have gone home for supper by now, and the colored lights, not to be lit until dusk Saturday, hang upside down in the twilight like slumbering bats.

She stumbles into the square and falls against the Wesley Tree, panting hard, trying to catch her breath. She squeezes her eyes together tight until she can see the shadow of her blood coursing through her brain.

"Dinah."

She keeps her eyes closed, hoping that the voice is in her head.

"Dinah gal, we all been lookin' for you."

Her eyes creep open. Addison Hilliard stands before her with a kerosene lamp in one hand, offering the other hand to her. She's still gripping the hunting knife in her fist and now raises it over her head. "You stay away from me!" she screams. Addison takes a step forward and she howls, like an animal with its paw caught in a steel trap, and plunges the knife into her lower abdomen.

Addison leaps backward but can't take his eyes off the girl. "My god gal," he mutters. "What have you done?" He recovers and steps toward her.

"No!" she shrieks, and cuts herself again. Addison bends down to help her. She raises the knife and stabs herself repeatedly until Addison stands up and starts to back away. He turns and bumps into Mrs. Dollar, who has come up behind him. Over Addison's shoulder she sees Dinah and her harsh face softens for an instant, before hardening again.

"I tried stoppin' her—" Addison says, but Mrs. Dollar cuts him off by lifting her hand. Neither of them moves. Dinah loses consciousness and the blade drops from her hand, clattering on the sidewalk.

"Get away from us," Mrs. Dollar says.

Addison moves aside, but Mrs. Dollar just stands there, staring at her daughter, watching the blood seep into a pool at Dinah's feet. Just then the posse of searchers comes upon the scene. They brush past Mrs. Dollar and rush to Dinah's side, but Dr. Riley pushes them back. He digs a set of keys from his pants pocket and hands them to Addison's father. "Baldy, run down the street to my office and get my pickup. It's parked out back. We've got to get this girl to the hospital in Broulet." There's no hospital in Abandon,

nor in all of Cullen County, a fact which usually is immaterial
since Dr. Riley can take care of most ailments.

Dr. Riley crouches next to Dinah to assess the situation. She has
a faint pulse and her breathing is shallow. Beneath her torn dress and
shredded flesh he finds half of a fetus swimming in an ocean of blood,
and covers his face with his hands in an attempt to suppress the tears.
Drunken women shooting off their toes he can handle, but this is
beyond anything he's seen in all his years of doctoring.

Baldy pulls up in Dr. Riley's pickup truck. He leaves the engine
running and steps out to help the doctor. "Addison," Dr. Riley says,
"there are some blankets in the seat. Spread them out in the bed.
Baldy, you grab her feet." The two of them lift Dinah's body. "Easy,
Baldy. That's it." They carry her around to the back of the truck and
set her down on the quilts Addison has laid out. "Good. Good." He
looks to the gathered crowd. "I need someone to ride in the back with
her. I think her family should be around her. Asa?"

"I can't, doctor. I've got to get to work or they'll fire me for sure."

"We'll go, Dr. Riley," Baldy says, pointing to himself and his son.

"Over my dead body," Mrs. Dollar says.

"Then you'll go?" the doctor asks Dinah's mother.

"No, no. I've left Reece alone in that house. Heaven knows
that girl's probably burnt it down by now. I need to go home."

"Good lord, people, this girl is dying!" Dr. Riley says.

"I'll go," Danny says, stepping forward. He hands his lantern
to his mother and kisses her on the cheek.

"No Daniel—"

"Yes mother," he says, climbing up into the truck bed. "She's my
sister." Dr. Riley slams the tailgate shut and gets behind the wheel.
Mrs. Dollar walks over to the driver's window and says a few words
to Dr. Riley, then steps back. Danny sits on the wheel hub and
holds Dinah's hand, swaying slightly as the doctor speeds away.

"How do you propose we get home, Asa?" Mrs. Dollar asks
her husband, crossing the road.

He points to a couple striding toward them, noticing for the
first time that his hand is shaking, that in fact he's shaking all over.

Finally Luther and Alfie Marvin reach the scene, having walked from their house next door to Dr. Riley's. "What's all the commotion down here?" Luther asks. He surveys the area, bends down and dips his finger in the puddle of blood spreading down the sidewalk from the Wesley Tree. "Oh my," he whispers, and wipes his hand on his pantsleg.

Alfie takes him by the shoulders and lifts him to a standing position. "He gets kinda woozy around the sight of blood," she explains. "Everybody okay here?"

They all nod.

"What happened?" Alfie asks.

Baldy and Addison Hilliard stare at the ground. Mrs. Dollar looks at her husband. "Well, she's your daughter. You tell them."

Asa stuffs his hands into the pockets of his work pants. "Dinah had an accident," he says. "Dr. Riley took her to the hospital in Broulet."

"Is she alright?" Alfie asks, patting her husband on the back. Luther is bent over with elbows on his upper legs and his head between his knees.

"We . . . we don't know."

"Well, I'm real sorry to hear about that," Alfie says. "If there's anything we can do—"

"As a matter of fact there is," Mrs. Dollar says. "We need a ride back to our house."

Luther lifts his head. "We'd be glad to take ya."

"We'll wait here."

Luther and Alfie go to fetch their car. When they're out of earshot Luther says to his wife, "They don't seem too broke up about it, do they?"

"Nope," she says.

"Didn't you say those Dollar girls came to see the doctor today?"

"Sure did," Alfie says. "That Dinah came in with morning sickness and cramping, half scared out of her mind. Ask me, I think she'd miscarried already, but Dr. Riley's not so sure." She shakes her head and clucks her tongue. "Nothing but poor white trash, they are."

*

Reece has been lying fully dressed on top of the bedclothes for hours, playing different scenarios over and over in her mind as to what might be going on out there in the woods. She longs to go downstairs and watch the television, or even to get her father's transistor radio and try to find the station that plays Halo Truly and Elvis Presley and Gene Vincent songs all night long, but she's afraid to move. If she moves her mother will come home and find her out of bed and tell her bad things about Dinah, things she's not ready to hear. Finally she hears a car pull up, two doors open and slam shut, and the car drives away. Then she hears another car door open and shut, an engine starts, and the car drives away. That must be Doodle leaving for work, Reece thinks, hurt that he didn't come up and say goodnight to her first. She hears the kitchen door open and people entering the house, but no one speaks. After a few minutes she hears her mother cock the shotgun and set it down on the kitchen table. She still doesn't move. She waits and waits for Dinah to climb the stairs and enter their room, and the longer she waits, the harder and louder her heart pounds until finally she can't take the sound anymore and shoves the pillow over her face to block out the noise, but it doesn't work because the racket is coming from inside. Eventually she can't breathe any-more so she removes the pillow and concentrates on listening for house sounds—creaking walls, popping windowsills, the scurry-ing pitter patter of little mouse feet—anything to distract her from the reality of her situation. After what feels like hours later she hears another vehicle pull into the driveway, what sounds like a pickup truck. Someone gets out of the truck, gets into a car, and both autos drive away. Reece is becoming confused now, with all these cars coming and going, she can't figure out who they all belong too, or even who is in the house at the moment. A few minutes later the same pickup truck pulls up, drops someone off and leaves again, then the kitchen door opens. She hears first Danny speaking to someone in a soothing voice, then her mother responding with a calm, almost docile tone Reece has never heard from her before. After a few minutes they climb the stairs together and their mother goes to her room. There's a knock on Reece's bedroom door, but before she can answer Danny walks in and shuts the door behind him. He sits on the edge of the bed and holds Reece's hand and tells her everything, how Addison found her first, propped up against the Wesley Tree, and how she stabbed herself in the stomach seven times, how they put her in the back of Dr. Riley's pickup truck and how he rode with her all the way to the hospital in Broulet, how she was in surgery for three hours and that the doctors there said she would live, but that she would be in the hospital for a few weeks. He doesn't tell her about all of the blood, or about the baby, or rather the half of a baby, that Danny saw in her stomach, because he doesn't think Reece would understand that, and he doesn't want to upset her. By the time he's finished the story the first glow of morning light is filling the room.

"I'm supposed to help Hilliards with their house again today," he tells her, "but they said I could take their truck and go see Dinah in the hospital, if I wanted. Do you want to go with me?"

Reece's eyes are nearly crusted shut with tears, but she manages to nod yes.

"Okay, but you know mom will never let you. So you go on to school and I'll pick you up out front before the morning bell rings."

She nods again.

Danny checks the watch on Reece and Dinah's nightstand. "I'm riding with Hilliards over to their place now. Don't forget to meet me in front of the school." He leaves the room and goes downstairs. Reece hears them trample outside, start up the truck and rumble away. She rolls over onto her right side and stares at the wall until it's time to get up.

She doesn't bother to change her dress or wash her face or brush her hair or teeth. When she hears her father return from work she climbs out the window and sneaks around the back of the house and up the hill. She takes the shortcut through the woods, wondering as she climbs over trees downed in the storm where Dinah had hidden, speculating if this sugar maple or that persimmon sheltered her sister from the demons inside her, if she'd crouched unseen behind the giant poplar that Jonah had said guarded the princess's castle. She wonders if Jonah had told Dinah the same fairy tale he'd told Reece. She hopes not. She likes to think that the golden castle was their secret and theirs alone.

At the base of the hill she's just steps from the courthouse square and from the Wesley Tree. She sees a small crowd gathered around the monument, some on hands and knees scouring the sidewalk with buckets of soapy water and scrub brushes, others supervising the operation. She sneaks away and makes it to the school without anyone she knows seeing her, slipping through dark alleys between shops and behind back fences of private homes.

Danny is there waiting for her in Addison Hilliard's pickup truck. She climbs in, stepping on the same pack of chewing tobacco that was there on the floorboard yesterday. But was it really yesterday? Since she hasn't slept, yesterday and today feel to her like the same day, like the longest day of her life. The thought makes her yawn so widely her jaw pops and Danny looks at her with concern.

"It'll take us a little while to get there," he says. "Why don't you try to get some sleep?" He lifts his arm and lets Reece snuggle under it, resting her head on his shoulder as he drives.

Reece is awakened by a bump in the road. She looks around but doesn't recognize her surroundings. "Are we there?" she asks Danny.

"Almost." At a four-way stop he turns right and Reece sees the hospital looming on the left side of the street, taking up a whole block. He pulls the truck into the parking lot and shuts off the engine. Inside there's no one sitting at the reception desk, so Reece starts to sit down in the waiting area. Danny pulls her arm. "It's okay. I know where her room is." She follows him to the elevator and he presses the button for the third floor.

The doors open and they step out into a blinding white, disinfected hallway. "This way," Danny whispers, leading the way to a room at the end of the corridor. He pushes open the door and they stare at two empty beds.

"She was—" Danny steps outside and checks the room number, then re-enters the room. "I don't—" He jogs back down the hall to the nurses' station. Reece follows him.

"Excuse me, ma'm," he says to the nurse on duty, who's typing a report. "We've come to see our sister, but she's not in her room. Can you tell me if she's been moved?" He flashes the smile that has charmed a hundred schoolgirls from Abandon to Cincinnati. "The name is Dollar."

The nurse checks her log. "You say she's your sister?" the nurse asks.

"Yes."

The nurse locates Dinah's name on a line in about the middle of the page and traces her finger across to the end of the line. "She's been moved, alright," she says, closing the log book.

"Can you tell us what room she's in?" Danny asks.

The nurse smirks at Danny as if he's the dumbest person she's come across this morning. "She's been *moved*. To Sister Cecilia's Hospital and Home for Wayward Girls." She swivels her chair away from them and back to her typing.

"Wait!" Danny says. "Why? Where is that?"

The nurse doesn't look up from her flying fingers. "That's all I can tell you." She zips the page from the platen, places it in a wire basket and loads the next report into the typewriter.

Reece looks up at Danny, bewildered. He shrugs his shoulders and presses the down button to call for the elevator. They don't speak until they're back in the truck and on the road.

"*She* did this, Danny," Reece says finally. Danny taps his fingers on the steering wheel. "I know you think she can do no wrong. But you don't know her like I do. Like Dinah and I do. You only

see her good side, what there is of it." Danny stares straight ahead.
"We should go looking for Dinah. We can rescue her and bring her
back home, where she belongs." Danny guns the engine and whips
around a tractor that's been slowing their pace. He snaps back into
his lane just before a car passes them going the opposite direction.
"She did this, you know," she says again. They ride the rest of the
way to Abandon in silence.

He stops the truck in front of the school. "Go on," he says,
when Reece doesn't get out.

"I don't feel like going in there today," she says. "Everyone will
ask me where Dinah is and I'll have to explain everything, or else
they'll know already, they'll know what happened to her and look
at me funny and whisper behind my back and the boys will lift up
my skirt and the teachers will look down on me with those pitiful
looks on their faces." She sniffs and puts her hand on the door
handle. "But I can't go home," she sighs. "Mom won't stand for
that." She flicks the handle and pushes the door open with her
shoulder. Danny takes her arm and yanks her back in.

"Come with me today," he says. "Maybe Baldy can find some
work for you to do." Gravel flies from the tires as he does a u-turn
in the school driveway and heads away from town, toward Hilliard's
farm. As they pass the Wesley Tree Reece cranes her neck out the
window, searching for any information about her sister. A few
townsfolk are still gathered around the monument, cleaning the
sidewalk and wrapping it with wire to protect it from the gifts to
be offered on Saturday evening. When they see Danny and Reece
drive by they stop their work and stare at them with what some
call the evil eye. Danny speeds up, throwing Reece against the
door. "Ow," she whispers, the sound cut off by the sobs rising
from her chest. She hides her face in her hands, letting the tears
fall between her fingers onto the pocket of her dress that holds the
sandstone and the arrowhead, the arrowhead she received in this
very truck just twenty four hours earlier. When she finally lifts her
eyes Danny is steering the truck between the gates of Hilliard's

farm, maneuvering the tires through the deep, jagged ruts that lead to the barn.

Baldy greets them by waving the navy blue handkerchief he always carries in the front pocket of his overalls. He steps up to the driver's side before Danny can kill the engine.

"How is she?" Hilliard asks. "How's that sister of yers?"

Danny and Reece get out of the truck. "Baldy, you got something to keep Reece busy for a while?" Danny asks his boss.

Baldy wipes his troubled forehead with the bandanna. "She gonna make it?" He glances at Reece. "I mean Dinah."

Danny shrugs and jerks his head in Reece's direction. "Maybe she can help Addison with something?"

The elder Hilliard squints at Reece, who's hanging back behind the truck, kicking at a hard piece of earth with a scuffed patent-leather toe. "Yeah sure, Danny. He's down at the springhouse."

Danny points to a squat, white building in the distance, its flat roof emerging from behind a rolling hill too high and round for planting or building on. Baldy has always believed the grassy hump rising from the earth was an ancient Indian burial mound and refuses to go near it, let alone plow it under. "Go on," he says. Reece watches the ground as she walks, carefully avoiding alternate piles of day-old manure and discarded lumber. She walks around the hill, not sure if she believes the Indian burial myth but not willing to risk it, and comes upon the springhouse. Its door is wide open so she steps inside and inhales the wet, cool aroma of clean water and cured meat. She hears the brook gurgling below her feet and stoops down, dipping her hands in the stream and gulping down the icy flow.

"Hey Dollar gal," a voice says behind her. She whirls around, splashing water on her dress and shoes. "Whatcha doin' down here? Shouldn't you be in school?"

Reece wipes her chin with her palm and licks the moisture from her lips. "Your dad sent me down here to help you."

"That doesn't answer my question, gal. Ain't there school today?"

She tries to step out of the springhouse but Addison moves forward, blocking her path. "Yes," she whispers. "But I—"

He puts a hand on her shoulder and lowers his voice. "I'm real sorry 'bout your sister. How's she doin'?"

Reece shrugs, mumbles "I don't know," and studies Addison's work boots. Years of farming this land, of wringing every kernel of corn from brittle stalks, praying the rain holds off and the price per bushel rises tomorrow, is embedded in the cracked chestnut leather. He carries his family's soil with him wherever he goes, breathes it in until it coats his innards like a coal miner with black lung. He coughs, then turns his head and spits. Reece's gaze drifts from the brown globule of snuff juice soaking into the ground up to his face, lines like dry river beds snaking prematurely across his cheeks and forehead and crusted with the same dirt as his shoes, and sees his slate eyes boring through her body. "You still got that arrowhead I gave ya?" he asks, noticing how one dress pocket hangs lower than the other.

She nods as he squeezes her shoulder and gently urges her backward into the darkness. He steps into the springhouse and shuts the door behind them. The odor of the ham drying beside her mixes with the smell of dirt and sweat and chewing tobacco, coating the inside of her mouth and nostrils with a sickly sweetness. He wraps his free hand around her waist and pulls her closer to him until there's just a whisper of space between them, and the area between her legs buzzes like a live electrical wire.

"How old are you now, gal?" he asks. "You fourteen yet?"

She forces down a dry swallow. "Saturday," she croaks.

"That's real good," he says. "Almost a woman now. A real pretty gal." He moves his other hand from her shoulder to her waist, then drops them both to the fleshy, upper part of her legs. She clenches as he strokes them gently until she relaxes. He takes a step forward and her face is immersed in his shirt front. Instinctively she lifts her quivering fingers to the buttons and undoes them from top to bottom. Her eyes are adjusting to the bit of light seeping in through the slats of the door and reflexively she traces her forefinger through the wisps of hair she can see on his chest. He emits a guttural moan and slips his hands under the skirt of her dress. She jerks her hand away and tries to escape but is trapped in the vise of his arms. She cries out but he clamps his mouth down over hers until she begins to kiss him back and hug his neck and stroke his hair. In her mind she sees the indelible picture of Dinah and Bernie writhing on the ground as she spied from behind a tree, but now the image has taken on a whole new resonance for her and she presses her lips harder into his. Still embracing, he slides one hand between her legs and prods them open until her breathing matches his, and he pushes his finger inside her. She screams into his mouth, biting the inside of his lip until she tastes blood, but he only pushes farther. When she tries to step away he finally removes his hand and with it pries her fingers from his neck and places her hand in that dark, forbidden region between his legs where she's never even allowed herself to look before, let alone touch. Their mouths still united, he shoves her hand down between the waistband of his pants and begins to sway as his kisses move down her neck and across her shoulder. With her other hand she finds herself unfastening his pants, slowly, slowly, unsure if this is what she should do or even wants to do, but the action pleases him because at that moment he

"Reece!" Danny's faraway voice pierces the dark air of the springhouse and they explode apart. She stands there, frozen, her insides burning and her skin clammy. Addison reaches out to brush a damp strand of hair from her cheek and she ducks under his arm and throws open the door. The sun's late afternoon rays burn the moisture from her arms and her entire body shivers as she runs on trembling legs into her brother at the top of the mound. He clasps her arm and pulls her behind him. "I've been calling you for half an hour," he growls. "Come on, we've got to get back home. Baldy'll drive us."

Reece stumbles along beside him, smoothing the wrinkles from her dress as she walks. It's later in the day than she thought and she tries to shake away the disorientation buzzing around her head like a mosquito. When they reach the house, nearly rebuilt now except for the roof, she veers toward its front door. "I need to go to the bathroom, Danny," she says. Her panties are damp and clinging to her waist and thighs.

"We have a bathroom at home, Reece. God, can't you wait ten minutes?" He pushes her toward the truck and they climb into the cab. "Mom doesn't like us to be late, you know that." He starts the motor as Baldy scrambles behind the wheel.

"What's your hurry, Danny?" he wheezes, having run from the barn when he heard the engine turn over.

"Our mother needs us. If we're late she gets very worried," he says, looking straight ahead out the windshield as Baldy steers them through the front gate of the farm. No one speaks for the rest of the ride. Reece fidgets the whole way home, attempting to surreptitiously rearrange her undergarments and hoping that what happened in the springhouse isn't plastered all over her face, because if asked about it she's not sure she could explain what took place there.

Walking into the kitchen Danny and Reece are met with a tableful of cakes, pies, casseroles, and breads of every sort, the kind of spread you only see when someone's died. Reece draws a sharp breath and clamps her hand over her mouth. She looks to her mother for some kind of sign but is met with the usual silence. "Is Dinah . . . ?" she whispers.

"Your sister is fine," Mrs. Dollar huffs. "That girl today has caused me almost as much grief as you have." She nods toward the buffet. "There's your supper. Fill a plate and take it to your room. Both of you." Danny pauses, unaccustomed to hearing that tone of voice directed toward him, but Reece does as she's told without a second thought. She sees her father eating from a t.v. tray in front of the television but goes upstairs without speaking to him, sick of the way he won't ever stand up to her mother.

In her room she takes a few bites of her food and sets the plate on the dresser. Even though it's early she rinses her face, changes into her pajamas and crawls under the covers. She's in that neverland between states of consciousness when there's a knock on the door.

Hoping she's dreaming, Reece doesn't respond. The door opens and Danny comes in and sits on the edge of the bed.

"Reece, are you awake?"

"Mmm."

He nudges her shoulder. "Open your eyes."

She looks at him with the one eye that's not buried in the pillow.

"Over at Baldy's today, when you were with Addison—"

Reece squeezes her eye shut again.

"Reece, listen! I looked up Sister Cecilia's in Baldy's phone book. It's in Vernon, Kentucky. I got the address." She opens her eye again and memorizes the number and street Danny has printed on a scrap of paper. He folds it up and puts it in his front shirt pocket. "Tomorrow—"

"Daniel? Daniel, come down here please," their mother says in a sweeter tone.

Danny stands up. "We'll talk about this in the morning," he says, slipping out the door and downstairs. A few minutes later her father enters her room, without knocking first, to say goodnight before he leaves for work.

"Reece m'dear?" he whispers. She pretends she's asleep and he knows it. He leaves without saying another word, pulling the door shut harder than usual on the way out. Reece has just drifted off when Danny enters her room again and squats down next to her bed. "What we talked about?" he murmurs. "Just forget it. Forget I mentioned it." He tiptoes out and climbs the stairs to his room in the attic. Reece knows that Danny changing his mind after speaking to their mother isn't a dream, and she reaches down the side of the bed and grabs the olive knapsack from underneath. In lieu of a stuffed animal or doll she pulls the bag close to her, nuzzling it against her damp cheek as she finally falls asleep.

*

Halo Truly's cheek and forehead are damp where he's been pressing them against the sticky vinyl seat of the Chevy. They've been stuck in this traffic jam for what seems like the entire ride from Memphis to St. Louis, and even though they have all the windows down, there's no air blowing through—it hangs before them in humid clumps. He's tried at least to get some rest during this downtime, but he's too anxious to sleep. If they don't get moving soon they're going to miss tonight's concert, and will most likely have to forfeit their fee. He hopes not, because they head home tomorrow and he'd like to surprise his mother by repaying her the hundred dollars she gave him just three months ago, at the start of this crazy ride.

"Just drive up on the shoulder, Kick," Rog suggests from the backseat.

"Why don't you just shut up?" Kick replies, then turns to Halo. "This is all your fault, Truly," Kick says. "We're gonna be late, and they're not gonna pay us, and it'll be all your fault."

Halo continues to rest against the seat and keeps his eyes closed. "Okay Kick, how is this my fault?"

"I'll tell you how it's your fault—" Rog says.

"Rog, dammit, I told you to shut up," Kick says. "It's your fault, Truly, because you think you're the king of the world and get to sleep in a bed. You don't think you have to pay your dues like me and Rog did. So I ended up sleeping on the floor last night, or should I say *not* sleeping because I was so damn uncomfortable, which caused me to be so tired this morning that I couldn't get up and we got a late start."

Halo turns to look out the window. "Whatever you say, Kick," he mutters.

"Hey, we're moving!" Rog says, poking his head over the front seat between Kick and Halo.

"Rog, I told you—"

"I know, shut up," Rog says and leans back again.

They make it to the venue in St. Louis—another high school, a gymnasium this time—with fifteen minutes to spare. It's just enough time for them to change their clothes and wipe off the sweat before they have to take the stage. Halo usually likes a little more preparation time than this, but strangely enough he finds the extra adrenaline helps, rather than hinders, his performance. His sneers and swivels and patented guitar-popping action have never been smoother or more successful. He knows the girls are screaming louder than they've ever screamed before because at one point he can't even hear himself singing. And the one time he glances over at Rog, the man actually looks as if he's enjoying himself. Five girls rush the stage tonight, but Halo manages to hang on to the jacket. He only needs to keep it intact for one more night, then he'll have his mother sew him some new ones for their next tour. It's beginning to smell a little ripe, anyway, and he's not sure how to clean lamé, so he'll probably end up throwing out the jacket on Sunday morning. Or maybe he'll donate it to the Smithsonian, he tells himself, and grins broadly at the idea, which, he thinks, may not be as far-fetched as it seems.

The show goes so well that Rog and Kick invite Halo to join them for drinks afterward, and even more amazingly, he accepts. They're recognized in the bar and talked into taking the stage for one go-round of "Love Me in the Morning," which even the house band knows and which turns into a three-hour jam session. As the three of them finally stumble into their motel room the sky is turning pale blue and rose at the bottom, and Kick offers Halo one of the beds. Halo almost refuses, not wanting to take any chances with the unpredictable Kick, then changes his mind. So what if Kick oversleeps again and they're late getting back to Abandon? To hell with that insignificant place and the stupid Founder's Festival. Tonight, with the bustle of the city and the buzz of the beer and the screams of the girls still clamoring in his ears, Halo Truly feels for the first time in a long time that he is already home.

CHAPTER NINE:
CHESTER LEE REECE—
SEPTEMBER 14, 1943

I remember the day Reece Dollar was born—September 14, 1943. It was Founder's Day, the Tuesday after my sixty-seventh birthday. I had just published my third book of poetry, *Alone But Not Forgotten*, which of course I believed to be my best work to date. I recall that the day was quite chilly-—the temperature never rose above fifty degrees, which for Indiana in mid-September is unseasonably cool. And the wind! To say it was brisk would be a terrible understatement. It was ferocious—whipping across the town square with such force that I feared we would all be swept away. Especially me, standing up there behind the podium, reading my latest work as the honored guest of the Founder's Festival. They only asked me to be the honored guest the years in which I published a new book of poetry, which, I will admit, stung my pride just a little bit, but I tried not to be petty and accepted their invitations graciously. After all, I was the most famous person Abandon had ever had in its midst, and everyone knew it.

Now before I go any further I just want to clarify a few misconceptions about me that have flitted about this town for years.

First, that bribery by alcohol was the only way I could at first get my poems published. Poppycock! My poems were graceful, airy fragments of brilliant light floating from my brain to the page and stand alone on their own merits.

Second, that my dear, sweet Mother was the true author of my poems, and that after she passed on her ghost inhabited the house in which we lived and I consulted her on a regular basis by means of the occult and such. Hogwash! My Mother was a beautiful, refined Southern Lady in the truest sense of the words, bred with a grace and dignity so rare here in the North (a land to which she was begrudgingly brought by her husband) but which she carried with her until the day she died. And while it is true that I loved her with as much force as any son can love his Mother, what kind of disturbed being would converse with a dead soul over the dinner table, as I was said to have?

Third, that I took certain . . . *liberties* with local boys during my time of residence in Abandon. Oh my, the accusation is so *reprehensible*, so *disgusting* that I am tempted to not even answer it. But I feel that I must, since this may well be my only opportunity. I believe this ugly rumor was started by a certain rival of mine, who shall remain nameless, but whom I know was extremely jealous of my talent and ability. Of course he and I weren't always rivals—in fact, we were good friends for many years as we both attempted to gain fame and fortune as poets of the first order. But I gained a national audience first, while his talent dried up as quickly as his insides did under the influence of the demon alcohol, until he could barely keep a weekly newspaper afloat—ah, but I've said too much. Suffice it to say he convinced those boys to bear false witness against me, using what devices I may never know. Whatever they say about me, *it is not true*.

But I digress. Looking back on the Founder's Festival of 1943, what I remember is that the Harvest Parade was not quite so bountiful during the war years. Yet it was one day of the year when the community could come together for a few hours of fellowship and forget about what was happening across the ocean, and hope that the day would pass without word of another county boy being killed.

It was after the parade, when the offerings had been placed at the base of the Wesley Tree, that I was to give my reading. As I made my way to the stage, I was accosted by a tall, thin man in dirty overalls and crew cut hair. He seemed to appear from out of nowhere.

"Excuse me, Mr. Reece?" the man said to me.

"Yes, yes, of course I am," I said, attempting to walk around him.

"Mr. Reece, I have always wanted to meet ya," the man said, extending his hand as if he intended me to shake it.

"Well, I am on my way to the stage now for a reading of my work," I said.

"I know, I know, but I just wanted to tell ya—" The man could not even look me in the eye, so he analyzed my shoes instead.

"Tell me what?" I asked, inching my way toward the podium.

"I just wanted to tell ya that I think you're the greatest poet who ever lived," he said, and I swear he was blushing. Suddenly from behind his back he pulled out a new copy of *Alone But Not Forgotten.* "Mr. Reece, would you mind signin' my book?"

I took the book from his hands. "Do you have a pen?" I asked.

"Um, no, I was hopin' ya—"

"Well, I certainly don't have a pen," I said. "Get me a pen and I'll sign the book."

"Yes sir, I'll get a pen," the man said as I rushed up the steps of the stage. He continued to talk. "My wife's set to have a baby soon—our fourth one, well really our fifth, but we lost—but anyway, if it's okay with her, I plan to name our child after you." At least that's what I thought he said. I was already concentrating on my opening remarks. I found out later that *is* what he said, that he named his newborn daughter after me. That girl, Reece Dollar, ruined my poetry reading.

I cleared my throat and began:

> When I was just a wee small boy
> Of only nine or ten,
> I caught a glimpse of Seamus Limp—
> A giant among men.
> And though he could not tell me why . . .

From the crowd just then came a woman's single, piercing note of agony, of pain. I tried to continue but a murmur had started circulating through the square which quickly drowned out my words, since I had not the luxury of a microphone. I banged my fist on the podium like a gavel, demanding quiet, so that attention could once again be paid to me and to my work—the best work of my career to date. But a circle had formed, apparently surrounding the woman who had howled. I heard someone shout "get Dr. Riley," and almost immediately the crowd parted as Dr. Riley came through. The doctor said something I could not make out and then I saw him and the tall, thin man in overalls who had approached me earlier carry a large woman across the square to Dr. Riley's car. At the time I thought the woman may have been pregnant, but her girth was such that I could not be sure. Of course later I found that she *was* pregnant, although only six months along.

I was sure now that the crisis was over and that all eyes and ears would once again turn upon me and my reading. But the spell I had so carefully cast had been broken, and the crowd quickly dispersed. Enraged, I stormed off the front of the stage and fell awkwardly on my ankle. After a few minutes of silent suffering a kindly woman, who identified herself as Alfie Marvin, a nurse, helped me to stand on my good leg and led me to her husband Luther's truck, and they drove me to the hospital in Broulet. Mrs. Marvin soothed me by repeating over and over that I would be alright, that it was probably just a slight sprain, nothing to get worked up about. Oh, if only she had known that it was not the ankle which had upset me so.

At the hospital they took x-rays of my foot and lower leg area and seconded Mrs. Marvin's opinion that I had suffered only a slight sprain. They wrapped it tightly in elastic bandages, gave me a pair of crutches and directed me toward the accounts payable window. When that nasty business was concluded I stumbled through the clean, white halls, searching for the Marvins and a ride back to Abandon. We found each other at the entrance to the obstetrics ward, although I was unsure how I had arrived there, since each section of the hospital looked exactly like the previous one.

"I am ready to go home now," I announced.

"Alright, Mr. Reece," Mr. Marvin said. "We'll be ready in a few minutes. We just want to check on Mrs. Dollar."

"Who?" I demanded.

"Mrs. Dollar," Mrs. Marvin said as if I were an imbecile. "You know, the woman who unexpectedly went into labor in the middle of your speech?"

"It was not a speech, it was a *reading*," I huffed. "And no, I did not know she had gone into labor. I hurt my ankle, remember?"

"Yes sir, we remember," Mr. Marvin said. "Why don't you come with us? They say the baby's in real bad shape and might not make it."

I realized I had no choice, so I followed them to the intensive care unit of the nursery. Behind the glass they pointed out to me a tiny creature in a pink cap—I couldn't believe it was human—lying in an incubator and hooked to a hundred machines.

"What's wrong with her?" I whispered.

"Premature," Mrs. Marvin said. "Three months. Even if she survives she's likely to have brain damage."

"Oh, that's awful," I said. One less person able to enjoy my poetry for years to come. "How's the mother?"

"Fine, fine," Mr. Marvin said. "Healthy as an ox."

"Luther, be nice," Alfie Marvin said.

"Yes dear." He turned to me. "Ready?"

"Certainly," I said. As we turned to go I glimpsed the name on the incubator—Reece Dollar. At least he didn't name her Chester.

CHAPTER TEN:
SEPTEMBER 13, 1957

Reece peels the stiff knapsack from her face, the olive canvas wearing the impressions of last night's tears. She awakens to a dawn so still and dark and cold it's not like dawn at all, but rather like another world, like what it must be to wake up on the moon, even though she knows it's ridiculous to even think such a thing. The viscous heat of earlier in the week is gone, broken loose by Tuesday evening's tornado and followed by a day or two of seasonal autumn weather. But now the morning, which usually rises with a warm smile and upturned palms, is coming down on Abandon with a wrought iron fist. As Reece stands a sudden breeze begins snapping the wild rose bush against the window until the petals swirl through the air like a silky fuschia scarf. In the distance she swears she can hear Cullen's Creek churn.

She strips off her nightgown and panties and stands completely naked in front of the wash basin, concentrating on the bowl of water in front of her. Even the slightest glance in the mirror will reveal Addison Hilliard's pawprints all over her body, like invisible ink that appears under a special light. She bathes carefully, with soap this time, making sure to reserve some clean water with which to brush her teeth. She even washes her hair a day early, rinses and dries quickly. She slips on a fresh pair of cotton panties with the least amount of holes, a pair of white socks, and what her mother calls her "best dress," a thin white number that used to be Dinah's. She stuffs two more dresses and two pairs of underwear into the rucksack, along with the old watch on the nightstand, her father's radio, the sandstone, and the five dollar bill Dinah keeps hidden

in the dresser drawer and doesn't think Reece knows about. She
fashions her wet hair into a ponytail, steps into her black patent
leathers, and surveys the room one final time. She picks up the
arrowhead from the dresser top and weighs it in her palm, starts to
set it back down, then puts it in the bag. She tosses the backpack
out the window and shimmies down the rose trellis, swooping up
the pack before it can blow away. Her skirt clings to her bare legs
as she runs headlong into the driving wind, over the tracks and
toward the bridge at Cullen's Creek.

When she reaches the school two miles later, she stoops behind
a bush to catch her breath, gritting her teeth against the stabbing
pain in her side. From between the boughs she sees the extra large
bus the school uses for field trips rattle to a stop at the front steps
and the extra large driver waddle up the steps and into the school.
Reece sprints to the bus and collapses into the half-seat in the last
row. She curls up with the knapsack beneath her head and falls
asleep. None of her eighth grade classmates would be caught dead
sitting in the "baby seat," so she knows she can ride here unnoticed
and undisturbed the entire way to Vernon, Kentucky by way of
Mammoth Cave.

The bus stops abruptly, brakes squealing, jerking her awake
and upright in the seat. She has to blink a few times for her eyes to
focus on the kids scooting from their seats, filling the aisle and
moving away from her in a crooked line. She scoops up her bag
and falls in behind them. Stepping off the bus she hears a familiar
voice call her name, and in a few seconds Roxanne is standing in
front of her.

"Where did you come from?" Roxanne says, pulling her friend
off to the side.

"I was in the back of the bus," Reece tells her.

"In the baby seat? What were you doing there?"

"Sleeping."

"Gather 'round," the Germ Man calls to the students.

"Come on Reece," Roxanne says, dropping Reece's arm and
taking a step toward the entrance to the cave.

Reece hesitates. "I forgot something on the bus," she says. "You go on."

Roxanne questions her friend with a skeptical look.

"Go on, I'll catch up."

"Okay," Roxanne says, "but hurry." She turns away. "Bo Cullen! Wait!" She runs toward a group of girls huddled together behind Mr. German.

Reece climbs up into the bus, the door having been left open when the bus driver tottered off to get a cup of coffee. Reece slumps in the front seat and watches her classmates until the last one has entered the cave. She slips the knapsack onto her back, sneaks off the bus, and heads toward the exit of the national park. On the road she stands with her thumb extended as five cars pass her by. The sixth one, a red pickup faded by the summer sun and rusted clear through from one wheel well to the other, stops and the passenger door opens. Reece hops up inside and studies the young man driving. "Can you take me to Vernon, Kentucky?" she asks, slamming the door and rolling down the window.

He scratches his day-old beard with fingernails that still carry dirt from years ago and nods. He shifts the truck into gear and drives away from the curb. Reece removes the rubber band from her ponytail, sticks her head out the window and lets her long blonde hair slap and sting her face.

"You got a name?" he says after they've passed through town and are cruising on a two-lane blacktop road.

"Reece," she says, finally bringing her head inside the cab and settling back against the seat.

"Reece? Ain't that a boy's name?"

She snaps her head to look at him. "I was named for Chester Lee Reece, the famous poet," she says.

"Well, I never heard of him," he says.

"He's very famous in Indiana."

He swallows with a *hmmph*, his colossal adam's apple dancing along the length of his tall, reedy throat. He speeds up suddenly and whips into the opposite lane, passing two cars before swerving back into the right lane just seconds before an oncoming vehicle whizzes by them, horn blaring in staccato honks.

"What's your name?" she asks, when she can no longer hear her pounding heart.

"Boggs."

Reece shifts in her seat, adjusting her backpack. "Is that your first name or your last name?"

"It's my name."

"Oh." She turns away from him and watches the landscape backslide along the road. In the distance she sees gentle hills rising like knuckles from a gauze-covered fist. In the foreground she notices that the close-cropped grass gives off a bluish tint, and realizes it must be bluegrass—that there *is* such a thing as bluegrass, that it's real, and not just some made up word like Hoosier. She thinks of Bill Monroe and his Bluegrass Boys, and unconsciously starts humming "Blue Moon of Kentucky," except she hums Elvis' hopped-up version. Her fingers tap against the door handle in time to the music in her head and she vows that tonight she'll stand outside and look up at the Kentucky moon and see if it has the same blue glow that the grass has. She can't wait to tell Dinah of her discovery when she sees her.

"You like Elvis?" Boggs is asking her.

She stops humming and looks at him. "Um, yeah, he's alright, but I really like Halo Truly. He's from Abandon, you know."

"Abandon? Abandon, Indiana? Is that where you're from?" Boggs asks.

"Yes," she says. "He was on The Blackie Harmony Show the other night, singing his number nine hit 'Love Me in the Morning.'"

"Oh. We don't watch that show," Boggs says. "Blackie Harmony's a Communist."

"Um, well, I didn't watch it either," Reece says. "We didn't have . . . our t.v. has been broken."

"Hmm . . . too bad."

Reece rolls her window up halfway. "Shouldn't you be in school?"

"Nah. I quit a couple years ago to help my daddy out on our farm. I figure I already learnt everything I was gonna learn in school." He removes one hand from the steering wheel and reaches across the cab. Reece's left leg recoils. Boggs flips on the radio. "You can sing along if you like," he says, replacing his hand on the wheel.

Reece looks down at her leg and swats at an imaginary bug, pretending that's why she moved it so suddenly. She scratches her calf until it's pink, then stops when she sees an empty tobacco wrapper wadded on the floor, the Indian chief's profile mangled and twisted. She tries to scoot closer to the door but finds she's already over as far as she can go. She leans her head back against the seat, closes her eyes and hums softly to the tune on the radio. Her body wants to sleep but her brain resists it, so she opens her eyes and soon sees a sign welcoming her to Vernon, Kentucky. She gives Boggs the address she memorized and in a minute he's pulling the truck into the parking lot of Sister Cecelia's.

"You want me to wait here?" he asks.

"No," she says, sliding her feet to the pavement. She turns and sticks her head back inside the cab. "Thanks for the ride." She slams the door.

"Welcome," Boggs says, and pulls out of the parking lot and into the street. She watches him go but he doesn't bother to look back at her. She puts the knapsack on her back and hugs herself, wishing she'd thought to wear a sweater. It's even colder here than it was at home this morning, and it seems the sun doesn't intend to shine today. Eyes to the concrete, she walks into Sister Cecelia's.

The windowless lobby is darker than the cloudy sky outside, and a constant draft flows from the ceiling. The mahogany reception desk is five feet tall with a crucifix on top that extends another foot, at least. Reece has to squint to make out the figures in the oil paintings on the walls, biblical scenes of howling virgins and headless babies and a storm of blood washing all their sins away. It takes Reece a few moments to realize there's no one behind the desk, so she slips around to the elevator. She scans the directory on the wall, presses the button, and rides to the second floor.

The usual hospital sounds are absent, replaced by a tension in the air not unlike that Reece felt during the tornado of a few nights ago. The two nurses on the floor, one pushing a medicine cart and one sitting behind the desk, seem to move in slow motion, their rubber-soled white shoes gliding along as if on a cushion of air. The one at the desk notices Reece and scrunches her eyebrows together.

"Yes?"

Reece moves forward, notices she's still hugging her arms, drops them to her side, doesn't know what to do with her hands, clasps them in front of her, then behind her, then stiffly crosses them in front of her chest. She forces her voice out. "I'm looking for Dinah Dollar."

The nurse scowls harder, takes a clipboard from a drawer and scans the list. "I don't see anyone here by that name."

Reece has been reading the list upside down at the same time and clearly sees Dinah's name at the bottom, the number 218 written beside it. She clears her throat. "I—"

"Can you find your own way out, or will I need to call security?" the nurse asks.

Reece shakes her head. "No. Thank you." She heads toward the elevator and pushes the down button. When the car arrives and the doors open Reece takes a step forward, then veers down the hallway. She can barely read the numbers as she flies past— 211, 213, 215, 216, 217 . . . 218! She turns the handle and nearly falls into the room. She quickly recovers her footing, shuts the door behind her and locks it, certain the nurse is not far behind. She turns toward the bed and hears an inhuman sound, like an animal taking its last resigned breath at the hands of its captor. She puts her hand to her mouth and realizes the sound has come from within her. She takes a few tentative steps until she's at her sister's bedside. Dinah's midsection is nearly double its normal size for all the bandages and tape wrapped around it, some of it pink and brown where fresh blood has seeped through. Tubes emerging from both nostrils are taped to her face; her half-open eyes swim under the broken elastic of her lids. Hearing the commotion she stirs; as her head rolls on the pillow Reece sees a tiny brown hole in each temple.

"Dinah?" she whispers. She touches her sister's hand. "Dinah?" she says louder.

Dinah's eyelashes flutter but her empty eyes are devoid of recognition, of life.

"Dinah, it's me. Reece. I . . . How . . . I . . ." She's not sure what to say next, so instead she strokes Dinah's wrist. Dinah slowly removes her hand from Reece's grasp and gradually, gingerly, digs her head into the pillow and rolls her shoulders and hips away from her sister until she's facing the wall. Reece lays two fingers on Dinah's spine, but her sister's body is cold to the touch and as still as the rock formations of Mammoth Cave a few miles away. Reece hears a key in the lock, followed by the nurse's voice.

"I've called security," Scrunched Eyebrows says. "You can wait in Sister's office." She pinches Reece's upper arm and drags her from the room. Reece keeps her eyes on her sister until the windowless, steel door slams between them with a finality Reece can't help but comprehend.

In the backseat of the security officer's car, Reece holds the knapsack between her knees and pulls out the sandstone. She turns it over and over in her hand but can barely feel its grit scrape against her palms. Her head buzzes when she presses her forehead against the cool window and gazes at the passing scenery, contemplating grass that is blue and underground limestone that is pink; Pre-Columbian mummies found floating in subterranean rivers (or so the Germ-Man had told the class—she'll never see it herself now) and smooth stones skimming the surface of Cullen's Creek; the odor of smoked bacon mixed with chewing tobacco and the scratch of a day-old beard against her innocent cheek.

The late afternoon sky hangs like a slate roof over the countryside, but it emanates a glow that pierces Reece's eyes until they begin to fill with tears, so she lets them fall shut. Her forehead taps the window with each bump in the road until her entire body is numb.

"Looks like they left without ya," the security officer is saying. Reece opens her eyes as the car pulls up to the entrance of the cave. The large school bus is gone. "Wait here," the officer says. He steps out of the car and strolls a lap around the area, leaving the car door open. An icy breeze gushes through the vehicle and tiny, shimmering snow crystals dot the windshield, then just as quickly melt away. Reece scoots forward, hoisting her bent knees against the back of the front seat, and covers herself with the backpack. The officer returns to the car and slams the door.

"I understand your family don't have a phone," he says.

Reece keeps her head down.

"I suppose I have to drive you all the way back home."

She doesn't move.

"You wanna tell me where that is?"

Reece mumbles directions as the man steers the car away from Mammoth Cave.

"You ever been to the cave?" he asks after they're on the road, watching Reece in the rear view mirror. She shakes her head no.

"Ya oughta see it sometime," he says. "Mighty impressive." He continues to glance at Reece in the mirror occasionally. The rest of the time he sighs and grunts and clucks his tongue as he struggles to see the road in the thickening snowfall. The wipers squeak across the windshield but manage only to leave a murky white smear. After they cross the Ohio River into Indiana the storm lets up momentarily and the officer clears his throat.

"That your sister back there?" he asks Reece.

She looks at him for the first time since they left the cave, suspicious and alarmed. She nods guardedly.

"Thought so," he says. "See that a lot. Don't you worry though, they fixed her up real good so she won't have no more problems."

Reece can see Dinah as clearly as if she's in this car right now, the two tiny holes in her temples, the glazed stare she gave Reece as if she didn't even recognize her own sister. Then Reece remembers her mother murmuring a few words to Dr. Riley before he drove Dinah to the hospital in Broulet, and she shivers visibly.

"You too cold back there?" the security guard asks and flicks a knob on the dashboard. The fan blows a burst of cold air on Reece's face.

"Sorry, my heater's not the greatest," he says to her in the mirror. Her eyes meet his. "When will she . . ." She's not sure how to finish the question, but the officer has heard this a dozen times before.

"Be comin' home?" he asks, chuckling. "She's not comin' home, miss. Sister Cecelia fixes 'em up and sends 'em away where they can't hurt themselves no more. Scrambles their eggs in more ways 'n one. It's best you just forget about your sister. Try to act like she never was born."

The officer's harsh words stab Reece like the icicles forming on the car windows, and she squeezes her eyes shut tight as the snow picks up again and increases in intensity the farther north they travel. By the time they pull into the gravel lane alongside the railroad tracks the tires squeak and slide through three inches of slick, sparkling cotton; the flakes are as wide as silver dollars and the tree branches sag under the weight of the wet, white stuff.

Reece is surprised to find she has fallen asleep and awakens slowly, peering out through the window with foggy eyes. She blinks a few times to clear her snowy vision until she realizes it *is* snowing, in September, the day before her birthday. She can't remember that ever happening before. In a more lucid state of mind she may have considered leaping from the slow-moving car at this point, but her head and limbs are as heavy as sandbags and she can barely move. She shifts to the left so she can see through the windshield and spies her father standing in the driveway before them. The headlights reveal him stooped over, shoveling a path so he can leave for work, even though the snow is not yet too high to drive through. The sight of his figure and his stiff, almost resigned, movements forces her fully awake as the car stops just inches from him. He leans on the shovel and squints back at them, shielding his eyes with a hand lifted to his brow.

Reece crawls out of the car and tromps toward the house, keeping her head down against the blowing snow and away from her father's stare. She hears him exchange a few words with the security guard before the officer turns the car around the drives off. Instead of entering through the front door, Reece decides to go in the way she left this morning. She climbs up the trellis, her hands growing numb and slippery from the snow gathered there, and lets herself in the bedroom window. In the dark she locks the window behind her and drags the nightstand before the door. She slumps down and lays her head on the bed, still clutching the damp backpack. Its canvas suddenly feels unbearably scratchy against her raw skin and she flings it against the closet door with a reverberating thud that seems to shake the whole room.

"Reece Dollar!" her mother yells upon hearing the noise. Her footsteps clomp up the stairs and stop in front of the door. "I know you're in there, you ungrateful, spoiled brat. I've given you everything and this is the thanks I get." She's pounding on the door now. "From the moment you were born you've burdened me with your foolish needs. But did you ever once consider me? No you did not. And today you disappear to god only knows where, your principal comes all the way out here to tell me you haven't been in school nearly all week, and that you disappeared somewhere into the depths of Mammoth Cave, and you're finally brought home from Kentucky by a strange man in a blinding snow storm, after the police in two states have spent their precious time looking for your sorry self." She gives the door a few kicks and the nightstand shakes but stays put. "Reece! Come out here now! You owe me an apology!" Reece closes her eyes and sees Jonah's face appear before her. He's crouched in a bunker on the MLR, the Main Line of Resistance against the Chinese, gripping his M-1 with frozen fingers, hugging the rifle against his bulky chest to keep from shivering. The snow is four feet high all around them and tinted with streaks of pink, like the fancy marble in the station where he boarded the train that took him to the bus that took him to the plane that took him to the jeep that brought him here. Here being just north of the thirty-eighth parallel, an invisible line he traced with his finger on the world map that hung on the wall at the post and found almost exactly bisected Cullen County. So he passes the time on his lookout pretending he's home, squatting in a tree stand in the woods behind his family's house, steadying his shotgun against his shoulder, aiming at a buck in the distance, squeezing the trigger and watching the majestic animal fall at half-speed, its steaming blood seeping through the cold white snow. He tells himself this is the same crappy winter weather they have at home, and he never seemed to mind it there, and that seems to help him through the late-afternoon shift. It's the worst time of day, that measureless, motionless time between day and night when everyone and everything seems to move in slow motion, especially the sun, falling into the horizon like a nickel into a jukebox. The countryside slips on a golden mask, rendering everything underneath opaquely invisible, and for a few brief minutes the soldiers in grimy fatigues and camouflaged faces that haven't seen a shower for four weeks are seemingly invisible too, and they let down their guard. That golden sheen can become deadly in an instant, sending an unsuspecting private face down in the snow before he ever realizes what hit him. Jonah can hear movement on the forward slope and knows the restlessness, the cockiness, is descending again, and prays that night falls without the sound of artillery. Here on the reverse slope he only has to hold his position for an hour more, maybe two, then he can take his rations from his rucksack, heat them with the flame from his Zippo and slurp them down with his fingers if he has to, lay out his bedroll and try to catch a few z's before the shelling begins again. The sky is darkening even quicker than usual, a sure sign that they're closing in on the winter solstice, just about a month away. He lifts his head a few inches, straining his neck to peek over the top of the hill. He scans the valley below, left, right, then left again, when out of his right eye sees something glittering in a clump of bare trees in the distance. He whips his head in that direction, then immediately curses himself for making such a sudden movement with his head sticking out where a gook can blow it clean off and not think twice about it.

Just then he sees it again, far away, a shining, glistening, golden light that seems to grow brighter as the sky grows darker. The glow seems to pulsate now, rising higher and higher past the tops of the trees, shimmering so brightly he can't believe anyone else on the hill has stopped to stare at this golden wonder. He rises to his feet and creeps toward the light, his rifle held out before him. He can almost feel Reece on his back, her tiny hands clinging to his neck. "Legend has it a fairy princess lives in a golden castle deep in these woods, among the poplar trees," he whispers, as though her delicate ear rests against his cheek. "They say she spends her days brushing her long, golden locks with a golden hairbrush, waiting for her handsome prince to return. Golden hair just like yours," he says, advancing on the light, feeling its heat on his face as he draws nearer.

"But you mustn't look directly at the princess's castle," he says, a bit louder now, "or it will disappear in a blinding flash of light. Instead, close your eyes tightly, and when I say so, open your eyes slowly and concentrate on the giant poplar that guards her home. You'll be able to see the castle's reflection on the tree."

He senses a sharp pain in his side as Reece swings her legs in anticipation. "Keep them closed," he says, squeezing his own eyes together. In this darkness he's created, a blinding flash penetrates his being and a rush of arctic air envelops his head. He rolls over and tastes a mouthful of wet, red snow. Able now to move only his eyes, he searches the twilight sky and sees his sister's face looking down on him from above. He manages to lift his head a few inches from the frozen ground and presses his lips against her cheek. *Don't . . . look at . . . the palace . . . Reece . . .*

"*Jonah!*" Reece screams, her head thrown back in agony as if she'd felt the fatal blow herself. At that moment the nightstand crashes over on top of her as the bedroom door whooshes open and her mother blows in. "*I told you, don't ever say that name in this house again!*" Mrs. Dollar roars, looming over her daughter and raising her right arm high in the air. She begins to bring a glinting fist down on Reece's head when Mr. Dollar appears behind her and grabs his wife's wrist. "*Rebecca!*" he shouts, pulling her backward.

A heavy object falls on the floor and rolls under the bed. Reece scrambles to her knees as her father forces her mother out the door and down the stairs. "Mother, what in hell's name are ya doin' to that child?" she hears him say as they enter the kitchen, but she can't quite make out her mother's muted response. She feels under the bed and her fingers run into a rough, bumpy sphere. She pulls it out and examines it in the snowlight under the window, finding it's really a sphere cut in half to reveal the glistening amethyst inside. *A geode,* she whispers, and wonders where it came from.

The screen door pops shut and she hears Danny return from his nightly, regardless-of-the-weather hoop-shooting session at the barn, dribbling his basketball hard against the bowed kitchen floor. Her father's voice rises for a minute and the bouncing ceases. "Ah, no," she hears Danny moan. "Come on, Dad. Do I have to . . ." Her father's voice rises again, even more insistent this time. "Okay," her brother sighs. She waits for him to come upstairs but he never does. A few minutes later her father does, however, and finds his daughter curled up against the wall, leaning her cheek against the cool windowpane. She's holding the geode up to her ear as if listening for the roar of the ocean in a seashell.

"Reece m'dear?" he says, stepping over the overturned nightstand. He bends down beside her and puts an arm around her shoulder. She stiffens and grips the geode tighter against her face. "I see you found your birthday present. I left it outside your door so you'd find it when you came home tonight. You like it?" Reece lets the stone fall to the floor. The rest of her body is perfectly still.

Her father pulls her closer to him. "You shouldn't have gone to see your sister," he says. "You've got to forget about her now. You two weren't that close anyways." Reece doesn't speak. "She did some bad things, Reece. Your mother knows—your mother and I know what's best here." When she doesn't respond he sighs deeply and squeezes her ribcage. "M'dear, I've got to go to work now. I'm late already." She wriggles free and goes to stand in the corner, head down, her arms folded in front of her. She rocks slightly back and forth.

"She'll kill me," Reece manages to say.

"Oh now," Mr. Dollar says, walking toward his daughter. "You're exaggerating. Besides, Danny'll be here, watching her. I've talked to him about it. Don't ya worry, she won't try to hurt ya no more."

"There's a gun in the house and she knows how to use it," Reece says.

Her father stops and scratches his chin. "I'll take the gun with me. I'll keep it in the car. How'll that be?"

Reece shrugs. "Danny'll make sure nothing happens to me?"

Mr. Dollar hugs her as much as she will allow. "Yes, m'dear," he says into her still snow-damp hair. He kisses the top of her head and leaves the room, closing the door partway. Suddenly exhausted, Reece stumbles into bed and burrows her head deep into the pillow. Shortly thereafter her mother and Danny ascend the stairs and draw back the covers on Mrs. Dollar's bed. Reece waits for Danny to pull down the stairs, but instead hears him climb in with his mother. The two of them whisper gently to each other for a long time.

Reece forces herself to rise and crosses the room. She picks up the geode from the floor and skulks back to the door. She clicks it shut and crouches behind it, the stone poised in her fist in front of her. She's still in this position a few hours later when the sun rises on her fourteenth birthday.

*

The sun is rising as Halo, Rog and Kick drive through the quiet streets of Abandon early on Saturday morning. Most of the booths are set up but are as yet unstaffed. As Halo suspected, they got off to a very late start leaving St. Louis because they just couldn't get Kick to wake up. So late that they ended up eating dinner and supper in the city and didn't start heading east until ten o'clock Friday night. Fortunately Kick has been in a good mood since the concert Thursday evening, and even offered to drive the entire way to Abandon. Halo hopes his mood will hold until after the show Saturday night, when the two musicians will get their last paycheck and head back to Nashville. Halo had been considering asking the record company if he could choose his own backing band for the remaining tours, but now he thinks he'll wait and see what happens tonight.

CHAPTER ELEVEN:
1943—1951

Dinah turned two years old on October 8, 1943, but there was no celebration and only one *Happy Birthday*, that from her father as he kissed the top of her head on his way out the door. At less than one month old Reece's condition was still critical and the doctors told the Dollars they would have to take it one day at a time.

Asa visited his baby daughter at the hospital every morning before he went to work, and again every evening on his way home from the forge. On weekends he would spend whole days there beside her incubator in the nursery, reciting his favorite Chester Lee Reece poems in whispery breaths, her tiny ears barely able to endure any noise louder than the turn of a page. Every day he asked Rebecca to come with him, to visit her daughter, even if she wasn't yet allowed to touch her. Rebecca snorted, waved him away and turned her attention back to her two sons, and occasionally to her older daughter.

When Asa returned home from the hospital on Christmas Eve, he came bearing a gift for the entire family. He let ten-year-old Jonah lift the blanket from the basket Asa carried to reveal infant Reece, whom Dr. Riley had released from the hospital in time for Christmas. The three children gathered around their baby sister, three months old but weighing only five pounds, her round, pink head covered with a blond thatch. As they stood over her she opened her eyes for a moment, and Danny asked his father why her eyes were a watery gray, instead of brown like theirs.

"All babies have that color eyes when they're born," he told them, as if this was an obvious fact everyone should know. "They'll turn in a few months, like a kitten's. Don't worry."

Jonah carried Reece in her basket to the living room and sat her on the floor near the wood stove—close enough to warm her but not so close as to harm her. He refused to leave her side for the rest of the evening, preferring to sit beside her and study her miniature features, sometimes putting her tiny hand in his and comparing the vast differences and the uncanny similarities between him and his new sister.

Rebecca returned to the kitchen without even looking at the infant. Asa, seeing Reece was in good hands with Jonah, followed his wife and started to speak, but she interrupted him.

"Shut up," she said. "Whatever you're going to say, don't say it. Just shut up. How dare you bring that child home—"

"What do you mean, Mother? She's our daughter, and she's healthy! She's gonna live! I thought—"

"Let me finish," she said. "How dare you bring her into this house on Christmas, on the day—"

"This should be a day for joy and celebration," Asa said. "Especially now—"

"Let me finish!" she seethed. "Christmas is the time we celebrate the births of our dear, lost Rachel, and Daniel, the sweetest boy his mother has ever known. There is no room in the house on Christmas for that . . . *child*."

Asa felt like he'd been punched in the gut and started to sit down, then thought better of it, knowing he could better fight this crazy woman standing on his two feet. He took a step toward her and grabbed her forearm, squeezing it until her hand turned purple. She tried to wrench free but his grip was too strong.

"*She is your daughter,*" he growled, "and you'll take care of her like ya do all your children. I'll make sure she's cared for, even if it means I have to kill ya. Believe me, woman, I'll do it and not think twice."

Rebecca jerked her arm away and laughed, low in her throat, in a way Asa had never heard before. "*You?*" she scoffed. "*You'll* kill *me?*" She laughed again, louder. "Your idle threats don't scare me, though they do amuse me." She crossed the kitchen to the stairs and turned to face her husband. "These little shows of force you pull occasionally? I've always seen them for what they truly are—weak, pathetic attempts to assert a manhood that was never really there. If you hadn't burdened me with these children, I'd go back to teaching and leave you here to die in this wilderness cabin, your bones picked clean by raccoons." As she climbed the steps she said, "But this is my lot in life, and I accept it, just as you must accept yours. Just remember that I've seen violence in my life, and the power it wields, and trust me, it doesn't change the outcome of things one bit."

Asa stood there in the kitchen for a long time, listening to the sounds of the house. He heard his wife change into her night-clothes and climb into bed, then the rustle of pages being turned in her bible as if the breath of god himself were blowing on them. He heard the laughter of his three older children as they huddled around their baby sister, and for a second he swore he heard the giggle of another child as well, a seven-year-old girl whose face he could not see but whom he imagined resembled that of a perfect doll—smooth, porcelain face, bright brown eyes, flowing mahogany hair tied back with a pink bow—as if the doll had been modeled on Rebecca Wonderman has she stood on her porch in Falling Star eleven years ago. Outside he heard the animals—Nanny the horse and Chester the cow restless in their stalls, the two hens unsettled in their coop—and was sure he could even hear snow beginning to fall. He opened the kitchen door as silvery flakes blew into his face, and he licked them away. Back inside the house he called to his children, "Time for bed, kids," and he saw Jonah pick up Reece's basket, ever so gently, and the four of them marched single-file up the stairs. He extinguished the oil lamp in the living room and carried the kitchen lamp upstairs behind them, Rebecca's reading lamp lighting the way in front of them. He pulled down the attic stairs and convinced Jonah to relinquish the baby's basket for the evening, then settled Dinah and Reece in their room as well. With-out a word he retrieved his pillow and blanket from the floor where Rebecca had thrown them and returned to the girls' room, where he made a place for himself on the floor next to Reece's basket-crib and turned down the kerosene lamp. His wife's lamp burned well into the night.

*

Asa Dollar and Archibald Hilliard had been casual friends since 1932, the year they both started working at the forge. Baldy and his wife Sarah lived on a small farm with their son, Addison, who was nine years older than Jonah Dollar.

Baldy was glad when Asa moved back to Abandon with his wife and son, although he certainly wasn't happy about the circumstances under which they had moved. Eventually the two families began to spend time together, usually evenings at the farm snapping the beans or shucking the corn that would serve as part of their supper, followed by a spirited card game of Five Hundred Rummy. On some Saturday nights, after an especially prosperous week at the forge, they would drive into Falling Star or Broulet for a movie—*The Good Earth* or *Destry Rides Again* or *Jezebel* or Asa's favorite, *The Grapes of Wrath*.

But when Rebecca became pregnant with Reece, she didn't want to be around people anymore, and even stopped attending church. She preferred to spend the summer of 1943 in the humid confines of the despised "wilderness cabin," leaving Asa to explain away her constant refusals of the Hilliards' invitations. After Reece was born he blamed it on something called post-partum depression, a term Rebecca had told him to use and which he didn't understand, but which seemed to satisfy Baldy and Sarah. They knew how certain events, or even the mere possibility of those events occurring, could turn a person's mind against itself.

They saw it on Addison's eighteenth birthday, when Baldy told his son to go get in the truck. He was taking him to register at the draft office, and he told him it ought to be the proudest day of his life. First Addison's face flamed up like a round red radish, then turned as white as radish flesh. His entire body quivered and his watery eyes seemed to be jumping out of their sockets. When Baldy stepped forward, one pleading hand outstretched, Addison actually growled at his father, a guttural, animal sound that rendered Baldy immobile. The boy hunched over and loped past the frozen man, out the door to the front porch and to the dead, dry cornfield beyond, which his father hadn't yet had time to harvest for animal feed. After a few minutes Baldy composed himself enough to go after his son, and followed a quiet rustling sound until he found him tangled among the dry stalks, picking grains from the withered cobs and stuffing them into his mouth. With stealth Baldy knelt down beside Addison, pulled him up and walked him back to the house and into bed, whispering the mantra *you don't have to go you don't have to go you don't have to go* until the boy fell asleep. Then he called Dr. Riley, who immediately came over with a supply of emergency syringes filled with tranquilizers in case it ever happened again, and a medical exemption printed on official-looking paper and signed by the doctor himself. He told Baldy to take that piece of paper down to the draft office in the morning and everything would be taken care of, and not to worry, he'd make sure no one ever found out what really happened.

So when Addison graduated from Abandon High School in the spring of 1943 he remained at home to run the family farm, which up to that point had been merely a part-time endeavor for Baldy. In less than a year Addison had turned the farm so profitable that Baldy could've quit the forge and still made a comfortable living, but he decided to stay on four more years and retire with full pension. Maybe his son wouldn't be a great war hero, but he had a strange, gentle way with the land that Baldy would never understand.

On Christmas Eve, after Dr. Riley had wrapped Reece in one of the hospital's pink blankets and placed her in a basket so that her father could take her home for the first time, he paid a visit to the Hilliards' farm. When Baldy met him at the front door the doctor removed his John Deere cap and apologized for intruding on them on this night, but he'd gotten Sarah's test results back and felt he should share them as soon as possible. Baldy said that's quite alright, doctor, and led him into the kitchen where Sarah was dusting sugar cookies shaped like angels with brightly-colored sprinkles. When she saw Dr. Riley she knew immediately it was bad news and a thunderous sound filled her ears, a rushing sound like thick, muddy river water overflowing its banks, so that she didn't hear him say that the cancerous growth in her stomach had already spread to her pancreas and her liver, and the disease was beyond treatment of any sort, unless they happened to believe in prayers and miracles.

Baldy quit the forge a week later in order to shepherd his wife through her final days. Sarah died on the first day of summer 1944 in the center of her flower garden, that season overgrown and untended for the first time since their life together began, where Baldy had carried her for one last view of their land. The crisp, green corn stalks already stood knee-high, portending a good harvest; tall silos brimmed with grain, their silver hoods shimmering with waves of heat; their only son spread seed to the chickens in the yard, dust rising from his shirtless back as he stood and lifted an open palm to her. She surveyed all that she and Archibald Hilliard had done together, squeezed her husband's hand, and was gone. She was thirty-seven years old.

*

With his mother gone, Addison decided to stay at home for as long as his father needed him. A few months after Sarah's death Baldy tried to hire back on at the forge, but they told him he'd lost his seniority when he quit and he'd have to start over, so he said no thank you. Business at the forge had slowed and the men didn't receive their cost-of-living raises for three years straight. Even with the extra money from his shift differential, Asa's salary barely covered the expenses of a six-person family. Still, he managed occasionally to bring home small surprises—a yo-yo, bits of bubble gum, a comic book, a deck of cards with an extra joker where the king of hearts should be. Every time Asa brought home one of these treats, Rebecca would ask him: How many pieces of bubble gum would it take to get electricity in this house? How many comic books would buy indoor plumbing? In response Asa would look at the children, roll his eyes so far back in his head that only the whites showed, stick out his tongue and leave the room. The girls would invariably collapse into giggles and follow him; the boys would always sneer and move to their mother's side.

The boys and their mother sneered in the fall of 1950 when a strange rumor began to circulate through the town of Abandon and into the valley beyond the hill where the Dollars lived. The rumor was that in the town of Artemus, exactly halfway between Abandon and the Kentucky state line, two men searching for heating coal in the side of a foothill at dawn had found a mass of prehistoric bones. They called the sheriff and by sundown a digging team comprising nearly all the men of the county had unearthed a nearly complete and intact skeleton of what the experts called a mastodon. It was the primary topic of conversation at the forge, at the Joshuas' general store, in the waiting room of Dr. Riley's office, at Patsy's Place, and at the school in Abandon, where Reece had just started first grade. She heard the older kids say that a mastodon was like a big, hairy elephant that lived two million years ago, but she couldn't even imagine such a thing. She looked up *mastodon* in the encyclopedia on her class's library day, but the article was filled with a lot of long words she couldn't understand and wasn't old enough to figure out on her own.

When she got home from school that afternoon, Asa was already up and had just started putting a new coat of deep red paint on the side of the old barn.

"What's wrong, m'dear?" Asa asked Reece as the children walked up the driveway. The other three went directly into the house but Reece sat on the ground near her father and watched as he worked.

Finally she said, "I want to see the mastodon."

Asa stopped painting in mid-stroke and looked at his younger daughter. He nodded his head as leisurely as a rocking chair and bent over at the waist to pick up the paint can. He carried the can and the brush inside the barn and closed its wide double doors behind him. "Me too," he said, and stood over her, offering his hand. She took it and he pulled her to her feet, and she didn't let go until they were in the car. Jonah saw them from the kitchen window and ran outside. "Where you guys going?" he yelled as he jogged down the driveway. When he reached the vehicle Asa motioned with his head for Jonah to get in the backseat. As he settled in Reece turned around and whispered, *Artemus*.

*

In less than a week the excavation site had flourished. As more bones were carted off in official-looking white station wagons, more volunteers and reporters and mere onlookers appeared. One entire side of the foothill was cut away to expose the dark cinnamon-colored soil beneath the surface, abundant soil which yielded more and more of the mastodon with each shovelful.

As the Dollars made their way to the edge of the site Reece was awestruck. She measured her steps, as if gliding to the wedding march, so as not to come upon the spectacle all at once. She wanted to examine each piece of the scene carefully before adding it to the larger picture that was forming in her mind, the only picture she would have to return to years later when she wanted to call up that day.

Asa and Jonah went on ahead, poking through the crowd to the brink of excavation site until soon Reece couldn't see them anymore. She was tempted to flatten her palms against her ears to muffle the sounds that were enveloping her, but she couldn't make any part of her body move except for her feet, which kept pushing her forward. The sounds were of people shouting and machinery pushing dirt aside and hand tools smashing and scraping against hard soil and rock and bone and motor vehicles snatching the discoveries away.

By then it was late afternoon, the day before the autumnal equinox, and the sun was beginning to grow larger and larger as it moved closer to the horizon. The scene shone of copper, of dust and of sweat, each person's outline clearly delineated against the backdrop of the setting sun, their features dropping away in shadow.

Reece stood on her tiptoes, seeking a glimpse of a leg bone or a tusk. Able to see nothing but the backs and shoulders of those standing in front of her, she circled around the crowd to an isolated spot near the digging site, a spot as yet untouched by human hands. She knelt in the dirt and with her hands began to scoop away clumps of grass and earth, forming a pile next to her that grew taller and taller as the hole became deeper and deeper. On the other side of the hole she stacked items she found that might be of value—things that looked like a bone chip, or part of a tooth—things that perhaps were the remains of a baby mastodon momentarily separated from its mother and preserved just yards away for nearly two million years.

She stopped digging only when someone tapped her on the shoulder. She turned around to find Jonah and an older man, a stranger.

"Reece, what are you doing?" Jonah asked, kneeling beside her. He picked up one of the objects in the buried treasure pile and brought it to his face, studying it with squinting eyes.

"I'm . . . I'm just looking," she said, suddenly ashamed of her child's folly.

"Reece, this is Dr. Conor," Jonah said, standing and gesturing toward the unknown man. She stood up to face him and he stooped over so they were eye-to-eye.

"Hi Reece," the doctor said. "Your brother tells me it was your idea to come here today, to see what we're doing."

Reece looked at Jonah, who nodded, so she nodded too.

"You seem to be very interested in paleontology," he said, motioning with his head to the hole Reece had made. The doctor saw the confused look on her face and quickly added, "Paleontology is the study of the prehistoric past through fossils—remains like we've found here. Are you interested in what we're doing?"

Reece looked at Jonah again, who smiled. She smiled back at him, then at the doctor, and said, "Yes."

Dr. Conor smiled as well. "I thought so." He began to walk toward the excavation site and Reece and Jonah followed him. "I brought my geology students down from Notre Dame to assist with the dig," he said. "Reece, would you like to help us?"

She thought the dizziness in her head would cause her to faint, if the pounding in her chest didn't give her a heart attack first. She wasn't sure if the professor would be able to hear her when she said, "Yes."

"Good. You can help us too, Jonah," he said, and led them to the supply truck, where he gave them each a pair of work gloves and gave Jonah a pick and Reece a miniature shovel. For the next hour Dr. Conor taught Reece the basics of archaeological excavation, and just as it was becoming too dark to see she found a piece of bone. She lifted it from the ground and held it up for the doctor to see, and he carefully brushed away the loose dirt and examined it for a moment and declared it be part of the mastodon's massive foot—a toe, Reece liked to think. Just then her father appeared beside them and when she showed him the "toe" he said, "That's real nice, m'dear."

She handed it to Dr. Conor and whispered, "Can I keep it?" but before the words were out of the mouth she knew what the answer would be, and the professor shook his head and took the bone from between her fingers.

"I can give you this, though," he said, and rummaged in the pockets of his jacket for a pencil and a scrap of paper. On it he wrote *Reece Dollar, world-renowned paleontologist,* folded it up and placed it in her hand where the bone had been.

"This will be you someday," he told her, "if you work very hard. I'm sure of it." He patted the top of her head and shook Jonah's and Asa's hands, then went to help the crew pack up for the night. "I'll see you again, real soon."

The three Dollars turned to go back to their car, Reece reading from the paper as she walked. Under her breath she repeated

over and over the word she had just learned and now saw written
before her, pronouncing again and again the word which she knew
would define the rest of her life. In the car she refolded the paper
and gripped it so tightly in her palm that it was damp with sweat
by the time they pulled into their driveway. That night she tucked
the paper under her pillow and dreamed of returning to the site
every afternoon after school, working side by side with Dr. Conor
and the students through the fall and even during the winter, the
heavy, wet snow soaking their hair and clothes, and still they would
work on until the following spring when the final piece would be
extracted by Reece herself, and the rest of them would circle around
her and cheer and chant her name, *Reece, Reece, Reece* and carry her
on their shoulders all the way out of the giant hole and out of
Artemus and away from Abandon forever.

*

Property taxes were due in Cullen County each year on September
tenth. Rebecca always assumed that Asa took care of the taxes, and
since they'd never received a delinquency notice or been asked to
vacate the premises, she assumed correctly.

But what she did not know was that every year, when Asa
would go alone to pay the property taxes, he would first stop in
at the Cullen County Bank and Trust which was catty-cornered
from the courthouse, visit the second-floor office of Orville
Steppenstohn, and take out a one-year loan for the amount of
the taxes. At the same time he would make his final payment on
his loan from the previous year. Then he would go across the
street to the courthouse and pay his property taxes, and Rebecca
would never be the wiser.

In 1950 September tenth fell on a Sunday, a day on which the
courthouse and the bank would be closed, so Asa needed to pay
his taxes on Saturday. All week he tried to think of a reason to go
into town alone and take care of this business without arousing
Rebecca's suspicions, but by Saturday morning he had come up

with nothing and had resigned himself to telling her the truth and facing her wrath yet again.

He was saved from such a fate by Rebecca herself, who on that Saturday morning decided she and the children would get an early start on the fall cleaning ritual, scouring the house inch by inch until it was as clean as was possible for such a structure. She welcomed the opportunity for Asa and Reece to be absent from this event, as her husband's laziness and her daughter's ineptitude would undoubtedly be even more of a hindrance to her than usual.

Driving into town, Asa tried to impress upon Reece the secrecy of their mission. "It's important ya don't tell your mom where we been," he said, poking her arm. "Are ya awake, m'dear? Are ya listenin'?"

"Mmm," Reece said, adjusting her position against the window. Asa smiled and left her alone until he pulled into an angular parking space in front of the Cullen County Bank and Trust.

"I'll be right back, m'dear," he said to his sleeping daughter, gently latching the door closed so as not to wake her. He took a breath so deep his shoulders heaved as he steeled himself for the walk upstairs to the second floor office of Orville Steppenstohn. After all these years the trip had never gotten any easier for Asa.

After about a half an hour he returned to the car, the cash in the front pocket of his work pants. Reece was awake and watching a mother and daughter window browsing at Dorthea's Dress Shop, just down the street from the bank.

"Reece m'dear, ya wanna go in with me?" he asked.

She nodded briskly and stepped out of the car, meeting him at the edge of the street and taking his hand. They crossed the road and climbed the limestone steps to the courthouse, Asa taking them one at a time in order to keep pace with Reece, even though he could easily take two or even three in one stride.

The morning was clear, crisp and bright, so that as soon as they stepped inside the imposing building they were temporarily blinded by the cool darkness. Reece had to blink a few times until her eyes adjusted, then could not believe what she saw. Immediately to her left rose a set of massive marble stairs, which wound up and around and up and around again, culminating at a stained-glass rotunda which extended nearly to heaven. Reece heard herself gasp and started to swoon as she stretched her neck back far enough to take in the entire breathtaking sight, and would have fallen over backwards had she not been holding her father's hand.

"It's real pretty, ain't it m'dear?" Mr. Dollar said. She could only nod in response. "I'll tell ya what. I'm goin' right over here to pay these taxes. Why don't you go on up those stairs and see if you can make it all the way to the top before I get back?"

Reece answered by sprinting to the steps and racing upward. She counted each stair as she stepped on it—fourteen, then a landing, turn, fourteen, first level. She stopped and peered over the railing, waved to her father below and then moved on again as he walked away. Fourteen more steps, landing, turn, fourteen steps, second level. Again she stopped and looked over the side, amazed at how high she was already. Gripping the rail as tightly as her sweating palms would allow, she looked up at the rotunda, just three levels away now, and lifted one hand as if to touch the colored glass. She began to sway and immediately grabbed the railing, then took off for the third level.

Fourteen, turn, fourteen, stop, look down, look up. On the third floor she took the time to look around her and saw a series of tall, dark wooden doors on every wall. One of those doors was ajar so she took a moment to investigate. She entered at the back of a room that contained rows of benches, then a divider with a gate, then two sets of tables, twelve chairs set off behind another divider, and a large desk with chairs on either side. She guessed it must be a courtroom, because one day last summer as she watched Jonah and Danny shooting baskets against the barn she had heard them talking about how they ought to put Erl Cullen V on trial down at the courthouse for stealing pieces of whittling wood from Luther Marvin's lumberyard, and that if the jury didn't find him guilty then the judge should, and they didn't care if he *was* eighty-two years old, stealing was stealing. She tried to imagine old Erl Cullen V teetering down the aisle on his hand-carved cane, shuffling all hunched-over toward the judge, and started to laugh. She stopped abruptly when she noticed for the first time the four stained glass windows which reached from the floor to the ceiling and were a perfect shimmering shade of blue, as if it were intended for there always to be a little bit of sky in the room, no matter what the weather or season. On that day the windows were especially beautiful, as the yellow sun shone through them and gave the room a green, eerie glow. Reece imagined that was what a church looked like, although she didn't plan to ever be inside of one.

She suddenly remembered Doodle's dare that she reach the top before he returned, and skittered out of the courtroom and back up the stairs. Fourteen steps, turn, fourteen, fourth level, look down, look up, go. Almost there. Fourteen steps, turn, fourteen steps, on the fifth level now. The top. Look down, look up, stop. stop. Stop. She looked down down down and was stunned at how small the people below looked. They were like tiny dolls carrying on in a make-believe world, going about their business without even realizing that a nearly-seven-year-old girl stood so far above them, watching them, almost feeling as though she could control them.

She didn't see her father down there, so she looked up at the stained glass dome above her, so close now she could make out the intricate patterns in the glass, peonies interwoven among cardinals and surrounded by the torch and stars of the Indiana flag. Again she reached up to touch the designs, stretching on her tiptoes but still falling just a bit short. She became dizzy just then and dropped to a sitting position, giggling and looking through the slats of the railing as if in jail for stealing pieces of whittling wood from the lumberyard. At that moment she saw her father below and shouted, "Doodle! Doodle, look up here!" and he looked up and waved and she waved back.

"Come on down now, m'dear," he said, motioning with his arm, and she popped up and circled back down the stairs as quickly as she could, forgetting to count the steps that time.

"Did you see me?" she asked, panting, out of breath.

"I did," Asa said. "Come along, m'dear, we're paid up for another year." He guided her out the door, down the limestone steps and to the car. "We've got one more stop to make," he said after he'd started the engine. "I got a little extra at the bank to buy a surprise for your mother. If she asks, ya tell her I said the taxes were less than we thought, so we had some money left over. Can you remember that, m'dear?"

Reece nodded and repeated, "The taxes were less than we thought, so we had some money left over."

Asa smiled and backed the car out of the parking space.

*

Rebecca certainly was surprised when Asa and Reece came home with a car full of meat. After they had left the courthouse Asa had driven to a butcher he knew in Falling Star, a fellow who used to work at the forge. He had told Asa to stop by anytime and he would give him a good deal on a side of beef, so Asa decided to take him up on the offer and stock up for the winter. He knew there was no way he could pay off the extra loan amount by next year, but he was counting on Jonah to begin working full-time just as soon as he graduated from high school at mid-term, just two months away, and that money sure would come in handy.

"What in heaven's name have you done?" Rebecca wanted to know as she watched Asa carry the meat from the car to the springhouse.

"Tell her, m'dear," he said.

"The taxes were less than we thought, so we had some extra money left over," Reece said.

Rebecca scowled. "What is the meaning of this?"

"Now Mother, don't get angry at the girl. She's tellin' the truth. We had some money left over, so we went over to Falling Star and got us a side of beef for the winter. Here." He handed his wife a package of thick steaks. "You can fix these for tonight."

"But—"

"No buts, Mother, it's done."

Rebecca sighed and looked down at the steaks in her hand. "How many steaks would put electricity in—"

"Mother."

She turned so fast that her skirt swirled around her knees and she stormed back into the house. In a minute Jonah and Danny came outside to help their father unpack the rest of the meat. When they finished Asa fastened the door shut with a wooden bolt. "Now I'm countin' on you boys to help me make sure this door is shut tight all the time," he said. "We've got to keep out the varmints and such." The boys nodded and ran back into the house, already thinking of the steaks they would have for supper that night.

All through the fall they would have had a different delicacy every night, if it had been up to Asa, but Rebecca prevailed, reasoning that they must ration the meat to last all winter. On Christmas morning, though, they all agreed that it was a special enough occasion for the largest roast in the lot. Just after dawn Asa trudged through the new, wet snow to the springhouse and had to stop, blink, rub his eyes, move closer and blink again to make sure he truly was seeing what he thought he saw. The wooden bolt was moved aside and the door stood slightly open. Mr. Dandy, the stray dog that had served Asa faithfully for nearly fourteen years, tore at a piece of red raw meat just outside the door, his full and bloated middle nearly touching the frozen ground.

"Get! Get away from there!" Asa cried hoarsely, his quivering limbs barely able to carry him forward. The dog looked up for a moment before continuing to eat. "I said *get away!*" Asa roared, this time kicking the animal squarely in the ribs and down into the driveway. He inched his way into the dark springhouse but could already tell it was empty, picked clean over by that mangy mutt. He turned to call to his sons but they were already walking down the path toward him, followed by Rebecca and the girls. Before Jonah or Danny could speak Asa exploded.

"*I asked ya to help me,*" he said. "*I asked ya to always make sure that door was shut tight, didn't I?*" When the boys answered silently by hanging their heads Asa repeated, *"DIDN'T I? Look at me, goddammit!"*

They kept they heads lowered but looked up at their father through their eyelashes, before shame forced them to look down at the snow again.

"Do ya realize how much this meat cost me?" Asa said, a bit calmer. "Do you realize what we've lost? Do ya, Jonah? You're almost eighteen years old now. I expect ya to be more responsible! How could ya let this happen?"

"Me?" Jonah wailed. "Me? It's your damn meat and your damn springhouse—"

"Don't use those words—"

"Shut up, old man. Don't try to blame this on me." At that moment Rebecca moved forward and took Jonah's arm, but he jerked it away.

"You were the last one in last night," Asa said. "That's how we've always done it. Last one in at night checks the locks and all outside. You left that door open. You were just too lazy to check it."

"And you are just too stupid to know any better," Jonah said.

"Come here, ya goddamn—" Asa lunged toward Jonah, his hand pulled back in a fist. Rebecca screamed *no* and tried to reach for her oldest son, but he escaped the grasp of both parents, his brother and sisters and took off running down the driveway, across the railroad tracks, down the unnamed road, across Cullen's Creek and into the cold Christmas day.

The remaining Dollars watched as Asa dropped to his hand and knees, hung down his head, and wept, his shoulders heaving as his salty tears made pockmarks in the snow.

*

"I curse this holiday," Rebecca said to Danny as he watched her wring the neck of one of their egg-laying hens. "Yes, it brought me you, my sweet Daniel," she said as she held the bird to the stump. "Careful, now." He lifted the axe and cleanly chopped off its head and feet. "That's good. I do wish you a happy birthday, Daniel, I only regret I have nothing to give you."

"That's okay, Mom."

"You're sweet," Rebecca said. "It was also the day my dear Rachel was born, may she rest in peace. No, pluck like *this*," she demonstrated, and Danny followed her lead. "But for the last few years this day had meant nothing but misery for me. Look at him," she motioned with her head toward Asa, still circling the springhouse obsessively as if he could say a magic spell and conjure up the meat again, or at least to turn back the clock to the previous night and make sure that door was locked. "Pathetic."

Danny said nothing but continued to pluck the feathers from the chicken. "At least we'll have a decent Christmas dinner," she said. "Lately her eggs were of poor quality, anyway. Tasted stale somehow, didn't you think, Daniel?"

He nodded, almost imperceptibly, still plucking.

"That's good enough," Rebecca said suddenly, rising and carrying the bare chicken into the house, where a pot of boiling water awaited.

Finally at dusk Asa came back into the house, just long enough to take the shotgun from behind the stove. Rebecca, Danny, Dinah and Reece heard one shot echo off the hill that rose up behind their house, and knew that old Mr. Dandy was no more, that he paid the price for Jonah's error.

The next morning Asa was the first one up, and by sunrise had contracted to sell both Nanny the horse and Chester the cow to Baldy for just barely enough money to pay the bank loan. When he returned from Baldy's he brought back an old icebox and a fresh block of ice that his friend loaned him, although they had nothing to place on its wooden shelves. He told Rebecca to kill the remaining hen for that night's supper and retired early without even reading a bit of Chester Lee Reece. It wasn't until well into the new year that Asa told Rebecca he had seen Jonah at Baldy's that morning after Christmas, that he had spoken to their son only long enough to learn that he planned to enlist in the army as soon as possible and was probably gone away to basic training by now. What he didn't tell her was that before he left he shook Jonah's hand and told him bring pride to the Dollar name, just as his grandfather Asa Dollar had in the Civil War and just as he and his father Arden Dollar tried to do in their respective generations. There was no use in making her even more upset.

Rebecca didn't bother to boot Asa from her bed that time— it made no difference to her anymore where he slept, because to her he no longer existed. In her mind he'd only been good for one thing anyway, and that one thing had burdened her with children she didn't love, or children she did love but who were taken away from her. From that point on she tried to live as if she were alone in the house, just she, her dear son Daniel, and the letters from her other dear son, Jonah, letters postmarked from a country far away, where the army had sent him to fight in a so-called police action.

*

On Thanksgiving Day 1951, the weather turned unseasonably warm and the countryside was pelted by days of unending rain. Cullen's Creek could not keep up with the precipitation and on the Sunday after Thanksgiving overflowed its already soggy banks. Soon the unnamed road was washed out, cutting off the Dollar's primary route into Abandon, although in a pinch they could take the shortcut over the hill. Rebecca, who stood vigil in the window of Dinah and Reece's room most of the day, watched the rising water with a dull, thudding dread in her chest. She had seen this before, watching the river from her house in Falling Star, and did not think she could endure that horror again. On Monday she forced herself to speak to Asa long enough to ask him if anything in the house or barn would float, and if not, if he could build something quickly in case they had to escape. Asa tried to assure her that there wasn't nearly enough water in little old Cullen's Creek to flood them out of house and home, especially since it hadn't even washed over the railroad tracks yet, but if worse came to worse they could just sit on the roof for a day or two. Rebecca did not appreciate his inappropriate attempts at humor, and would have made some derogatory comment to him to that effect if only she'd thought it worth her time and energy. At that moment she felt that, as the only rational and sane member of the family, all her time and energy should be devoted to saving herself and her Daniel from the raging flood waters. Naturally the rest of the family were not as concerned, as being trapped in their home meant they did not have to attend school or work, and they were actually enjoying their extended Thanksgiving holiday.

On Tuesday, as Rebecca watched the flood's progress from her daughters' window, it seemed to her the creek surely had reached its crest. The rain had stopped, the creek didn't appear to have moved any higher over the last few hours, and she had almost allowed herself to feel a bit of relief when, from out of nowhere, a large yellow finch came flying at the speed of sound directly into the window at which Rebecca was standing. It hit the glass with such a *crack* and a *donk* that the rest of the family downstairs heard the noise and thought that a bomb had gone off. Rebecca gasped, then shrieked, holding her hands first to her heart and then her head as she realized what had happened. As Asa and the children rushed upstairs they found Rebecca lifting up the sash and sticking her full upper body out the window in an attempt to see the bird lying lifeless, its neck broken on the ground below. When she pulled back into the bedroom, her face was drained of all color.

"We're doomed," she said.

"Don't talk crazy," Asa said, moving toward her.

"Stop!" she said. "Stay away! Someone is going to die."

"Mom, what are you talking about?" Danny said, trying to sound reasonable.

She huffed as if asked to answer a stupid question. "It's common knowledge, Daniel. When a bird flies into a window, it means someone is going to die."

"Mother, that is just an old wives' tale," Asa said.

"It has been proven to be true," Rebecca said to her husband, rather calmly. "I can only hope it is you who is due to expire."

"Mother, ya don't mean that," Asa said.

"Don't I?" she said. Her face had regained its color and she strode from the room, taking Danny's arm as she passed. "Daniel, why don't we sit downstairs and await your father's death?"

Danny looked at Asa, shrugged, and escorted his mother down the stairs and into the living room.

On Wednesday evening, the creek had returned nearly to its normal level, the roads were passable, and Rebecca had grudgingly accepted the fact that Asa was still alive and would be for a long while. Just after supper Baldy knocked on their kitchen door and burst through before being properly asked in.

"I'm sorry for bustin' in, Rebecca," he said when she glared at him for his lack of manners, "but I just heard some great news I wanted to share with you all. I heard on the radio that over there in Korea they just signed a thirty-day cease fire. Ain't that grand?"

Rebecca hugged Danny, and Reece hugged Asa, leaving Dinah to hug Baldy in an uncomfortable embrace. "That is good news, Archibald," Rebecca said. "Thank you for letting us know. I'm sure I'll be hearing from Jonah in a day or two and he'll tell me all about it. Thanks again, and goodnight." She practically pushed him out the door.

The telegram came the next day—Thursday. Just seventeen simple words: *We regret to inform you that Jonah Dollar was killed in action on Tuesday 27 November 1951.* His final letter arrived on Friday, the letter Rebecca had expected would bring the glad tidings of the cease fire. *Dear Mom,* it began, *Another freezing day on the front line, even with the sixty-five layers of clothes I wear twenty-four hours a day. I haven't had a bath for four weeks, but I do manage to change my socks at least once a day. It's amazing how a good pair of clean, dry wool socks help to keep you warm, even when the nights get down to about thirty below. I can't* wait to get back to the reserve area, peel off these dirty rags and step into a hot (or at least lukewarm) shower.

An early winter storm blew in two nights ago, dumping almost four feet of wet, heavy snow on us. We spent most all day yesterday clearing the stuff, and I promise you when I get back home I'll never complain about shoveling snow again!

We're burrowed into the backside of Hill 702, which means it's 702 meters tall. That's about 2,500 feet to us Americans—sure is a lot bigger than our little hill behind the house! And here it's considered a small hill. The way we've dug into it kind of reminds me of when they found those dinosaur remains in Artemus. Do you remember that? I wonder what ever happened to those old bones.

We had a bit of a scare this morning. There hasn't been too much action lately from the other side, so I guess we got a little careless. Webb Wood, this knucklehead from Seattle, got it into his head to start a snowball fight. Pretty soon we were all into it, throwing and ducking and running, until all of a sudden we heard scattered rifle fire from the gook side and everyone hit the ground. We hadn't noticed in all the ruckus that another fellow, South Schrieber, had slipped over onto the forward slope, right out there in the open. We call him South because he's got a real heavy southern accent—come to think of it, I don't know what his real name is. Maybe I'll try to find out. Anyway, the guy was what you call a sitting duck out there, and I hate to say it but it served him right for not being more careful. He caught a bullet in his shoulder, but he'll live. It sure shook us up for a bit, and made us remember real quick why we're here and what waits for us just on the other side of the ridgeline.

I hope I didn't frighten you by telling you this, but I think you have a right to know what's going on over here. Don't worry about me, even though I know that you do. I'll take care of myself. And please tell Dad again that I'm real sorry about leaving the way I did, and when I get home I'll pay him back for everything that he lost. Write back as soon as you can, and tell everyone hello and that I send my love.

Jonah.

His body and personal effects arrived on Saturday, and Baldy drove all the way to the Cincinnati airport to bring him back in his pickup truck, since Gracious Sider the mortician refused to drive his hearse any farther than the hospital in Broulet.

At the visitation on Monday, Rebecca told Asa and Dinah and Reece to stay at the back of the room, that as Jonah's mother she was the most appropriate person to receive the condolences of the community. She held Danny to her side and wept just the right amount at just the right moments, having learned from Rachel's death what the townsfolk would and would not tolerate from one in the throes of grief. There were only two people from whom she did not accept sympathetic words or handshakes or hugs.

When Rev. Calder stepped toward her in the receiving line, she kept one hand at her side and with the other pulled her surviving son closer to her. "Rebecca," he said, "I know not what forces drove you from the church, but I do know that in times like these one who had suffered a loss such as yours can be comforted—"

"The loss of my parents and my two oldest children, an idiot husband and the birth of two ungrateful daughters, for starters," Rebecca said. "Haven't I been punished enough in this lifetime?"

"Rebecca, God is not out to punish you. If you only come back to Him and ask—"

"I'm through asking him for what I want, because with each request he has laughed in my face and spit in my eye." She squeezed Danny's shoulders. "I have my salvation here beside me. *He* will never forsake me. Isn't that right, Daniel?"

Danny nodded solemnly at Rev. Calder, who simply shook his head and moved to the back of the room, where one by one he took the hands of Asa, Dinah and Reece.

A few minutes later Baldy Hilliard stood in front of Rebecca and began to tell her how sorry he was, how he knew what it was like to lose someone close to you. She cut him off with a wave of her hand.

"How is it you know about my loss?" she asked. "How is it that your only son was exempted from war and is still alive? How is it that at the age of twenty-six he is unmarried and still living at home?" Before Baldy could answer Asa was at his wife's side.

"Calm down now, Mother," he whispered, but she tried to shoo him away. He refused to budge. "Be nice to Baldy. He's been in a world of hurt since Sarah died."

"Don't keep throwing that in my face," she said to Asa, although she looked straight at Baldy. "That happened a long time ago, and I'm sick of hearing about it. Frankly, right now I wish I were dead."

"Mom, don't say that—"

"I'm sorry, Daniel, but it's true. There's nothing left in my life now but you, son, and you're growing older every day." She finally looked at Asa. "I blame my cold, cruel, unjust misery on you. You drove Jonah away. You killed him." She went over to Jonah's casket and stroked the top of his hand as it lay folded over his chest. Asa attempted to pull her arm away and she swatted at him, then turned to leave the mortuary. "You killed him," she said again, whispering under her breath. "And you finally killed me. Tomorrow I'll be gone and can be teaching again by the start of the new semester." She left the room and stepped out into the bitter December wind in only her thin dress. Danny took her coat from the rack and raced outside to wrap it around her shoulders. Together they walked home, Danny tugging at Rebecca's hand and entreating her not to leave, nearly succumbing to the tears he felt behind his eyes but which he knew his mother would never tolerate. The next day when he awoke and went downstairs, she was there fixing his breakfast as usual.

CHAPTER TWELVE:
SEPTEMBER 14, 1957

Reece awakens in a sitting position, leaning against the back of her bedroom door. Her arms are empty and dead. She rubs her right arm against the door frame for a few minutes until it regains feeling, then uses that hand to lift her paralyzed left arm and massage the life back into it. She winces as numbness gives way to prickling needles under her skin. The pain finally subsides as she rises on stiff legs and wobbles her way to the window. She has to shelter her eyes from the zealous sun which has already melted last night's snow. Or perhaps it didn't snow at all—Reece can't be sure of anything now. The nightstand is in its usual spot against the wall, next to the bed, all of her personal items exactly in place where they should be. Reece takes a closer look at the nightstand, then in the closet and the dresser drawers, all of which are eerily empty. Every last one of Dinah's things have been removed from the room. It's as if she never existed.

A howl of anger and frustration, of loneliness, despair and fear bubble up from Reece's stomach, piercing her heart and screaming up toward her throat. But there it loses its momentum and is swallowed down in a bitter gulp of resignation. She scoops up the olive knapsack, still lying where it landed against the closet door last night, and pulls out the wristwatch that serves as the bedroom clock. The shattered face can't hide the fact that the hands are not moving; she has no idea what time it is, but judging by the shadows outside it's either very early or very late in day. She guesses it's nearly sunset; the sun is low enough to take shelter behind the hazy blanket that hovers just above the ground, which, the Germ

Man explained to them in class one day, is why sunsets are so brilliant. She accepts this explanation and wonders why no one in the family woke her up before now.

The house below her is silent, so she reasons it's safe enough to venture downstairs. But first she digs through her dresser drawers until she finds her blue jeans, "the devil's drawers," her mother calls them, which she is forbidden to wear unless participating in chores that will cause one of her dresses to become completely "filth-infested" (her mother's phrase again). She pulls them on and tucks her nightgown in like a blouse, slips on her sneakers and treads lightly down the steps.

The kitchen windowshade is drawn, casting an umber pall over the room. At the foot of the stairs the dinner table is practically sagging under the weight of vegetables from their garden, some of which Reece is sure her mother harvested weeks ago. She wonders where she must have been storing them all this time. She walks around the table, inspecting the piles of onions and carrots, green peppers and radishes, potatoes, beets and green beans. Each stalk, each leaf has been carefully removed; each vegetable washed and neatly stacked in preparation for this evening's Harvest Parade. Reece can't remember her mother ever going to so much trouble before. "It's nothing but a poor white trash tradition," she usually says, standing in the garden with her arms crossed against her chest, until Mr. Dollar whispers a few words in her ear and she relents, plucking a few scrawny tomatoes from a vine and agreeing, albeit reluctantly, to march in the ceremony.

Last September fourteenth, and every September fourteenth that she could recall, Reece would nearly tumble downstairs to find three small, wrapped presents waiting for her on the kitchen table (when Jonah was still with them there would be four gifts). She'd open them hastily, despite her father's admonitions to unwrap them slowly, then the family would drive to the Founder's Festival. They'd come home early for cake and ice cream, treats reserved for special occasions, then her parents would have their little discussion in the garden, and finally they would walk back to the school to participate in the parade. Reece searches the kitchen for any sign of a gift or a cake, but sees nothing.

A dull *thud* draws her attention back to the table, where a head of lettuce has rolled away from the congregation of vegetables and dropped to the floor. Reece stoops to pick it up and return it to its place when she instead darts to the door, kicks it open and with a banshee whoop hurls the green, leafy ball up the hill with more force than she's ever exerted in her life.

She stands perfectly still for a moment, watching it land on the hard ground and roll back down a few feet, then explodes into laughter, an almost hysterical yet completely freeing laugh that seems to burst from every cell in her body. She scrambles back into the house and with both hands sweeps the sum total of her mother's harvest onto the floor. Using her arms for leverage, she springs up and then crashes down on the food with both feet, again and again, crushing the firm, round objects as if they were empty peanut shells. She kicks small, squashed, shattered pieces against the walls and under the pie safe and against the stove, then scoops up an armful and spins around and around, head back, and throws the load up into the ceiling and cackles as it falls onto her head and around her feet. She scoops up another two handfuls and, forcing the door open with her shoulder, skips down the stone path, flinging bits into the fading sunlight as she goes.

At the end of the path Reece stops, arms empty. She sees her father's car rolling toward her and she stands there, carefree now but not careless, legs apart and hands clasping her elbows at her waist. She guesses it must be six o'clock.

Her father swings the car into the driveway and brings it to a stop in front of the house. The three of them climb out of the vehicle and stare at Reece, still standing defiantly a few yards away. Mr. Dollar begins to walk toward her until Mrs. Dollar mutters a sharp command and he halts. She puts her hand on Danny's back and they turn to enter the house when she notices the trail of vegetable parts littering the path. They follow it inside, then Mrs. Dollar quickly storms back into the yard, slamming the screen door so hard Reece can actually see the house shake. Danny trails behind her. Mr. Dollar bends down to pick up the remains of a radish, then flings it into the grape arbor. Reece walks forward, arms hanging loosely by her side at first, then swinging with purpose.

They all meet beside the car. Mrs. Dollar immediately raises an open hand against her daughter but Mr. Dollar restrains her. Danny glares at Reece and moves next to her, but makes an obvious effort not to touch her or the space around her.

"*What is the meaning of this?*" Mrs. Dollar seethes.

"Yeah Reece, what'd you do that for?" Danny asks, leaning his face near hers.

"Do what?" Reece asks with exaggerated innocence.

"Do what?" Mr. Dollar asks, in true innocence.

"Come on Reece, you've got food in your hair!" Danny says, glancing first at his father in contempt and then at his mother with amusement.

She points her plump finger at Reece. "Once again your mere existence is a curse to me," she says. "All I wanted to do was to march in our town's fine Harvest Parade, sharing my bounty with those of my friends and neighbors, and you set out to destroy—"

"You're such a liar," Reece says, practically spitting out the words. "I see right through you. Everyone sees through you." She looks at Danny, who won't meet her stare. "You hate the Harvest Parade. Every year you say you won't march with the poor white trash. Isn't that right, Doodle?"

He studies the ground and tightens his clutch on his wife.

"You don't care about anyone but yourself. Not Doodle, or me, or Dinah or Jonah—"

"Reece Dollar, don't you—" she begins, her voice rising, but Mr. Dollar cuts her off, finally starting to understand what happened.

"Reece m'dear, ya can tell us why ya did it," he says. "We won't get mad."

"In jesus christ's name, Asa, of course we're mad!" Mrs. Dollar shouts. "That evil girl's got the devil in her heart!" She wrestles free of her husband's grip and lands a heavy blow on his cheek that makes him stagger backward a few steps. Before he can recover she lunges toward her children. Danny steps aside and she pushes Reece's shoulders to the ground and straddles her. Reece can't move under the weight and takes five or six slaps to the face from her mother before Asa is able to pull her off.

"Danny, why didn't ya help you sister?" he pants, struggling to keep mother away from daughter.

Danny shrugs and steps in between his parents, taking his mother by the arm. He whispers in her ear and strokes her hand until the two of them are chuckling softly, heads pressed together in conspiracy. Mr. Dollar helps Reece up and checks her face for injury. She's stunned and her inflamed cheeks sting with humiliation, but she'll survive.

Mrs. Dollar and Danny stroll into the house and return in a few minutes with some vegetable scraps, which they've formed into passable resemblances of whole vegetables. They climb into the backseat of the car. "Come on Asa, let's go," Mrs. Dollar says through the rolled-down window.

"Mother, what are ya talkin' about?" a puzzled Mr. Dollar asks, his arm still around his daughter's shoulders.

"We've got to make an appearance at the parade," she huffs. "Start up this car now." She settles back into the seat and takes Danny's hand.

"You know we're not allowed to drive to the parade," he says. "Tradition says we've got to walk to the school, then march to the monument."

"Asa, we're going to miss the entire thing if you don't get in this car immediately!" she says, releasing Danny's hand and leaning her elbows out the window. "We can park in the alley behind the courthouse and join the parade like we've been there all along. Now let's go!"

Mr. Dollar starts to move forward but Reece holds him back. "No, Doodle," she whispers, her eyes shouting with fear. "Can't we stay here?"

"*Can't we stay here?*" her mother mimics. "Not another word out of you, young lady. You look a mess and you stink to high heaven. When we get there you go off with that Roxanne girl. We'll collect you when we're ready to leave."

Asa literally has to drag Reece into the passenger seat. He gets behind the wheel, starts the car, and the four of them ride in silence to the courthouse alley.

The town square shimmers in the golden shadow of the setting sun. Scattered pools of melted snow reflect the drooping white lights—battered by last night's snow storm—that border the plaza. The filigree lampposts that line Main Street are decorated as well with twinkling colored lights that pulse with the rhythm of the townspeople as they make their way to the monument. The Wesley Tree seems to stand taller than usual in its gilded glory, illuminated for the first time this year with permanent spotlights buried near the base that will light up the tree year 'round. The Harvest Parade is wrapping up as the Dollars approach; the last stragglers add their gifts to the assemblage until the entire town has formed a semi-circle in front of the monument. There Mrs. Dollar gathers up the remains of her vegetables and links her arm in Danny's. They walk ahead of Reece and her father, who shuffle a few steps behind, hiding their bruised faces with their hands.

"Reece m'dear, the day you were born was the happiest day of my life," Mr. Dollar says. "First I met Chester Lee Reece, who was so nice and kind and friendly to a nobody like me, and then later that night you came along. I wanted to get ya something more for your birthday than just that geode, but ya know I just can't afford it," he says, slipping his arm across his daughter's shoulders as they walk. "I hope ya liked it, 'cause it's not right, a girl havin' a birthday without no—*any* presents. Happy birthday m'dear." He stops and swoops her up in a hug.

She stands on her tiptoes and squeezes his neck in return. "Thank you Doodle." She avoids his eyes, fearing he'll discover there that she hasn't seen the geode since it rolled under her bed the night before. They start walking again and watch Mrs. Dollar kneel solemnly before the Wesley Tree monument, mouth a few words and place her offering there, tucking it behind vegetables better formed than her own. Despite the best efforts to scrub clean the concrete around the monument, a few purplish stains remain from the bloody scene three nights before, but now they've been covered completely by the offerings of the townspeople. Mrs. Dollar stands up, brushes her hands on the front of her skirt and turns to Danny. Over their shoulders they glance back at Mr. Dollar and Reece and simultaneously begin to laugh.

At that moment the crowd is silenced by an electronic squeal followed by the sound of Erl Cullen VII clearing his throat into a microphone. Mr. Dollar pulls Reece into an empty booth which earlier in the day sold baked goods to benefit the high school band.

"Do you think he'll mention Dinah in his speech?" Reece asks her father.

He glances at two of the figures in the crowd gathered around Erl beside the monument. "Not with your mom and Danny standin' there givin' him the evil eye."

"Welcome people of Abandon to the Founder's Festival," Erl Cullen VII shouts into the microphone, reading from a tattered, dirty piece of paper. The people of Abandon break into applause and whistles. "This is a mighty special year for everybody here, but 'specially for us Cullens." The applause dwindles to murmurs. "It was a hunerd and fifty years ago that my great-great-great-great grandpa founded Abandon by the banks of Cullen's Creek. Course it weren't called Cullen's Creek then," he ad libs with a chortle. The mumbles grow louder—the people of Abandon have heard this story many times before. "Why, if my great-great-great grandpa hadn't found the markings on the Wesley Tree here, we wouldn't even *live* in Abandon today." He pauses for dramatic effect. "We'd all live in *Broulet!*" His attempt to invoke civic pride falls woefully short and is met by a smattering of grumbles and boos, which he ignores.

"We've come a long way in a hunerd and fifty years," he continues. "Fought in the Civil War . . . went from ridin' in horse-

drawn buggies to drivin' cars . . . got electricity in all our houses . . ."
He flicks his eyes across the first few rows of the people of Abandon.
" . . . Well, most of us did, anyway." The crowd erupts in laughter.
Mrs. Dollar scowls at Erl, then jerks her head in Danny's direction.
Erl nods. "And more and more of our youngsters are goin' off to
college than ever before. In fact, just today we got word that one of
our local boys got offered a full-ride scholarship to go play basketball
at the University of Kentucky." Oohs and aahs ripple through the
crowd. Heads turn to try to identify the lucky boy. "Danny Dollar,
come up here." Wild applause fills the square. Teenage girls push
their way to the front to get a better look. Young boys who shoot
baskets on the sides of their barns in the dark look upon Danny's
lanky figure in wistful awe as he tries to make his way to the tree.
Reece sees her mother tear at Danny's shirtsleeve but he escapes
and steps toward the tree. "Say a few words, Danny," Erl says,
putting his arm around his shoulders. Danny stares down at the
microphone and shrugs. "Nah," he says, then quickly disappears
back into the crowd.

Reece looks at her father. "Did you know about this?" she asks.

"Nope," he says. "But it's good news for Danny, ain't it?"

Reece watches the crowd collapse onto her brother, offering
congratulations, attempting to touch any part of him, hoping some
of his magic rubs off on them. "I guess so," she says. "But I—"

"But what, m'dear?"

She sighs. "Nothing."

"Congratulations, Danny," Erl Cullen VII says. "On a more
serious note, as most of you probably know by now, our town's
first honest-to-gosh famous person passed away last week. Chester
Lee Reece lived his whole eighty-one years here in Abandon, and
as a matter of fact he'd started to write a special poem to be read
here tonight in honor of our hunerd and fifty year anniversary. If
you all will be quiet for just a few minutes, I'd like to read it now."
He pulls another wrinkled piece of paper from his pants pocket
and clears his throat more forcefully than before.

"In Abandon did Erl Cullen, age nine
A stately withered beech tree find
And beside it, the sacred creek ran
Through virgin woods unseen by man.

"Now in twilight's silver glow I see
Gliding like ghosts through walnut trees
Faint shapes of generations past
Phantoms of a childhood gone too fast.

"Oh, Abandon Indiana!
We will not abandon ye,
Although you have no mountains
Although you have no sea
Except for Cullen's Creek.

"That's it," Erl Cullen VII says.

When he finishes the few people actually listening applaud politely and then continue their conversations. Asa and Reece clap loud and long until noticing that they're drawing attention to themselves by still applauding. Only Miss Corliss, the English teacher, realizes instantly that in his final days Chester Lee Reece was forced to plagiarize at least the first stanza of his unfinished epic, and she cringes at the ragged meter. Giving him the benefit of the doubt, however, she thinks perhaps he, like Coleridge, had tried to invoke the poem in a drug-induced state, but of course he failed miserably. She also suspects that Erl Cullen VII added those parts about the Cullens himself, so she cannot in good conscience take the poem at face value. She leaves to get a cup of punch.

Erl Cullen VII steps up to the microphone one more time.

"And now, as a special treat, Abandon's newest famous person has come back home with a song that's almost at the top of the record charts," he says. "If you ask real nice, maybe he'll play that 'Love Me in the Morning' song, you think?" The girls erupt into screams. "So here, on this stage right now, is Halo Truly!" The screaming intensifies as Halo, Rog and Kick take the stage. "And here's to another hunerd and fifty years of Abandon," Erl Cullen VII says, but no one listens to him now as the first notes of music begin.

The band doesn't play "Love Me in the Morning" right away, but instead begins to play a song Reece has never heard before. Soon girls in poodle skirts and saddle shoes are dancing with boys in rolled up jeans and penny loafers, with various adults patrolling between the bodies to limit contact to a minimum. Despite last night's snow and the chilly weather of earlier in the morning, the temperature has risen to a comfortable level and soon jackets and sweaters are discarded in piles up and down Main Street. As Halo Truly sings he looks out over the crowd, into the eyes of swooning girls and their jealous boyfriends, of those who mocked him all through school, who tried to break his guitar or called him a sissy-girl for playing music instead of basketball, and smirks as he thinks, who's the sissy-girl now?

"Hey Reece!" Roxanne Joshua says, bounding up to her friend. "Hi Mr. Dollar."

"Hi Roxanne," he says. "I'm gonna go find Baldy," he tells Reece. "Meet ya back here later?"

"Sure Doodle," she says.

"You look terrible!" Roxanne says. "I can't believe your mom let you out of the house like that."

"She doesn't care," Reece says.

"So are you in trouble?" Roxanne wants to know as soon as Reece's father is out of earshot.

Reece sees Danny get swept into a throng of zealous well-wishers and vicarious thrill-seekers. His forlorn mother drifts away from the crowd and toward the street, her eyes scanning the faces. Reece steers Roxanne away from her mother to a hiding place behind a tall stack of speaker cabinets set up next to the stage. Before she can speak she spies a most unbelievable sight and is forced to re-focus her eyes. "Is that Dr. Riley with—"

"Vernie Cletis, yeah," Roxanne says without looking.

"How did you know?"

"God, Reece, the whole town knows," she says, rolling her eyes. "Dr. Riley let Vernie stay at his house the night after she blew off her toe. Just to keep an eye on her, I guess. Once she sobered up they got to talking, and . . ." She turns toward Abandon's newest couple just as they stop walking and kiss tenderly, but passionately, under a low-hanging string of burnt-out lights.

"Eww," Roxanne shudders, then turns back to Reece. "Nice try, but you're not changing the subject," she huffs. "Now tell me: Did You Get In Trouble?"

"Why would I be in trouble?" Reece shouts over the music, the volume of which seems to increase with each note.

"Why?" Roxanne says, amazed. "You ran away from Mammoth Cave. The police had to bring you home."

"He was just a security guard," Reece says. "And besides, how do you know all that?"

Roxanne clucks her tongue. "Everybody knows," she says. "The police called the Germ Man at Mammoth Cave and told him they had you in custody and that they were bringing you back right away."

"So what did the Germ Man say?"

"He told them he couldn't guarantee we'd still be there when you arrived, and that he wasn't responsible for whatever happened to you."

Reece shakes her head. "The Germ Man is a jerk." The music stops and the word *jerk* reverberates through the square.

"Reece!" Roxanne says, then drops her voice. "It wasn't his fault you ran off. Where'd you go, anyway? Nobody in your family would say."

The band starts up again, another tune Reece doesn't recognize. "What do you mean?" she yells.

Roxanne cups her hands around her mouth. "Today at the Festival. Whenever anyone asked your dad or Danny where you were, or how you were doing, your mom would butt in before they could answer. She'd say everything was just fine and change the subject."

"Did she mention Dinah?" Reece asks.

Roxanne peeks around the speaker as she checks out the dancing kids spilling out of the square and into the street. "Um, no. Look. There's Mark Isaac. He's coming over here." Her eyes glaze over and she leans against the cabinet, arms folded in front of her.

"Hi Mark," she purrs.

"Hey Roxanne," he says, sidling up to them, hands stuffed in the pockets of his black leather jacket.

"Hey Mark," Reece says, stepping slightly in front of Roxanne.

"I'm still mad at you, Mark Isaac," Roxanne says, planting her hands on her hips in an exaggerated manner.

He stares at her through the lock of oily hair that hangs from his forehead.

"You said you'd meet me at the monument at two o'clock today, and we'd walk around together," Roxanne says. "Did you forget?" She tucks a stray wisp of hair behind her ear.

"Uh, yeah," Mark mutters, then in a move quicker than the eye a hand shoots out from a pocket and leads Roxanne by the arm to the middle of the square. Before they disappear into the squirming mass of teenagers Roxanne looks over her shoulder at Reece and sticks out her tongue.

Reece feels the bottom of her stomach drop away like a trap door, leaving a gaping hole through which her heart falls hard and fast down to the cuffs of her devil's drawers. Tucking her chin into her chest she turns to flee to the safe haven of the family car and instead runs headlong into Baldy Hilliard.

"Hey girl, slow down," he says, steadying her by the shoulders. "Here she is, Asa."

Mr. Dollar walks up beside Baldy, followed by Addison Hilliard. Reece starts to gasp, then swallows it down.

"Ya okay, m'dear?" her father says.

She nods and swallows again, harder. "Yeah."

"Well, ya don't look so good. Why don't ya go lay down in the car for a while?"

"The car? You drove?" Baldy says. "How come?"

"Long story," Asa says. "Reece, ya go on now. Baldy and me're gonna go try to find your mother, but Addison'll walk with ya. Won't ya, Addison?"

Addison snags Reece's hand up in his. "Sure thing, Mr. Dollar."

Asa slaps Baldy on the back of his overalls and grins. "That's a fine boy ya got there, Baldy. Now Addison, ya take good care of her." The two old friends stroll off to the other side of the square.

"I will, Mr. Dollar." He tugs on Reece's hand a few times until her feet finally shuffle forward. "Come on gal, I don't bite." He grins so that his teeth show even in the dimmed festival lights. "You like this song?" he asks. Reece strains her ears and finally recognizes that Halo Truly is playing "Love Me in the Morning."

"Yeah, sure," she says, and starts to hum along. All the way to the car Addison walks a bit ahead of Reece. She tries with every stride to extract her hand from his but he matches her effort step for step until they reach the alley. With his free hand he pops open the door to the backseat, then motions *after you* with an upturned palm. She considers trying to break free one last time but suddenly her legs seem to collapse beneath her and the backseat looks so inviting that if she can only lie down for a minute or two and close her eyes or maybe even sleep for just a little while then maybe when she wakes up her blood will have stopped pounding against the inside of her skin and she'll be at home in her bed and Dinah will be lying beside her and upstairs Danny and Jonah will be bouncing the basketball against the floor and she'll be convinced that the ceiling is going to fall right in but of course it never does so she lets him pick her up oh so gently and place her carefully on her back and he climbs in after her and lets the door fall shut with a *clack* and as she sinks into the seat she lifts her chin until she's looking upside-down at the panel above and behind her and watches the pillar light wondering why it never comes on even when the door is open and remembers doodle said it needed a new fuse but she imagines if she stares at the creamy white rectangle long enough she can make the light go on just by thinking about it at least that way she won't have to think about the day-old beard scraping against her cheek her neck her ear her cheek again and maybe if she keeps humming love me in the morning quietly to herself she won't hear the zipper of her jeans slowly creeping down down down tooth by tooth until the waistband is somehow around her ankles and she feels a breeze like the window is open but she doesn't dare take her eyes off the darkened light so she can't know for sure but what she does know now is the taste of his flannel shirt in her mouth its scratchy cotton filling her dry mouth until she can barely breathe and she begins to take deep heaving frantic breaths that he mistakes for something other than suffocation and he begins to breathe the same way and she can smell water like it's raining but she knows that it's not and she can smell smoked bacon and she wonders why because they closed the food tent at the festival hours ago but then she recalls that time in the springhouse which seems like a long time ago and then she remembers how she felt down there and she realizes she feels that way again and she likes it but she doesn't want to like it she's not supposed to like it so she keeps her eyes on the white rectangle come on light come on come on COME ON she feels as though hot liquid metal is being poured inside of her like when doodle took her to see where nanny's shoes were made and the blacksmith poured the glowing liquefied lead into a mold and as it cooled and hardened he took his little hammer and banged it into shape that's what it feels like now but she won't cry she'll just hum a little *love me in the morning my angel of the night cover me with kisses after dawn's first light has swept away the teardrops from the sweet earth fresh with dew oh love me in the morning and forever I'll love you* and keep looking at the dark place where the light should be come on come on come on light come on come on there it is! there's the light! but it's moving it's moving all around the inside of the car and she hears her name being called far far away reece! reece m'dear! jesus christ reece! and she hears the door open and though the hot metal stops pouring down she's still burning inside but she won't cry and she won't move even though the car is shaking and swaying and the door is swinging open and shut open and shut and now it's open because she can feel a breeze again and it feels good against her bare skin so that she can take her eyes from the side panel of the car and she makes her eyes follow the light that's still flitting around outside the light is coming from doodle's hand and now it's gone and she hears a woman's voice cry whore whore and she knows the voice it's familiar but still she doesn't recognize it but then she hears danny's voice clear as day say what's wrong mom and the voice cries get away from here your sister's a whore both your sisters are dirty harlots and then *he* says *he says* they learnt it from you gal you sure did like it when i did it to you fourteen years ago least you acted like you did but ever since then you been real mean to me and my pa too and in fact to just about everybody and i never could figure out why and doodle says rebecca? and she says yes yes it's true he came to the house when you were at work and had his way with me and later Reece was born and then she lets out an ungodly howl even worse than the old dog mister dandy did the night doodle had to put him down for eating all the meat in the springhouse when really it was jonah who should've been put down cause it was his fault and then doodle calm as anything comes into the back of the car and reaches under the seat and pulls out a long shiny thing and it makes a click-clack sound and he says move out the way mother and she hears baldy's voice she knows it's baldy's voice cause he just spoke to her a few minutes ago and she's a little more clear headed now the fresh air is helping her to be more clear headed now and she hears him say for the love of god asa don't do it he's my only son you lost a son and you know how it hurts but you still got one son left don't do it but doodle can't hear anything but his wife's animal moan and can't see anything but his daughter who's not really his daughter after all lying there in the dark backseat and the gun goes off and she scrambles out of the car and stands over *his* body lying there on the ground and she looks into his eyes propped open with death and that's when she sees for the first time what it was about him that seemed so familiar and it was his eyes those gray eyes just like hers but now she guesses hers were like his and then in her mind she starts to sees the faces of others like bo cullen who she realizes had gray eyes too and while she's standing there over the dead man her father sets the gun down on the grass and sits inside the car not on the seat but down by the running board with the door still open and his head down and his elbows resting on his knees and his arms dangling between his knees like he's worn out from doing something usual like chopping firewood or milking a cow and he sits like that until the town marshal comes and leads him away but not in handcuffs because he says a man in his position has to have *some* dignity.

CHAPTER THIRTEEN: HALO TRULY

I was in Hollywood when Asa Dollar finally went on trial for shooting Addison Hilliard at the Founder's Festival. Our new manager, Benjy Strassman, had gotten Rog, Kick and me a bit part in a movie called "High School Juvenile Delinquents Rock." It was about a gang of juvenile delinquents in reform school who get their friends on the outside to smuggle in some musical instruments, then convince the superintendent of the school to let them put on a talent show. There was also a subplot about the delinquents' girlfriends, all tarted up with teased, bleach-blonde hair, red lipstick and tight sweaters, who have to fend off the advances of the rival gang across town. For the finale the incarcerated gang members whip out their instruments and blow the roof off the place with a blistering rock 'n roll number, which of course was my second single, "Bitter Sun:"

> *My woman left me*
> *On a cold winter's day*
> *She left me no note*
> *She had nothing to say*
>
> *As I walked down her street*
> *Past the house where she lived*
> *That bitter sun laughed*
> *With no mercy to give*

Oh that pale, bitter sun
Setting low in the sky
Hung heavy on my heart
As I told her goodbye.

The song sets off a riot in the school, whereby the boys overwhelm the guards and bust out into the streets, taking over the town. The guards, realizing they are powerless to stop them, start laughing and dancing and singing in the streets to more rock 'n roll music, including, of course, my first single, "Love Me in the Morning," and pronounce that everyone is free to go. The End.

Rog and Kick and I played three of the juvenile delinquents in the band. Rog and Kick's characters didn't have names; they just milled about in the background the whole time. My character was "Heartless" Hap Highgate, a harsh high school car thief who also plays a mean acoustic guitar. I had two lines: "Yeah, Daddy, you can't stop kids who want to rock!" and "Come on, Daddy-O, show us what you got!", both times addressing one of the uptight reform school guards.

When Benjy told us about the movie he said we should strike while the iron was hot, that we should hurry up and try to fill the empty spot Elvis left when he joined the Army. "Out of sight, out of mind," Benjy said. "With Elvis away in Germany, you'll be the one those little girls are seeing everywhere instead of him. They'll never know what hit 'em! Ha *Hee!*" Benjy always said "Ha *Hee!*" whenever he was excited about something, which seemed to be most of the time. I thought he sounded like a sick donkey whenever he made that sound, but of course I never said anything. Because ever since Benjy introduced himself to me after a show we did in Ft. Wayne, Indiana and offered to be our manager, he made Rog and Kick and me, but mostly me, a whole lot of money.

That show in Ft. Wayne was just a week after we played the Founder's Festival in Abandon, where, of course, Mr. Dollar shot Addison Hilliard. It seemed like everywhere we went in the tri-state area people were talking about the incident, and when they found out I was there that night they wanted to hear all about it. At first I told the truth, that I was on stage at the time and didn't see anything. But soon I noticed that the girls paid even more attention to me when they thought I was involved in the scandal in some way, so after a while I started embellishing my version of what happened. Each night I remembered another new piece of information that I had somehow forgotten about before, until it ended up this way: After I heard the first gunshot over the music, I leapt offstage and ran in the direction of the sound, just in time to see Asa Dollar preparing to take a second shot. I lunged at him, knocking the shotgun out of his hands and wrestling him to the ground, holding him there until the sheriff came. Fortunately they didn't call me to testify at Mr. Dollar's trial, or else I would have been found out as a big old liar.

By the time of the trial I was in Hollywood with Rog and Kick and Benjy Strassman, filming my scenes in "High School Juvenile Delinquents Rock." But I never even saw the finished cut of my movie debut. At the wrap party after our last day of filming we all went to this club on the Sunset Strip called the Weeping Willow which I called the "Weepin' Willa" til everybody told me the right way to say it so I wouldn't sound like the hick I was. As soon as we walked through the door somebody put a shooter of whiskey in my hand, and somebody else kept it filled all night long. There was music and dancing and these women, one right after the other, all looking more and more like Jayne Mansfield or Marilyn Monroe with each whiskey blast and each one beckoning me to the back of the club. When I finally got back there someone shoved me through a trap door hidden behind the bar and into a secret room. There were things going on in that room that I was sure didn't go on in Abandon, or even anywhere east of the Mississippi River. The next thing I knew someone had cut up some white powder on the tabletop, sniffed a line of it into each nostril, and motioned for me to do that same. Whew! All I had to say after that first hit was "The King is dead! Long live the King! Me! Ha *Hee!*" and fell back against the red vinyl chair. When I came to a few minutes later I asked them to hit me again, and they did, and that went on for the rest of the night. Or so they tell me.

About three a.m., no, it must have been two o'clock because the bartender cried out "last call," we headed outside. Benjy was letting Rog and Kick and me stay at the house of a friend of his, somewhere high up in the Hollywood Hills. I got behind the wheel of my brand new baby blue '58 Chevy, and made my way up those twisty, turny hills. Rog and Kick were crashed out in the backseat. All of a sudden the road, which had been snaking around toward the right, veered off toward the left but I kept going to the right and going and going until the car CRASHED into a big, ugly, dead-looking tree, which looked more like a cactus to me but what did I know, I was just a small-town boy from Indiana. I crawled out from behind the steering wheel and shook Rog and Kick by the shoulders to make sure they were okay. They were alive and breathing but still heavily under the influence of the evening's pharmaceuticals and wouldn't be waking up for a while. I knew we needed help so I started walking. Every time a saw headlights approaching on that deserted road I stuck out my thumb, but no one stopped. Finally I heard what sounded like a truck coming down the road, so I took an extra step into the roadway to be sure the driver saw me. He didn't, until it was too late, and I was flattened under his wheels, another pretty face gone too soon.

That was twenty years ago, yet I remember it like it was yesterday, and I'm still the most famous dead person in Abandon. More famous than even Chester Lee Reece.

Right, Chester?

[Sigh] *Right, Halo.*

Whose grave gets visited by more people, even after all these years?

[Sigh] *Yours, Halo. But tell me, Halo, what have you done since you've been here?*

What do you mean what have I done? I don't have to do anything here! No one does!

We don't have to, but it doesn't hurt to remind the supreme one what we did down there, understand?

No.

Allow me to explain. Exactly how many songs did you write in your life?

Two.

Two. How . . . prolific.

At least I wasn't a plagiarist.

Ah, yes . . . I only resorted to that once. Besides, it didn't matter—I was about to take my last breath. None of those simpletons knew the difference anyway.

Miss Corliss knew.

That spinster? I knew she would never tell. She took great satisfaction in knowing she was the only one in town intelligent enough to recognize it. And at least I, unlike you, worked right up until the end.

Hey, give me a break. I had a short life.

That's no excuse. Your song lyrics were no better than my poetry.

Maybe not, Chester, but when I set my lyrics to music, the kids didn't care. Besides, I would rather write two perfect songs than spend a lifetime writing mediocre poems, know what I mean?

I do know what you mean. Before, the poetry unraveled in my brain like fancy, decorative threads weaving into a beautiful tapestry. But as soon as I began to write down the words, the magic was lost and the cloth became rumpled and ratty and threadbare and torn and ugly and—

Okay, I get the picture.

—and it was never what I meant to say. I felt as though I had a million beautiful poems inside of my head that I could never give voice to. I kept trying, though, until I ran out of time.

I know. [Sigh] I know.

CHAPTER FOURTEEN:
DECEMBER 25, 1958

For the second Christmas in a row, two of the nuns at Sister Cecelia's Hospital and Home for Wayward Girls come to Reece's room at dawn and rouse her from troubled sleep. Once she is dressed, they take her to the front door, put her in the backseat of a long black car and make her lie down in the back. They tell her to either go to sleep or cover her face with her coat. They don't want her to see where they're going, although this year Reece has a pretty good idea it's the same place the took her last Christmas—to visit her mother.

The car finally stops moving after about two hours. The nuns open the back door of the car and lead Reece into a large brick building, shielding her eyes from her surroundings. They take the back stairs to the second floor and walk down the hall to Rebecca's room.

Mrs. Dollar sits in a chair by the open drapes of the window, but stares down at the open bible in her lap. She doesn't look up when the door opens.

"Rebecca? Your daughter is here," one of the nuns says. She waits for Mrs. Dollar to answer, but when she doesn't, says, "We'll be out in the hall if you need anything," and they leave the room.

Reece moves towards the window and sits on the edge of the bed, facing her mother who, in the past fifteen months, has lost nearly half her body weight. "Merry Christmas, mom," she says.

Rebecca continues to read her bible.

"How are you?" Reece asks. Still Rebecca says nothing. Reece can't stand the silence in the room, so she begins a one-sided conversation.

"The trial was a few months ago," she says. "Of course Doodle confessed to it, and there were plenty of witnesses, but they had to decide whether or not he went to the Founder's Festival *planning* to kill Mr. Hilliard." Reece feels the tears and the tingly feeling rising up from the center of her chest. She's never spoken of these events aloud, but she thinks her mother should know what happened. "To make matters worse, his was the first case ever for the public defender assigned to him. Have you ever heard of him? J.L. 'Lucky' Luckinger?" She stares at the top of her mother's head as it bends over the bible. "Me either," Reece says. "I was there all three days—the nuns took me. I was even called to testify." Reece fidgets on the bed. "The jury deliberated for just four and a half hours. They found Doodle guilty of second degree murder. They said he didn't go to the Founder's Festival with murder on his mind, but when he raised that shotgun to his shoulder he surely intended to shoot to kill." Reece sighs deeply and continues. "The judge sentenced him to forty years in the State Prison in Michigan City. His lawyer was at least smart enough to offer to appeal, but Doodle said no, he'd do his time." Reece searches for any sign of awareness on her mother's face. "Mom, he's fifty-four years old. He'll die in there. Don't you care?"

With these words Rebecca looks up. "Danny?" she asks.

Reece's imminent tears change instantly into rage. "You don't care about anyone but yourself and your precious Danny!" she screams. "Don't worry about Danny; he'll be just fine. He moved in with Coach Winthorp and his family. He's all set to go to Lexington and be a big basketball star, just like you wanted him to be."

Reece swears she sees the hint of a smile on her mother's face. "I, on the other hand, am not doing as well," she says. "Sister Cecelia's is cold in the winter, hot in the summer and the food, what there is of it, is awful. I have to wear hand-me-down clothes and all the other girls make fun of me, and I don't even know why. I plan to leave there as soon as I can get away. Thanks for asking."

Mrs. Dollar turns the page in her bible and begins to read a passage. Reece shifts her position on the bed again. "Will you at least tell me where Dinah is?" she asks her mother.

Rebecca lifts her bible toward her daughter and points to the lines she just read. Reece takes the book and reads them herself.

"'The time has come,' he said. 'The kingdom of God is near. Repent and believe the good news!'"

Reece hands the bible back to her mother, who still has not yet looked upon her daughter's face. "You want me to repent?" Reece asks. "For what? Being born? I didn't ask to be born. If anyone should repent, it's you, for the way you treated everyone around you. Because look where it's gotten you! I'm only here because they made me come. Are you even listening to me?"

Mrs. Dollar is rocking back and forth in her chair, hands folded in front of her face, eyes closed, smiling broadly now, whispering *repent, repent.* Just then the nuns enter the room.

"Reece, it's time to go," one says.

"Gladly," Reece says, striding toward the door.

The other nun grabs Reece's arm. "Go kiss your mother goodbye," she snaps. Reece glares at the sister but goes back to the chair by the window and skims her mother's sunken cheek with her lips. She practically runs out the door and down the stairs to the car. At this moment her realization becomes a decision—she no longer has a family. She is an orphan. She is alone and always will be.

CHAPTER FIFTEEN:
JONAH—JULY, 1978

The road shooting away from the northwest corner of the state is long and gray and barren, each mile as dismal as the last. As the bus rumbles south down that road, the grimy industrial monuments which loom over the region—the steel mills and the auto factories and the prison—give way to green, silky cornstalks and shiny blue silos and crisp red barns with iron basketball hoops nailed to the sides.

He watches the passing landscape through cool, tinted windows which give the scene an eerie purplish glow, distorting his view of his first hours of freedom. This morning the guard had roused him from his bunk an hour before wake-up, gave him a beat-up cardboard box and told him to pack up everything in the cell that was his. Five minutes later the guard led him to the out-processing area, and in less than half an hour he was on the street, beholding his first free sunrise in twenty years. Most of the time he hadn't allowed himself to think about this day; he was never sure if it would come. But once in a while, when the thought slipped into his mind before he could stop it, he tried to imagine how he would feel out there, breathing in the air, taking in the sky and the trees and the people and wondering if they could tell just by looking at him where he'd been for the last twenty years, if they could see in his eyes that he was capable of killing a man. But when he boarded the bus and took his seat no one even noticed him, and he immediately turned his attention to the world outside his window.

Now he jerks awake when the bus stops for fuel in Columbus, barely realizing he'd fallen asleep. He disembarks to stretch his legs and rambles across the parking lot toward a mom-and-pop diner. But he stops in mid-step when across the street he notices an imposing brick building looming behind an ornate iron gate. The sign out front reads *Fields of Green Home for the Infirm*, but the only green fields he sees are masses of overgrown weeds spreading from the weather-beaten gatepost to the building's battered facade. With a shudder and a grimace and a low shake of his head he shuffles back to the bus.

For the rest of the ride he contemplates what sort of people might live in a place like that, and by the time they pull into the station at Broulet he's concluded that, all things considered, it couldn't be any worse than the place he's lived for the past twenty years. He figures they're the lucky ones—at least most of those folks don't have the mental capacity to realize where they are, or to remember the circumstances that brought them there in the first place. Meanwhile his mind and his memory seem to have grown sharper and clearer with each passing year until he thinks his brain will literally explode with the excruciating images of that night at the Founder's Festival.

He takes his cardboard box from the overhead storage compartment and steps down off the bus. He wants to stop right there and take a good look around to try to determine what has changed and what has stayed the same after all this time, but is afraid if he stops now he might never get moving again. He learned that up north—always keep moving or you won't get your food or your shower, your exercise or your television privileges, but you might get a surprise from your cellmate. Always keep moving.

After the bus pulls away he turns to face the road and extends his thumb. He tells the driver of the first car that stops where he's headed and enters the passenger seat, stowing his box on the floor between his feet. The driver is a man probably the same age as his passenger but whose oily black hair and unlined face make him appear twenty years younger. He tries numerous times to start a conversation, ceasing only when he realizes his passenger hasn't listened to a word he's said; he's been watching the towns speed by his window the entire time. The driver sulks for the rest of the ride, and when they finally reach their destination he stomps on the brake just long enough for his passenger and his box to leave the car and then accelerates again, hard, before the door is even shut.

Immediately the passenger senses there has been a mistake and whirls around to hail the driver, but he is long out of sight. He turns back to the dilapidated building that he swears used to be Patsy's Place. He may have been gone for twenty years, but he had spent enough time at Patsy's to know where it was supposed to be, even now. He shields his eyes with one hand against the sun, just now reaching its noontime peak. Sweat trickles down the back of his wool shirt as he swings his gaze up and down the street, searching for something familiar. Not finding anything, he plunks down on the sidewalk in front of the old building and right there on the street changes into the light cotton shirt he stuffed inside his box earlier this morning. The intense humidity begins to coat his lungs and eventually he has to force his head between his knees just to breathe, panting like a dog there on the sidewalk.

*

The day is typical for July in Indiana: temperature in the 90s, humidity over ninety percent, the air hanging like a wet blanket over the entire state. Her '73 Monte Carlo has no air conditioning, so that every inch of exposed flesh is superglued with sweat to the vinyl seat. Not very professional or glamorous for a world-renowned paleontologist, she thinks. She thought it was hot back home in Texas, but she'd forgotten how unforgiving the Indiana summers can be.

Soon after crossing the state line the round, knobby hills of the south begin to come into view. Continuing north, she finally stops the car at a gas station in Columbus. As the attendant fills the tank and swabs the windshield she heads through the parking lot to a mom-and-pop diner to buy a sandwich and a soft drink. On her way she notices across the street a massive but crumbling structure hidden by an overgrowth of weeds behind an iron gate. A sign at the front reads *Fields of Green Home for the Infirm*, but she imagines no one could possibly live there today, judging by its exterior condition. It seems familiar to her but she knows she's never seen it before. Despite the overwhelming heat and humidity her body shudders and she forces herself to look away. She begins to feel light-headed until she opens the door of the diner and the cool rush of air hits her in the face.

A plump, middle-aged waitress makes eye contact and points her toward an empty booth. "Seat yourself," she says pleasantly, rushing by her with an empty coffee pot. "I'll be right with ya."

Instead she stands at the curved, formica counter behind lonely men in seed company caps and grimy work boots hunching over warmed-up coffee and rhubarb pie and watches images from a lifetime ago flash across a small television hung high in the corner. A superimposed voice is saying that today is the twentieth anniversary of the death of Halo Truly, an Indiana boy who had two hit records and a small part in a movie before dying in a tragic accident at the age of 20.

All at once she's thirteen again, curled up under the covers with the radio to her ear and a photo torn from a yearbook under her pillow, being sung to sleep by the mysterious boy with the soothing voice. She knows this should strike some sort of emotional response, but what she feels is all she's ever felt since the night of her fourteenth birthday—utterly, completely numb.

Above her the television displays a montage of Halo Truly footage intercut with twenty-year-old scenes of hysterical, grief-stricken women and girls wiping their tears as his casket is carried out of the school gymnasium, where a public memorial was held, to the hearse for the ride to the Abandon cemetery. She sits on an end stool and sees Halo Truly as a young man, shaking Blackie Harmony's hand and nodding humbly after his second appearance on the man's television show, and immediately she's back at Sister Cecelia's twenty years earlier. Flimsy silver tinsel adorned the door frame of the long t.v. room that connected the residential and hospital wings; a few loose, glittery strands littered the cold linoleum floor. She wore the frayed, pink cardigan given to her by Sister Cecelia herself, the two sides of the sweater stretched as far as they would go in an attempt to cover her bursting chest. She knew she should be thrilled, after all those months finally able to watch the moment, even if it was a rerun, to see the boy she missed the first time he was on The Blackie Harmony Show and whose picture she still kept under her pillow, one of the few items she was allowed to bring with her. She'd left behind most of her belongings, including Jonah's rucksack, because they smelled of that house and she just couldn't bear it. But despite her excitement, when Halo Truly sang the first line of "Love Me in the Morning" an inadvertent, guttural howl escaped from her like steam from a locomotive and Sister Mary Theresa and Sister Mary Elizabeth had to take her back to her room in the residential wing and gave her a shot in the thigh like they did every night for the first month she was there, when they kept her in the hospital wing in a room right down the hall from where they had kept Dinah.

"Is this gonna be to go, hon?" asks the waitress, whose nametag reads *Veulah* and is pinned crookedly to a light blue polyester blouse that strains across her chest.

"Yes, a hamburger, fries and a Coke," she says, her heart still pounding from the memory she just experienced. While she waits she stares at faces that pass over the television screen: Elvis on the Ed Sullivan Show; Elvis getting his hair cut, then boarding a ship to Germany; Elvis marrying a young girl with stiff, tall hair and black-rimmed eyes; Elvis in a white, studded jumpsuit on stage in, according to the trail of letters at the bottom of the screen, his last concert ever, held up the road at Market Square Arena in Indianapolis just more than a year ago. The announcer is now making the inescapable comparisons between Halo Truly and Elvis Presley, who died almost one year earlier.

The heels of Veulah's orthopedic shoes squeak when she returns a few minutes later with a white paper bag spotted with grease stains and a tall white styrofoam cup. "Here ya go, hon," the waitress says. "I threw some salt and ketchup in there for ya." She waves a green slip of paper. "I can ring you up over here," she says, making her way to the cash register up front.

She pays the check, takes her food and goes back to the car, her gaze purposely avoiding the foreboding brick building across the street. If she allows herself to start thinking about the people who live there, perhaps children traumatized in ways no human being ever should be, she knows she'll never make it through this day.

She pays the service attendant, starts the engine and turns up the radio. In recognition of the day, "Love Me in the Morning" segues into "Bitter Sun." She flips off the radio and zooms away from the station, eager to let any sort of breeze, even one hot as a dragon's breath, flow through the open windows and break up the stagnant air inside the car. She turns away from the interstate into the eastbound lane of a two-lane highway. She eats half of her sandwich and puts the rest back in the bag with the uneaten fries.

Soon she is winding alongside the river, racing a coal barge floating down from West Virginia. Finally she pulls ahead, leaving the barge behind in the muddy stream. Just before she comes to the town of Falling Star she takes a sheet of paper from her purse and double checks the address of her destination. The excavation site is located in the side of a steep hill behind the old Presbyterian Church, and she can see the towering brick structure as she enters the town limits. Even from here she can see the heavy white line on the side of the building, eighty feet up, which marks the highest level the river reached during the flood of '37.

Paying attention to the church in the distance instead of the road ahead, she almost doesn't notice the gaunt figure of a man shuffling down the sidewalk carrying a cardboard box. His shoulders hunch over so far that the box practically drags the ground, and he appears short of breath, as if each step is a struggle.

She passes him and continues on the road toward the church and the dig site until something makes her check her rearview mirror. At that moment the old man raises his chin just enough for his eyes to meet hers, and that familiar numbness overcomes her for the second time today. Still she keeps driving, although the quivering of her entire body makes it difficult to steer the car. She starts to slow down, then speeds up again, brakes, accelerates, then pulls over to the side of the road and stops. She puts the car into Park and takes a deep breath, then another, then one more. She knows she should go back, but she suddenly is paralyzed. She literally cannot move, even to turn her head and look behind her. She wishes she could snap her fingers and instantly disappear, but her hands won't leave the wheel. She *knew* she shouldn't have taken this assignment; regardless of the clout this excavation and its subsequent discoveries will bring her, she does not want to be here. She'd much rather be leading a dig in Montana or Mexico or Morocco, or even sitting on the front porch of her home in Austin, doing nothing but slapping away the mosquitoes and watching the bats alight from under the bridge at dusk. Anywhere but here, at this moment.

She squeezes her eyes shut, hoping for invisibility, when she senses a presence beside her. She opens her eyes and looks beside her.

The old man is stooping beside the passenger door and looking through the rolled-down window.

"Reece? Reece m'dear?" he says.

She opens her mouth but no sounds comes out. Finally she swallows, looks ahead through the windshield and says, "Please don't call me that. I'm not thirteen anymore."

"I'm sorry, m—Reece," he says. "It's just that I didn't expect—what are ya doin' here?"

"I'm working," she snaps, then immediately softens her tone of voice. "They found some prehistoric remains in the hill behind the Presbyterian Church," she says, nodding her head in that direction. "Basically, I'm going to see what I can dig up."

"Is that right," he says. "I always knew ya would end up doin' somethin' like that. Ya always liked that sorta thing. Remember when they found that thing over in Artemus, what was it?"

"A mastodon."

"Yeah, a mast-o-don. Remember when I took you and Jonah—"

"Yes, I remember," she says, cutting off his words. She feels his eyes examining her face.

"I almost didn't recognize ya," he says. "I haven't seen ya since—I mean, ya look so different. You're all grown up now."

She flicks her head in his direction. "I grew up pretty fast," she says, spitting out the words as if they were spoiled milk. "I had to."

Mr. Dollar sighs and looks down at the rough, gnarled hands that grip the box. "I'm sorry 'bout that," he says. "I know—"

"How could you possibly know what my life's been like these last twenty years?" Reece seethes. "Why don't you just spare me what you *think* you know."

The old man straightens up. She hears him speaking over the top of the car. "You're right," he says. "I got no claim to ya and no right to be wastin' your time." He resumes his shuffling pace down the sidewalk.

Reece watches him walk away, each step tentative and seemingly painful, and smacks the steering wheel with an open palm. *Damn it*, she mutters, and gets out of the car. It only takes her a moment to catch up with him.

"Do you need a ride?" she asks. She can hardly believe how small and frail he is. Growing up he seemed to her the biggest and strongest man she would ever know. But now he is the one who looks up at her—she finally gained her mother's height, while his six foot, four inch frame diminished a few inches over the years.

"Aw no, I don't want to trouble ya—"

"It's no trouble," Reece says. "They're not expecting me at the site for another couple of hours." She walks back to the driver's side of her car. "Come on—let me take you somewhere." She notices his tender gait as she watches him make his way to her vehicle. "You okay?" she asks after he's crawled inside and set down his box.

"Sure, sure, I'll make it," he says.

She doesn't even ask him where it is he wants to go. She shifts into Drive and heads away from the river. "If you're hungry, there's half a sandwich and some fries in the bag," she says. "You're welcome to them."

Mr. Dollar takes the bag. "Thank ya. I appreciate it," he says.

When they hit a stretch of open road Reece takes her eyes from the road and really looks at Asa for the first time today. He's lost weight since the last time she saw him, as well as most of his hair. What's left is pure white and is still fashioned in his trademark crew cut. Aside from his eyes, that's how she knew for sure it was him. His skin is not as smooth as it once was, especially the area around his eyes; the wrinkles there are even more pronounced by the thick horn-rimmed glasses he now wears. His back is straight but his shoulders slump forward and his chin rests on his sunken chest.

"Did—" Reece begins. "Did you just get out—I mean—today?"

He doesn't even look at her. "Yep," he whispers. "I've been a free man for less'n a day now."

Reece shakes her head. "Where will you—what do you plan to do now?"

He stares out the window. "There's a place in Madison they say hires men with records like mine, some apartment complex or somethin'. If I do maintenance work for 'em they'll give me a room to live in. I'll go there in the mornin'."

"You're going to work?" she asks, incredulous. "But you're seventy-four years old."

His shoulders sink even farther into his body. "Yep."

"But that's crazy," Reece says. "Can't you—" But she realizes she doesn't know what other options a seventy-four-year-old ex-convict has.

"Don't ya worry 'bout me," he says, reaching over to pat her on the knee, then thinking twice and returning his hand to his lap. His words hang in the air already thick with humidity until the silence is too much to bear, and she turns on the radio.

"Oh yeah," she says. "Did you know that it's twenty years ago today since Halo Truly died?"

He squints at her, trying to place the name. "Halo Truly," he says, then his eyes stretch open in recognition. "Oh yeah, he was from Abandon, wasn't he? Died twenty years ago? He must've been young."

"He would've been forty, had he lived."

"Forty, is that right?" Mr. Dollar says, taking off his glasses, scratching behind his ear and replacing the frames. "When I was forty, you were just a year old. Jonah was still alive, but we'd already lost little Rachel." He stares out the window, stroking an imaginary beard. "So much livin' yet to do when you're forty. Shame, it is." He looks over at her. "Ya always did like that Truly boy, didn't ya?"

Reece nods.

"Yeah, I remember how upset ya were before I got us that t.v. Ya couldn't watch him on The Blackie Harmony Show like all your friends . . ."

"I didn't have any friends," Reece mutters.

"Well sure ya did," he says. "What about, what was her name? Roxanne. Roxanne Joshua?"

Reece snorts. "She ended up marrying Mark Isaac, the boy I really liked. Her brother was the one who got Dinah pregnant. And she never once came to visit me at Sister Cecelia's. I wouldn't consider her my friend."

Mr. Dollar continues to stroke his invisible beard, a deep line furrowing his forehead.

"You knew that, didn't you? That Bernie Joshua was the one who . . ."

"Sure, sure. Never mind them," Mr. Dollar says. "What about that Cullen boy? Erl the whatever?"

"Erl VIII," Reece sighs. "He had a crush on me, that was all. I didn't much get along with those Cullens, anyway. Mom would've said they were—"

"Poor white trash," Mr. Dollar says. "I know. But ya must've made friends later, at the . . . home?"

Reece adjusts her rearview mirror, then the side mirror. She turns down the volume on the radio, then turns it off altogether. With her palm she wipes a layer of dust from the dashboard and wipes her hand on her shorts. She settles back into her seat.

"There was no use making any friends there," she says softly. "Most of the girls didn't have much to do with me, since I tended to break into fits of screaming hysterics without notice. The ones I did get to know would get adopted and leave, and then I'd have to start all over again. So I mainly just kept to myself."

Mr. Dollar slumps even farther down in his seat. "I'm real sorry ya had such a hard time," he says. "I wish I could've made a better life for ya all."

The two of them stare straight ahead at the road as it twists and curls and rises and falls and grows more and more narrow the closer they get to Abandon. The air is cooler here; leafy trees grow next to the roadway, their branches bending over and brushing the tops of the cars that pass by like a harem of attendants fanning their queen.

Mr. Dollar leans his head out the window and closes his eyes. "This breeze feels mighty good," he says.

"Aren't you hot in those clothes?" Reece asks, considering the heavy navy blue pants and the medium-blue, long-sleeved uniform he's been wearing since this morning. "You could roll the sleeves up at least, couldn't you?"

"Nah," he says. "I'm used to it. In fact, this weather reminds me of the forge. It'd get so hot in there in the summertime, men'd be keelin' over left and right. It's a wonder I didn't collapse myself. Sometimes I thought I would."

Reece looks over at him as long as the curving road will allow. "You never let on how miserable it was," she says.

He opens his eyes and lifts his head. "It wasn't your concern, m'—Reece. I did what I had to do for my family." He faces forward. "All I ever tried to do was look after my family the best I knew how." He swallows hard and bends over at the waist, pretending to tie a loose shoelace.

Reece focuses on the road ahead. "I know you did," she whispers.

After about a minute Mr. Dollar sits up and looks out the open window, trying to regain his bearings. "Here!" he shouts, waving a wild finger at a dirt road up ahead and to the right. "Turn here."

Reece whips the car into the lane, immediately slowing down

as a dust cloud envelops them, the grainy particles coating their throats and clogging their eye sockets. As the granules settle to earth she sees where they are. Smooth granite slabs jut from the thirsty ground in jagged rows, the brittle grass rasping against the bases of the tombstones like a three-day beard.

Ahead of them a row of parked cars snakes along the dirt path, and a large cluster of tourists and gawkers are gathered around Halo Truly's simple tombstone, into which is etched only his name and the years *1938-1958*. Folks take turns posing for photographs next to the grave; some make pencil rubbings to take home. A handwritten sign speared crookedly into the dirt beside the granite stone gives fans directions to the Halo Truly birthplace home and museum, just two miles away.

She brings the car to a halt and shuts off the engine, leaving the key in the ignition. Mr. Dollar opens his door and uncoils his stiff frame. He walks forward a few paces then stops, turns, and bends over, hands on his knees, until he can see Reece through the rolled-down window. "Ain't ya comin'?" he says.

Without looking at him she nods and steps from the car. At the front of the vehicle she pauses, leaning her palm heavy against the hood until the fiery heat forces her to pull it away.

"Come *on*, Reece. You've got to pay your respects to your family." He extends his hand to her but she sidesteps him and circles around to the far side of the cemetery, keeping her head down and her eyes locked on him as if he is an unsuspecting gazelle and she is a savanna lioness who hasn't eaten in days.

He watches her, maintaining a safe distance between them, knowing sooner or later she'll come around to the Dollar plot. He's not sure if she's been here at all during these intervening years or not. He was last here more than twenty years ago, when only three graves, his mother's and Jonah's and Rachel's, stood alone in this farthest corner of the cemetery. Yet he knows exactly where to find them, even though tombstones taller and more ornate have sprung up on all sides.

She stops and backtracks, studying a group of seven matching pink granite markers. She bends down in front of one and traces the carved letters with her finger.

Mr. Dollar walks up behind her, puzzled by what he reads on the headstone.

Dinah Dollar
October 8, 1941—September 12, 1957

"She didn't . . . Reece, what's the meanin' of this?"

Reece remains in a crouched position, keeping her back to him. "I spent fifteen years trying to find her," she murmurs, almost growling. "But Mom made sure Dinah got lost in a sticky ball of bureaucratic red tape, in a catholic conspiracy of lies and dead ends. And when Sister Cecelia's burned down five years ago, all the records were destroyed."

Mr. Dollar reaches out, his hand just barely brushing her shoulder when she stands up as if catapulted. "If she's still alive out there somewhere, I'll never know it," she says, smacking imagined dirt from her palms. "So I had this marker put up. Because in my mind my sister died there under the Wesley Tree that night." She turns to see Asa's eyes glossy with tears. "All these years . . . you didn't know where she was, did you?" she says. "I never asked you because I assumed—"

As he shakes his head the tears dribble onto his cheeks. "I begged her," he says, gulping back the sobs attempting to escape his lips. "I begged her not to be so harsh on the girl, on both ya girls. They could've taken care of her at the hospital in Broulet just fine. But I knew as soon as I watched Dr. Riley drive her away in the back of Luther Marvin's old pickup truck that we'd never see her again." He sniffs and pulls his shirtsleeve along his nose. "I couldn't stop her—"

"I know," Reece says, longing for a moment to comfort him with a pat on the arm or back before thinking better of it. "No one could stop her."

Mr. Dollar rubs a hand across the top of the stone. "It's nice, though," he says. "Ya did your sister good."

Reece slips her fingers into the front pockets of her jeans and shrugs. "I just called up and asked for one to match the others," she says. "Today's the first time I've ever seen it."

He rubs the stone harder, scratching his palm against the corners. "How's that?"

She squints as she reads the words again and again. "I was in Mexico on a dig when I just decided to do it, kind of a spur-of-the-moment thing. I asked Danny to help me. He told me who to call, how to arrange everything, even though he thought it was a bad idea. Like putting up a gravestone after all these years, for someone who may not even be dead, is the same as opening a door as wide as it will go so the bad things can just walk on through. Of course I couldn't pay for it, either, so I asked him to. Money always seemed to be a sticking point with him. So one day I got a letter from him that said, *The damn thing is up and paid for and don't ever speak to me again, you soulless ghoul. I hope you die before I do so you won't be tempted to dig up my bones like you do everyone else's.*"

"Ya haven't spoken to your own brother since then? Your own flesh and blood?"

She shrugs again. "It's no big deal." She starts to walk away, but stops in front of Jonah's grave. She pauses for a moment and smiles to herself before moving on to the next marker. Upon seeing her mother's name she gives it a small but sharp kick with her toe and keeps right on walking.

Mr. Dollar rushes up behind her and grabs her by the shoulders. "Don't ya do that, young lady!" he seethes in her ear. "She gave birth to ya so that ya could be here today. Ya show her some respect!"

"Do you think I want to be here today? Do you think I asked to be born? Especially into this family?" She jerks free from him and walks faster toward the car. He begins to chase her but stops at a tombstone between his wife's and his mother's. His name and birthdate are engraved in the granite; a blank space remains for the date of his death to be added later.

"Ya can't wait to get ridda me!" he cries. "Then ya can finally be all alone, just like ya always wanted to be, hidin' between the vines of the grape arbor or runnin' off by yourself to the crick to look for rocks. Well I ain't dead yet!" He looks around, making a sweeping gesture with his arm. "Where's your empty grave, young lady? Or Danny's?"

She turns toward him but continues to walk away, backward. "Danny's going to be buried next to his wife," she says. "I plan to be cremated, and my ashes scattered over whichever archaeological site I happened to be working in when I collapse and die."

Asa shakes his head. "Don't ya have a husband? A family of your own?"

"God no," Reece says. "I figured out a long time ago that all the problems in our family started because of love, or lust, or a combination of the two. Love causes nothing but trouble for all involved. So it's better I remain on my own." She reaches the car, gets in and starts the engine. "Let's go, old man."

He gives her a dismissive wave, mutters under his breath and stumbles down a row to another gravesite. He stands there for a few minutes, head bowed, and from the car Reece sees his lips moving. She squints against the sunlight, trying to read the name on the stone until the realization hits her as heavy as a falling tombstone that Asa is paying his respects to Chester Lee Reece, and when he finally gets back in the car she knows where to go next. He started this, she figures, imploring her with his sad, watery eyes and weary voice to take him back home again, so she'll make sure she finishes it, once and for all.

She screeches away from the graveyard, gravel dust and dirt exploding under the tires. She turns right onto Cemetery Road and almost immediately presses the accelerator to the floor, coaxing the Monte Carlo with her entire mind and body to make it up this vertical road. At the top the car seems to pause for a split second before rushing down, her stomach following a few seconds later. She lifts her right foot from the gas pedal and rests it on the seat, under her thigh. She sneaks a glance at the passenger next to her and finds the reaction she was looking for—he's pressing an imaginary brake pedal on the floor, gripping the vinyl dashboard with translucent fists, one eye clenched shut, the other keeping a watch out for inevitable disaster. At the bottom of the hill she negotiates a tight turn without braking, then blows through the stop sign at Wellever Road, the road that leads to downtown Abandon. Not a single time in her life has she ever seen another car at this intersection, and she doesn't expect to see one today. She thinks she hears a wheezing gasp across the seat but doesn't turn to look. She places her foot back on the gas and accelerates to seventy miles an hour for the final minute or so of their journey. Up ahead the road ends in a T and, again without stopping or barely slowing down, she steers the car to the left. After several seconds the pavement ends and they're snaking along the unnamed road. A few of the houses, much smaller than she remembers, still remain but are boarded up and falling down. The one exception, of course, is the Cullen place, in need of a fresh coat of paint but otherwise in fairly good condition. The home has doubled in size, additional rooms having been added on to accommodate the growing brood, and Reece wonders just how many generations reside in the house; what roman numeral they're up to now. As she drives over the one-lane, concrete bridge that crosses Cullen's Creek she suddenly sees *it* up ahead, and begins to slow the car down. But she doesn't have enough power to propel the car up the final small hill that will take them across the railroad tracks, so she presses her foot down mightily and they shoot across the tracks. Once over, she turns right onto the gravel road that runs alongside the tracks. The path seems much more narrow that she remembers, and at that instant she realizes, like a scientist at the moment of discovery or a saint at the moment of epiphany, that it was never a road at all but rather more of an emergency lane, a shoulder, a mere extension of the railroad. It was never meant to be driven on by a full-sized automobile, and she is stunned. Somehow the lack of electricity and running water had always seemed almost natural, almost bearable; but not even having a real road to take you home seems now to Reece indecent. Intolerable. Inhuman.

These thoughts have distracted her; she's driven the entire

length of the path on mental autopilot. At the end she makes a u-turn into the driveway, coasts for a few yards and stops. The Dollar home slouches before them. Most of the shingles are gone; some lie scattered in the yard. The slanting roof of the side porch, just off the kitchen, is propped up by a rotting two by four; the leaded glass kitchen window, which faces out toward the driveway, winks at them, threatening to dissolve altogether in the blistering afternoon heat. Just then, as if signaled, the sun moves behind a cloud, casting an eerie gray-green shadow over them like an eclipse. Reece shuts off the engine and listens to the silence.

She expects to hear remnants of her childhood, anything from the time she spent here. She strains, trying to coax even a fragment of remembrance from the hill that rises up beside them, from the cistern in the front yard, from the water well and the grape arbor to their right at the base of the hill, from the flagstones that lead to the detestable outhouse. She only hears the silence.

She senses a slight movement beside her and turns to look. Mr. Dollar stares straight ahead, swallows hard, opens the car door and begins walking in a slow, lumbering gait toward the house. When he reaches the kitchen porch he stops and turns, squinting at her through the windshield flecked with pieces of dead insects, summoning her with his gaze as he used to when she was a child. She leaves the car and joins him on the porch. He takes her arm for support, forcing open the blighted door with the other arm. Together they walk across the threshold.

Everything remains in place—the propane-powered cook stove, the pie safe and ice box, the kitchen table with its six mismatched chairs. Ahead of them the sofa, recliner and television—the much-revered television—stand as they have for twenty-one years. A thick, greasy layer of dust coats the surface of the furniture, the appliances, even the walls and ceiling, and the buckled floor is poised to fall into the crawlspace at any moment. Reece walks to the sideboard and picks up the drinking ladle, still floating in the pail in a soupy mixture of water and wood beetles and chunks of debris that have fallen from the ceiling. She swirls the ladle around and replaces it, imagining the taste of the heavy tin in her mouth, wondering how, after all these years, she still tastes a residue of metal whenever she drinks a glass of water.

She turns and finds Asa gone, then hears footsteps above her. She makes her way to the stairs, hoping they'll hold just a little while longer. She sees him kneeling before the bed he shared with her mother, smoothing the stiff sheets with his rough palm, and leaves him. She moves along, swatting at the long string that hangs down from the door in the ceiling, the trap door that leads to Danny and Jonah's old room, then enters her and Dinah's bedroom.

A leaky roof has caused most of the newspaper lining the walls to peel and melt away and lie in damp shreds along the baseboards. The musty odor that permeates the house is especially strong in this room, and immediately Reece feels a bit lightheaded. She takes two steps forward, the floorboards squeaking below her feet, and she reaches out to steady herself on the bed. The furniture is remarkably intact for having stood unused in this damp house for more than twenty years.

Everything is still in place—the sheets, though now slick and stiff, clinging to the mattress; the blue willow bowl and pitcher, filled with yellow, standing water, atop the washstand in the corner; the dresser, the top of which is nearly bare except for Dinah's schoolbooks, still stacked haphazardly as she had left them. Reece touches the cover of the top book, English Literature, then moves it aside to reveal the U.S. History book underneath. The pages practically crumble under her hand. At the bottom of the stack is Dinah's notebook, the cover emblazoned in teenage script *Dinah Loves Bernie . . . Dinah-n-Bernie . . . DD + BJ . . . Mrs. Bernie Joshua . . . Dinah Joshua.* Reece traces the words with her finger, then suddenly sends the whole stack of books skittering across the top of the dresser and onto the floor with one abrupt sweep of her arm.

Asa hears the clatter and comes into the room. "Reece m'— what's goin' on?" He sees the books scattered over the floor and bends down to pick them up. He reads the titles of each one, spending an extra moment or two looking at the notebook, then carefully replaces them on the dresser. "These are all you've got left of your sister, Reece," he says softly. "Ya ought to take—"

"Ought to what?" Reece shouts. "Take better care of them? Take them with me? Don't you think I carry her around inside of my head every day of my life? I don't need a book to remind me of what happened here."

"I understand," Asa says, reaching out his hand. Reece slaps it away.

"No, you don't understand! You weren't here. You didn't see it! You didn't see her sitting on this very bed in agony, miscarrying before my eyes, only I didn't know that's what it was at the time. You didn't see her in the hospital, that look in her eyes, like there was no one there, just an empty body . . . You haven't seen what I've seen."

Asa walks to the window and stares out, his gaze crossing over the tracks and down the road to where Cullen's Creek is just visible. "Remember, Reece," he says in a deep voice, deeper than Reece has ever heard before, "I was in prison for twenty years. I've seen things, too." He's almost whispering now. "I saw ya in the backseat of that car." He swallows hard. "I've seen plenty. Enough to last me two lifetimes." He turns around to face Reece with eyes shiny with tears and walks toward her. "Tell me what ya saw," he says. "Tell me everything."

Reece sits down on the bed and pokes at a hole in the floor with the toe of her shoe. After a few minutes she looks up at him, still standing in the same place by window. She pats the bed and he sits down beside her.

"Where do I start?" she asks.

"Start at the beginnin'," he says.

Now *she* stands and stares out the window, pressing her forehead against the pane thick with age and grime, until she can see the barren stalks of the wild roses that used to flourish below. "I saw the looks," she says to the glass. "The looks in everyone's eyes. Pity, in the eyes of the cops when they led you to the police car.

Shame, in Mom's eyes when she looked at you, then at me, then down at the ground as some other cops put us in an ambulance to take us to the hospital in Broulet. More pity in the eyes of the doctors and nurses and the child welfare workers who came the next day to take me to Sister Cecelia's, without even asking me if I wanted to go. Complete and utter disgust in Danny's eyes, his face, his entire body when he came upon the scene that night, his family's ugly truth exposed in front of the whole town on a night when the triumph should have been his. That was the last time I ever saw him, his face contorting in total emotional devastation as he turned and ran away. I tried to convince him to come to your trial, but he refused."

"I remember that," Asa says, almost whispering, stroking one cheek and then the other with his palm. "It meant a lot to me, ya bein' there."

"Good god, old man, they *made* me go," Reece says. "If you recall, they put me on the witness stand to testify to the brutality of the . . ." She swallows and starts again, her voice a bit lower now, and calmer. "A lot of good it did."

"Forty years," Mr. Dollar says. "To me that was a life sentence. If it weren't for the parole . . ." He closes his eyes, shakes his head as if rattling the vision loose from his mind and opens his eyes again, fixing them directly on Reece. "Like I said, it meant a lot, even if ya didn't want to be there."

Reece shrugs. "What I wanted was for Danny to be there, for my family to be with me."

"But I—" Asa literally bites his tongue until tears form in the bottoms of his eyes. He releases his teeth's grip but the tears remain. "Can't say I blame the boy," he says finally, quietly.

"Don't let him off that easy," Reece says, snapping her head in his direction. "He's done all right for himself. Played basketball for four years in college on scholarship and got a high school teaching job right after graduation as far away from here as he could get. Became varsity coach after two years and has the winningest record ever at the largest high school in California. Rumor is he'll be

hired by a Division I program within the month. And through all
of that it's always been obvious where his priorities have been,
especially after Mom died."

"They sent me a telegram telling me your mother had passed
away," Asa says, standing. "They wouldn't give me any details. I
wrote to Danny, but my letters were always returned unopened.
So I wrote to you, askin' . . ."

Reece resumes her watch out the window. She longs to move
about but the room is so small and crowded with the two of them
in there that she would rather stand perfectly still until her joints
stiffen and her legs fall asleep.

"She was in the sanatorium for three and a half years," she
says. "She spoke maybe ten words from the night they brought
her there in the ambulance until the day her heart finally gave out
and they took her away in a hearse. Every Christmas the nuns
would take me to visit her, which involved her sitting there staring
at her bible and me babbling like an idiot for an hour until it was
time for me to go. The strange thing was I never knew where they
were taking me—they made me lie down in the backseat so that I
couldn't figure out where we were going. All I knew was that it was
a big brick building. Then at the end of the visit they would force
me to kiss her goodbye, and I would press my mouth against that
cheek so dry and thin I feared it would crumble like a dead leaf
beneath my lips."

"They wouldn't let me go to her funeral," Asa says. "Been my
wife for twenty-eight years and I wasn't allowed to say goodbye."

Reece sits down on the bed beside him. "She wore her blue
dress—you know the one I mean? The one she only wore on special
occasions."

Asa stares straight ahead and nods. "I'd like to've seen her buried
in her weddin' dress, but I imagine she hadn't been able to fit into
it for years." He loses himself in a momentary daydream. "Was her
hair down? Spread out across the pillow?"

Reece shakes her head. "Pulled up like it always was. I never
saw it any other way."

Asa looks at Reece. "Your mother was a beautiful woman," he tells her. "I wish I had a picture to show ya. All the men in Abandon and Falling Star put together were after her. She could've had any man she wanted and she chose me. And we were happy for a lot of years."

"Until I was born," Reece says.

"No! No," Mr. Dollar says. "Children shouldn't ever blame themselves for their parents' troubles. You're an adult, m'—Reece, ya should realize that."

Now Reece stares straight ahead. "I think our family's situation was a bit different," she manages to say. "I shouldn't have to remind you that you lost three children by the ages of eighteen, and I say three because Dinah was as good as dead the night mom chased her from the house calling her a whore. Then you killed your best friend's son because of me. You went to prison, Danny ran away and mom became catatonic before she died. All of that was my fault." She puts a hand over her mouth to keep from spilling her tears over the both of them.

Asa wants to hug her, but determines that no physical contact at all would be best. He does stand, though, to try to gain some perspective on the situation. When he finally speaks his voice is surprisingly steady, considering his entire body is shaking.

"Don't ya ever say that again," he says. "Don't even think that. What happened to our family was nobody's fault. It was just the way it was supposed to be."

Reece looks at Mr. Dollar, incredulous. "You mean to tell me it was simply our *destiny* for everyone to either run away, go to prison or die? I don't buy it, not for a minute. After Jonah died Mom used to always say it was god's fault. Even that explanation is more plausible to me than to say it was all just some cruel twist of fate."

Asa's forehead wrinkles as he tries to sort through Reece's words. "Your mother had a complicated relationship with god," he finally says. "She gave him the credit for all the good things that happened and the blame for all the bad things, especially what happened with her and Add—" He swallows hard and continues. "A long time ago she was convinced god had sent me directly to her to fill up her empty life, to make it complete, to give it meanin'. Years later she swore god had sent me directly to her to make her life a livin' hell on earth."

"Sounds goddamned familiar," Reece mutters.

"You ought to watch your language," Asa says. "That's no way for a lady to talk."

Reece shoots up from the bed. "I'm sure you heard worse in prison," she says. "You should be used to it."

"Not from you," he says, turning his back on her and heading toward the stairs. "Where did ya pick up such a filthy mouth?" He starts down the steps.

Reece begins to follow him, but turns first to take one more look at the room. She thinks she sees something glimmering under the bed, but when she looks again she sees nothing and is convinced that the emotional side of her brain is playing a game with the logical side, and they're both playing a trick on her eyes. She slams the door closed and runs down the stairs after Mr. Dollar.

"I'll tell you where I picked up this filthy mouth," she says to the back of his head, pink skin showing through the close-cropped, white hair as he makes his way to the living room. A piece of the ceiling just below her bedroom door drops into Asa's old recliner as he prepares to sit there. He steps aside with a start and looks up, studying the origin of the falling plaster.

"On the streets, that's where, ever since the day of my mother's funeral, which, I might add, Danny didn't bother to attend, either," she says, standing with her hands on her hips as Mr. Dollar sweeps aside the plaster dust and sits down. "They were filing us out for the procession to the cemetery. I turned on the waterworks and asked if I could go to the restroom to compose myself. Of course the nuns were going to let the poor girl go. It was one of the few times they ever left me alone for more than a minute or two, and I took advantage of it. I climbed out the bathroom window at the funeral home and was gone. I was seventeen years old with no money and only the charity clothes I was wearing, and I hadn't been so happy in years. Probably not since Jonah was alive."

"What happened to ya?" Mr. Dollar asks.

"I started walking down the streets of Broulet in broad daylight and nobody cared," Reece says. "I don't know how many miles I walked that first day, but I crossed the river into Kentucky at dusk. Just past the bridge an old, faded red pickup truck pulled up alongside me, driving real slow as I walked. Finally I stopped and looked at the driver as he brought the vehicle to a halt, and I realized I knew the man inside. The last time I'd seen him he'd been just a boy, but of course I'd been just a scared thirteen-year-old girl myself. I couldn't believe it was him, in that place, at that time, after all those years, and at that moment I knew that whatever I did from that point on would work out alright."

Reece sits on the floor at Mr. Dollar's feet. "When I opened the passenger door huge chunks of rust fell onto the pavement, and I started laughing. The young man gave me a strange look and scratched his day-old beard with grimy fingernails, then he started laughing too, and we couldn't stop, even after I'd climbed up in the cab and he'd driven away from the curb. I stuck my head out the window and let my long blonde hair slap against my face until it stung, laughing the whole time. Finally we calmed down and when I pulled my head back inside the truck he said, 'You got a name? and I said, 'Reece,' and he said, 'Reece? Ain't that a boy's name?' and I said, 'I was named for Chester Lee Reece, the famous poet,' and he said, 'Well, I never heard of him,' and I said, 'He's very famous in Indiana,' and he just made this strange sound deep in his throat that made his adam's apple bob in and out, and then he said, 'You don't remember me, do you?' and I said, 'Sure I do, Boggs,' and he smiled a little bit, and I said, 'Is that your first name or your last name?' and he said, 'It's my name.'

"We didn't speak any more for a long time after that, until finally he said, 'You're not going to Sister Cecelia's again, are you, cause it's just up the road,' and I said, 'God no, I want to get as far away from that place as I possibly can,' and he said, 'That bad, huh?' and I didn't say anything else, except to ask him if he had a knife, and he pointed to the glove compartment. I opened it up and he had a big old hunting knife in there, and I took it out of the sheath and grabbed a fistful of my hair and sawed it off right there in the truck cab, and flung handfuls out the window and watched them fly away behind us in the night, and I tried to laugh again but found I couldn't make any sound at all. When my hair was as short as Boggs' I replaced the knife and as I looked up we were pulling into someone's driveway. He said, 'Don't worry, my mama and daddy won't mind,' and he was right, they were about the nicest family I'd ever met."

"So you knew this Boggs character?" Mr. Dollar wants to know.

"Yes," Reece says. "He gave me a ride to Sister Cecelia's that day I skipped out on the class field trip to Mammoth Cave, right before . . ." She swallows hard and continues speaking in a louder, higher voice. "His family fed me supper and gave me a clean bed to sleep in, and the next morning Boggs drove me to the library so I could look something up, and that night his mama helped me write a letter to Notre Dame. Do you remember that professor we met in Artemus that night we went to see the mastodon dig? Dr. Conor?"

"Sure I do," Mr. Dollar says.

"I remembered him too," Reece says, "and I remembered he was from Notre Dame. I wanted to go there and study under him. He wrote me back and told me Notre Dame didn't accept women students! This was 1961, and I couldn't believe it. Right then I could hear mom cursing the Catholics like she always did, and I'm ashamed to say that for a moment I joined in."

Mr. Dollar shakes his head but doesn't say anything.

"After I calmed down I did some more research and ended up writing to the University of Texas," Reece continues. "The family let me stay with them that whole summer, helping out on their farm, until I received a reply from the UT admissions office, telling me I'd been accepted to study paleontology and that I qualified for enough financial aid to put three people through college.

That fall they drove me to the bus station and right before I boarded they gave me an envelope filled with what must have been their life savings. I told them I didn't want it, but they said I'd earned it working for them that summer. They treated me like family and that whole time they didn't know me from Eve. I never forgot their kindness, and I tried many times to repay them, but they wouldn't hear of it. I always intended to visit them, but I ended up spending my summers digging up and down the Texas hill country and somehow never made it back to Indiana. When I graduated I wrote them and the letter came back unopened and unforwarded. I never heard from them again. To this day I have no idea what happened to them."

"That's too bad," Mr. Dollar says. "They sound like real good people."

"They were," Reece says. "But I've been in Texas ever since, and I love it there. I appreciate the fact that for the most part everyone just leaves me alone to do my job."

She sees the concerned look on Mr. Dollar's face and adds, "Don't misunderstand, I have friends—other professors at the university, in the radiocarbon lab—but I've found it's just easier to disconnect from the human race as much as possible. Because whenever you find someone you can trust, they go away."

Asa's thin, wrinkled eyelids drop over his eyes and he doesn't move, or even acknowledge that he's heard what she's just said. Reece leans over and jabs her finger into his shoulder and he looks down at her, the corners of his eyes and mouth literally turned down.

"How can ya have such a—" he searches for the right word—"*bleak* view of the human race? How can ya go on livin' without lettin' anyone get close to ya?" He closes his eyes again and shakes his head. "Just like your mother," he mutters. "That's no way to live, without someone to love ya."

"It's easy," Reece says. "You just shut down. Besides, it's better than the alternative."

"What, bein' dead?" he asks.

"No," she says, shaking her head. "Being with someone. Because once you let 'em get you into bed, it's all downhill from there."

"God, you are vulgar, young lady." Asa practically spits the words. "I don't know how this conversation got so dragged down, but it stops here." He stands and slaps pieces of ceiling from his pants legs. "I was wrong. You're not like your mother—she was never so vulgar. If she were here she'd be ashamed."

"I'd venture to say she'd be proud," Reece says. "Or at least justified that her opinion of me was accurate."

"I'll tell ya what," Asa says, pointing at her, punching the air again and again with his finger. "Your mother would never use such filthy language when speakin' to *her* father."

Reece opens her mouth to correct his misstatement, but instead closes her mouth and stares at the floor, the cracked linoleum peeling up around her feet.

"Let's just go," Asa says. "I don't know why ya brought me here exactly, but ya can drive me to the bus station and be on your way back to the dinosaur site in an hour." He pushes past her and heads toward the stairs. He turns and says, "Give me a few minutes up here. I want to take one more look around. Prob'bly be my last chance." Reece starts to protest but he holds up one hand. "I'll meet ya in the car," he says.

"Okay—" she says aloud, standing up and crossing the kitchen—*Doodle*, she adds under her breath as she walks out onto the side porch. Behind her a piece of the kitchen ceiling falls to the floor as Mr. Dollar walks above, and she closes the screen door gently, using two hands.

She follows the stone path to the grape arbor, the once-lush leaves and branches now mere twigs and stems. She leans against the trellis and surveys the property all around her, absolutely stunned at how small it all has become, how the landscape has collapsed upon itself as the old man in the house has. The hill which once loomed so large behind her childhood home looks to Reece as if it could be covered in three large strides. The cistern in the front yard which captured rainwater for laundry and which seemed like a bottomless pit, especially when she and her brothers and sister leaned over the side and caught their reflections and shouted their names down into the hole and laughed as the echo bounced back at them, now seems to be a miniature model of the real thing. She studies the patch of land behind the grape arbor where the springhouse once stood, before Mr. Dollar tore it down, and can't imagine any structure fitting into such a small space.

She looks back at the house and, seeing no movement inside, decides he might be in there a while. So on a whim she sprints across the yard, over the tracks and down the road to Cullen's Creek. Without bothering to take off her shoes she wades into the low water, which barely covers her ankles. She walks hunched over, her hands planted on the tops of her knees, searching the creekbed for a unique specimen to take back to the lab in Texas. After all these years she will finally know the true history of Cullen's Creek, of Abandon, and it can all be found in a fragment of fossilized limestone that she can hold in her palm or slip into her pocket.

She squats closer to the surface of the water, even dips her fingers in a few times, but comes up empty-handed. After fifteen minutes she hasn't found a single rock that looks promising enough to dislodge from its resting place. As she slogs up the slight creek bank and across the road she looks up at the house in the distance, then has to blink and look again. It appears to be sitting crooked, slanting downward as if a corner of the foundation were sinking. Then she notices that one side of the roof has completely caved in, and she emits a *yip* and covers her mouth with her hand. Water sloshes in her sneakers as she runs across the tracks but she doesn't notice. She keeps her eyes on the house but can only watch help-lessly as it crumbles before her in slow motion. It seems to her that the nearer she comes the faster the walls and rafters and shingles fall, so she slows up until she is standing in the driveway in front of her car, her hands shielding her eyes as if from the sun even though dark clouds have formed. She tries to shout but no sound comes from her mouth, and she realizes she doesn't know what name to call anyway. Mr. Dollar is too formal, Asa too familiar.

Suddenly she finds her voice and yells over the roar of crumbling wood *Doodle! Doodle!* and she knows she should run inside and try to save him, knows his frail body is no match for this force, but also knows it's too dangerous, and also that it's too late. She's still shouting his name when the rumbling stops, and when she finally quiets down she hears no other sound, not even a bird or insect nor even the bubbling waters of Cullen's Creek, a sound which many a night used to soothe her to sleep.

She stares at the remains of the home for a long time, then her instincts and training take over and she walks forward until she's right in the middle of the rubble. She knows how to do this—she's dug up most of Texas and good portions of Mexico as well over the last few years—so from a practical standpoint she understands which pieces to move first so as not to disturb what's underneath without hurting herself in the process. But it's easier when it's just old dirt you're digging up and sifting through, when the anticipation of not knowing exactly what you'll find burns you up inside until you think you can't stand it anymore, yet you continue to dig and dig because that's what you do, that's all you know how to do.

After half an hour she feels as though she's made no progress, perhaps because she has lifted and moved and stacked and resettled each piece as if it were bone china. But then her hand touches a mass of wet newspaper and she knows which room she's exploring and she wants to stop because she knows what she's bound to find, but she can't stop now. And then, there it is, the rough canvas scratching her already raw skin, and she lifts up the olive knapsack and holds it out in front of her as if admiring a painting. She sits down in the grass next to a stack of beams, unzips the bag and sorts through its contents. Two ratty dresses and two pairs of even rattier underwear. Mr. Dollar's old watch, standing forever at 3:29. His radio, the back sticky where the batteries have leaked. A five dollar bill. A chrome Zippo lighter, the only item remaining from when Jonah owned this bag. A scrap of paper, on which are written the words *Reece Dollar, world-renowned paleontologist.* She nearly chokes when she reads these words, a declaration she hasn't seen in years, and slips the paper into the pocket of her shorts. She lays out the rest of the items on the grass beside her, but the bag is still heavy. She slips her hand inside and pulls out a sandstone, then an arrowhead, the latter poking into her palm and puncturing a layer of skin. She remembers still the day Addison Hilliard gave it to her in the cab of his pickup truck, and resisting the urge to fling it far away from her, instead sets it and the sandstone down with the other items. She takes a deep breath and plunges her fist into the bag one final time and her hand wraps around a hard, rough sphere. Slowly she removes her hand and pulls out the geode, her fourteenth birthday present from the man she thought was her father, the object with which her mother tried to bash her head in when she cried out Jonah's name from a nightmarish vision. She weighs the stone in her palm, gently tossing it up and down like a baseball, then throws it hard onto the ground. She rushes into the rubble, covering over again with beams and boards and shingles and splinters of soggy wood the places she earlier exposed, and when she runs out of material she starts grabbing handfuls of earth and filling in the rest of the open spaces. Soon the remains of the house are barely recognizable as such for all the mounds of dirt and grass that cover it.

Finally she stops and straightens up, supporting her lower back with one hand. Oblivious to how much time has passed, she looks around the homestead and is surprised to see the first star of the night in a sky a million gradient shades of indigo. She disembarks from the heap she's made and reaches around to grab the knapsack, brings it to her nose and inhales deeply, its instantly familiar odor mixing with the clean evening air and filling her entire body. She lifts her face away from the bag and gulps down one more swallow of fresh air, then slowly gathers the contents of the knapsack that are scattered about her and stuffs them inside, saving the arrowhead for last and clutching it in her palm. She stands and surveys the site around her, which is becoming more difficult to see in the waning light. She knows even if she found him at the bottom of this pile she probably would not be able to move him by herself, and even if she could, what would she do with him? Where does one take a dead man at dusk? So she decides to leave him there, buried under the house his father built and where he and his wife raised four children. As she turns to go she hangs the knapsack on her shoulder and tosses the arrowhead onto the heap, her two fathers joined together in the cold Abandon dirt.

As she stands there she suddenly feels exhausted, realizing all at once just how tired she is of the nomadic life of a paleontologist, chasing dinosaur bones from one end of the continent to the other. She thinks of Dr. Conor at Notre Dame, how she has crossed his path a few times through the years, and that she has heard he is preparing to retire. If that is the case there will be a position opening in the department, and this time, in 1978, being a woman won't be an automatic disqualification.

Eyeing the rubble before her, everything seems much clearer now, yet she senses she's not quite finished here. She reaches into the knapsack and pulls out the Zippo, flips open the top and whispers Jonah's name as it lights on second try.

She steps forward, kneels before the remains of the house and places the flame on what's left of her childhood bedroom. Staring into the growing flame she thinks of the sister who was lost before she was even born, closes her eyes and breathes Rachel's name.

She opens her eyes and thinks of the brother who is still alive, but lost to her just the same, and she utters Danny's name as well.

She hesitates, then imagines her mother as the fire jumps and spreads. Silently she takes and holds a deep breath, in her mind forms the words *I forgive you,* and exhales.

Asa Dollar, she then whispers into the flame, *Doodle, I always loved you. I'll miss you.*

Just then, as she thinks of her sister, the one whose grave down the road lies empty, a vision flashes across her mind. It is a picture of the *Fields of Green Home for the Infirm,* the imposing brick building she saw earlier today in Columbus, and immediately she knows with complete certainty that that was the secret place where the nuns took her to visit her mother. She also knows it is where Dinah has lived for the past twenty-one years, and where she must stop before heading north to Notre Dame.

Invigorated by this revelation she leaps to her feet, tosses the Zippo high above her head and catches it. She looks up, past the tops of the hill, past the darkening Indiana sky and the scattered stars that are beginning to appear there, and she smiles. And out of all the lights aglow there on earth that evening I spot that one, the flame engulfing our old homestead, floating higher than all the others. As I look into the center of the flame I smile too, and finally now I can see the present, rushing up to meet me like an eager child. Then, miraculously, there is the future, standing where it has been all along, in the darkness, and I see my sisters Dinah and Reece, and I see that they are alive.

The End

BVG